**"It's your turn to fly the kite, Callie."
Chip left the children gripping the string
together and sauntered over to her.**

She took the hand he offered, and he pulled her to her
feet. They stood inches apart, their hands still linked.
His was warm and strong, his grip firm but gentle.
She glanced up at him, hoping for a smile. Instead, his
serious side had reappeared. His gaze swept over her
face, coming to rest on…her mouth?

Was it possible Chip wanted to kiss her? What would
she do if he tried? Part of her wondered what it would
feel like to have his lips pressed to hers, but the more
sensible part—

"Don't you wanna do it, Miss Callie?" Jasper's question
shattered the moment, which was for the best. Chip
wasn't ready to court anyone.

The trouble was that the more time she spent with
him, the more Callie found herself drawn to him.

Award-winning author **Keli Gwyn**, a native Californian, transports readers to the early days of the Golden State. She and her husband live in the heart of California's Gold Country. Her favorite places to visit are her fictional worlds, historical museums and other Gold Rush–era towns. Keli loves hearing from readers and invites you to visit her Victorian-style cyberhome at keligwyn.com, where you'll find her contact information.

Books by Keli Gwyn

Love Inspired Historical

Family of Her Dreams
A Home of Her Own
Make-Believe Beau
Her Motherhood Wish

KELI GWYN

Her Motherhood Wish

HARLEQUIN® LOVE INSPIRED® HISTORICAL

Recycling programs for this product may not exist in your area.

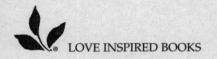 LOVE INSPIRED BOOKS

ISBN-13: 978-0-373-42516-7

Her Motherhood Wish

www.Harlequin.com

Printed in U.S.A.

For every house is builded by some man;
but he that built all things is God.
—*Hebrews* 3:4

In memory of my dad, Carl Lannon, who welcomed
me into his heart and his life from the very start.

Acknowledgments

My heartfelt thanks to those who have
made such valuable contributions to this story…

My perceptive editor, Emily Rodmell,
who takes a rough version of a story and gives me
insights into how to polish it until it shines.

My agent, Rachelle Gardner,
who deals with all the publishing details
and offers support and encouragement so
I can devote myself to writing my stories.

My AAA Team:
Adri, Amanda and Anne, who read the story
at various stages and gave me excellent suggestions on
how to make it even stronger.

My husband, Carl,
who gives me the male perspective, fuels my creativity
with delicious homemade scones, and listens to me
go on and on and on about my stories.

My friend Jessica Scharffenberg,
an ob-gyn nurse, who answered my medical questions.

Chapter One

March 1875

The sight of the golden-haired beauty stopped Chip Evans in his tracks. He hadn't seen the lovely Miss Caroline Hunt since he'd returned to Placerville. But there she stood, shielded from the California sunshine by the hotel's balcony as she rummaged in the beaded handbag dangling from her wrist.

He drank in the vision with the eagerness of a man who'd been stranded in the desert for days. The Plan didn't call for him to begin courting a lady for another three years, but a fellow couldn't pass up the opportunity to feast his eyes on such a striking specimen of femininity, could he?

Callie, as everyone called the petite woman with the smile as warm as a spring day, could have walked out of the pages of one of those fashion magazines at the mercantile. Her light pink gown, with its form-fitting bodice, hugged her in all the right places. The rosiness in her cheeks added a nice splash of color, drawing his attention to her exquisite features—clear blue eyes, a pert nose and petal-soft lips. Or so he imagined.

He gave himself a mental kick. Although he'd welcome the opportunity to kiss Callie, he had no business thinking such a thing. Sure, she'd agreed to dine with him. Once. They'd enjoyed a delicious meal with delightful conversation, but that was the extent of it. Entertaining romantic notions could be a distraction and keep him from reaching his goals.

Why he'd asked her to join him in the first place remained a mystery. One minute she'd been seeing to his order at the Blair Brothers Lumber Company, where she worked as a clerk, and the next he'd issued the invitation. Giving in to an impulse wasn't like him.

Callie snapped her reticule shut, spied him and started. She composed herself, lifted a gloved hand to shoulder level and gave a demure wave, appearing almost shy. Odd. The Callie he knew exuded confidence.

Chip sauntered across the wide main street to the Cary House, his boot heels thudding against the hard-packed earth. He stepped onto the plank walkway and struck a casual pose, leaning against one of the pillars supporting the balcony overhead. "Where are you off to all fancied up like that?"

She blinked in rapid succession. "Fancied up? If you intended to compliment me, that's not the way to go about it."

"No, but you look cute when you're piqued."

"So you admit to intentionally irritating me?"

He would admit to no such thing, even it was the truth. "I'd say you look stunning—" which she did "—but you'd probably accuse me of being too forward."

The hint of a smile lifted the corners of her mouth, but

the irksome woman wouldn't let it break free. Normally, she was easygoing. "Although I appreciate the thought, I'm unclear as to the reason behind your flattery. Was there something you wanted?"

Since admitting the sincerity behind his compliment could be telling, he chose to answer her question instead. "You're standing at the stagecoach stop, and you were smiling when I first saw you. It appears you're going somewhere and are looking forward to your trip. Am I right?"

She swept her gaze from his slouch hat to his boots and back again. "Not that it's any of your business, but yes. I'm going to visit my brother."

"Is he still in Shingle Springs?"

Her trademark smile burst forth in all its radiant glory. "You remembered."

"Of course."

"I'm sorry. It's just that…" She brushed the toe of her boot over a knothole in the walkway, the leather sole rasping over the rough pine.

"Go on."

"I told you where my brother is living when you took me to lunch. That happened six months ago, and since you lef—" She winced, a slight gesture he might have missed, if he hadn't been so focused on her every movement. "Since I wore your ears out that day, I'm surprised you were able to recall anything I said."

He remembered their conversation in detail. They'd started off talking about the lumber business but quickly moved on to more personal topics. They discovered that they'd both lost their parents during childhood.

Unlike other women, Callie was easy to talk to. She might wear fancy dresses on occasion and carry herself with the bearing befitting a society lady, but she didn't put on airs.

"I'm headed to Shingle Springs, too. I have a job down that way. If you don't mind riding in my wagon, you could go with me."

To her credit, she showed no outward sign of surprise at his abrupt change of subject, other than a brief pause. "I'd like that."

"Good. It's parked behind Dr. Wright's office. I've already filled my wagon with lumber, so we can set off right away." He was tempted to offer Callie his arm, a gentlemanly courtesy he would normally think nothing of, but refrained.

Although he would enjoy having her hand wrapped around his elbow, he wasn't in the habit of strolling with a lovely lady. Since he'd asked her to lunch during the last week of September the previous fall, showing a lapse of judgment on his part, she might get the impression he'd taken an interest in her. He would keep things nice and friendly-like this time so there would be no misunderstanding.

Chip swept an arm toward Coloma Street, opposite the hotel. "Shall we go?"

They arrived at his wagon minutes later. She accepted his help climbing aboard, rewarding him with a friendly smile and simple thank-you.

Perhaps his earlier concern was unfounded. She'd been pleasant company that day at the restaurant, but her reaction to seeing him today proved she hadn't set her cap for him. The reception she'd given him the past July, when he'd taken second place in the horse race at Placerville's Independence Day celebration, had indicated the same thing. The first- and third-place winners had each received a kiss from the ladies who presented their ribbons. All he'd gotten from Callie was a businesslike handshake.

The springs of his new buckboard creaked as he climbed aboard. He no longer needed to rent one, thanks to having achieved the first of his two yearly goals, the other being the completion of his kitchen. With the hefty load he was carrying under the tarpaulin today, his recently acquired team of workhorses would earn their oats.

He took his place on the bench seat, leaving a respectable distance between Callie and him, grabbed the reins and got underway. Her rigid posture and lips pressed firmly together gave him the impression she didn't care for his company. "If you're not comfortable riding with me, just say so."

She sent him a parlor-perfect smile, stiff and insincere. "It's fine."

"Really? You look as relaxed as my thoroughbred before a race."

"How is Dusty?"

"He's doing well. I'd stop by my place and let you see for yourself, but we need to get underway. If you're still willing to join me, that is."

"I am. I appreciate your offer." She raised a delicately arched eyebrow. "I'm just not sure why you made it."

He chuckled. "Because we're going to the same spot. Why else?"

"Yes. Of course." She faced front once again, as tense as before.

His experience with his female customers had taught him that women didn't always say what was on their minds. Perhaps if he helped out Callie, she'd give him a clue what she was thinking. "It's not like you to be on edge. Is something wrong?"

She fidgeted with her fan. "Since you asked…I didn't think *you* cared for *my* company."

"What gave you that idea?" He enjoyed spending time with her, more than he should.

"You left town so abruptly. We'd dined together just two weeks before, and yet you didn't even tell me you were going away until the day you rode off."

A warning gong sounded inside his head. He hadn't realized his departure would matter to her. The fact that it had proved his earlier decision not to offer his arm had been a wise one. Although Callie made a wonderful companion and possessed many of the qualities he would seek in a wife, he had three years to go before he would be ready to go courting. He wasn't a cad, though. "I'm sorry. As my friend, you deserved to know. Can you forgive me?"

The momentary drooping of her lovely lips followed by a genuine smile told him his message had been received. He'd accomplished his goal, so why did his chest feel so hollow?

Friend? Callie hadn't known where things stood between them. Now she did. Chip hadn't asked her to lunch because he harbored feelings for her. He'd made that clear when he'd failed to let her know he was leaving town until the last minute. His standoffishness earlier that morning when he hadn't offered her his arm reinforced the message.

A lady couldn't help but hope a man as accomplished and attractive as Chip would take an interest in her, though, could she? She longed to marry and have a family. She'd wondered if the powerfully built carpenter with the broad brow, thick brown hair and adorable lopsided smile could be the answer to her prayers. The charming man was a bit too regimented for her liking, but he was hardworking, generous and oh, so handsome.

She drew in a calming breath in an attempt to slow her racing heart. Why it had taken to thumping so wildly was beyond her. It wasn't as though there was anything between them.

Although Chip could be a mite exasperating at times, his engaging personality and ready laugh made him a delightful companion. Since she enjoyed his company and wasn't likely to see much of him once she began her new job in Shingle Springs—provided she got it, of course—she would make the most of this unexpected opportunity to spend a few hours with him.

Conversation flowed freely, just as it had when they'd shared a lunch all those months ago. He urged the horses into a slow trot, and the miles flew by.

A familiar screech rent the air. Callie put a hand above her eyes to shield the sun and peered at the sky, where a large bird circled. "Just what I thought. It's a red-tailed hawk."

"I didn't know you watch birds."

"I don't, but my brother does. Isaac can identify most species. It's one of his many talents."

"You don't talk about any other brothers or sisters. Was it just the two of you?"

She nodded. "Mama and Papa wanted more children, but that wasn't to be. What about you? Did you come from a big family?"

"Big enough. And noisy. There were four of us boys, although I'm the only one left. Alexander was the oldest.

I was second in line. Jeremiah came next, and Montgomery was the caboose kid, as Pa used to say." He gazed down the road, a sorrowful look in his eyes.

"I'm so sorry." Although she wanted to find out what had happened to his brothers, she couldn't come up with a question that suited her.

Chip sent her a too-bright smile. "It was a long time ago, but I have good memories."

She followed his lead, avoiding a subject he obviously didn't want to dwell on. "You must have had a lot of fun together."

"That we did. I look forward to the day my home is filled with the joyful shouts and laughter of my children." He cast her a quizzical glance. "What about you? Do you look forward to having a family one day?"

She did, very much, but the question never failed to shake her sense of peace. Chip's emphasis on the word *my* breathed life into fears she fought to suppress. Most men had a strong desire to father children of their own, just as most women dreamed of becoming mothers.

But what would happen if a woman couldn't bear children? The elderly doctor who'd treated her after the accident when she was a girl of six said she couldn't.

A muffled sob coming from behind a thick stand of manzanita bushes spared Callie the need to answer Chip's question. "Did you hear that? It sounds like someone's crying."

Not just someone. A child.

Chip brought his wagon to a halt, jumped to the ground and looped the reins around a low-hanging branch of a scraggly oak. His team shifted restlessly, causing the heel chains on their harnesses to jangle. "It's all right, fellows. I just need to have a look."

Callie climbed from the wagon and stood beside Chip. Although she listened intently, she heard nothing but rustling leaves. "The crying seems to have stopped, but I'm certain there's a child out there somewhere. We have to find the poor dear."

He beckoned. "Follow me."

They rounded the plentiful shrubs. He stopped and pointed toward a downed tree in the distance, where two youngsters sat huddled together, their attention on each other. "Look."

"I'll try to get closer without scaring them." She approached slowly.

A twig snapped under Callie's foot. The little fellow, who appeared to be all of five years old, pulled the small girl to his side and stared at Callie, wide-eyed.

She held up her hands in the classic surrender position. "I'm not going to hurt you. We're here to help."

The boy froze, but the slip of a girl broke free and ran into Callie's open arms, dangling a doll in one hand. She pulled the child to her in a tender embrace. "I've got you, sweetheart. Everything's going to be fine." Or so she hoped.

Left alone, the young fellow's gaze darted from Callie to something over his shoulder. He was shaking. What could have happened to terrify him so?

Chip drew closer to the boy. "It's all right. We won't let anything happen to you."

"No." The lad's lip quivered. "The bad people left us here and made Papa drive away, but what if they come back? I gotta keep Ruby safe."

Chip's features tightened, but he spoke with admirable calm. "Ruby's a nice name. What's yours?"

"Jasper."

"That's a great name, too. You said the people took your father, Jasper? When was that?"

The young fellow shrugged. "Not too long. One of the bad men hollered to the others and told them to get back on their horses when you come along."

Thank the good Lord they'd shown up when they did. These children could be in danger. It sounded like their father was. Callie joined Chip, cradling the frightened girl to her chest. "Do you know where they went?"

"Over there." Jasper pointed to the north, where a cloud of white smoke crested the trees.

Callie inhaled sharply. Something was on fire!

Chip leaned over, putting himself on the boy's level, and spoke with such tenderness that Callie stifled a sigh. "I need you to stay here with my friend Miss Callie while I look for your father. Will you do that?"

"Y-yes."

"Good." Chip straightened, assumed a take-charge manner Callie found reassuring and spoke beside her ear. "I don't like leaving you and the children alone, but I have no choice. Take them back behind that log—" he angled his head toward the downed tree where Jasper and Ruby had been hiding "—and keep out of sight until I come back."

Although she did her best to keep her voice level, it cracked. "I'll do that. What about you? They're sure to be armed."

"I have what I need." He flipped open his jacket, revealing a revolver strapped to his hip.

Callie nodded. "Go on then. We'll be fine."

He left, and she hustled the children to their hiding place. She held Ruby in her lap and pulled Jasper to her side.

"What's the tall man's name?" the boy asked.

Callie replied in a hushed voice, using the informal manner of address preferred by the owners of the Double T orphanage, where she hoped to work. "Mr. Chip."

"I never heared that name before."

"I'd never *heard* it, either, until I met him." It had to be a nickname, since his parents had given his brothers longer names. "I like your name. Did you know Jasper is a special stone?" If she could keep him talking, perhaps the traumatized boy would relax.

He scoffed. "'Course I do. Papa told me. He makes pretty things out of stones like that."

"Oh, is he a jeweler?"

"Yep. He's gonna start a jewelry store up in Placerville. Have you ever been there?"

"I live there." But if her interview went well, she'd be moving to Shingle Springs.

Jasper's face pinched with worry. "When will Papa and Mr. Chip come back?"

"I don't know, sweetheart. We must be patient."

"Why did the bad people take him?"

She wished she knew. "I'm sure we'll find out shortly."

The rapid-fire questions continued until Chip returned. Alone. Callie approached him with Ruby on her hip, eager for good news.

Jasper raced around the log and faced Chip, with his legs spread and arms folded, scowling. "Why didn't you bring Papa back? You said you would."

Chip squatted and rested a hand on the boy's shoulder. The kindhearted man spoke with such compassion that Callie's eyes misted. "I looked for him like I said I would, but I'm afraid I have some sad news, Jasper. Your papa won't be coming back. He's…gone."

The boy's face paled. "You mean he's dead, don't you?"

Blood rushed in Callie's ears, drowning out all other sounds, much as it had the day the robbers burst into her parents' house and took their lives all those years ago. She clutched Ruby to her and pressed a kiss to the girl's mass of blond curls.

No, Lord, no! How could You let this happen to these precious children?

She drew in a calming breath. Giving way to sorrow would do no good. The days ahead would be difficult ones for the children, but things would work out for them, as they had for her.

With her composure restored, she became aware of her surroundings once again. Chip stood nearby, holding the brokenhearted boy tightly, his features drawn.

Ruby clung to Callie, soaking her shoulder with tears. How much did the darling girl understand? She couldn't be more than two or three years old. How could she grasp the harsh realities the way her brother had?

Jasper had told Callie about his mama going to heaven not long after Ruby learned to walk. With their father gone, too, they were orphans. Callie could empathize with their pain, as could Chip. How like the Lord to put the two of them on the road at the precise time Jasper and Ruby had been left alone.

Chip set the boy down, held his small hand and looked into Callie's eyes. "I suggest taking our young friends to the Abbotts' place. I know space is limited, but from what Spencer said, Tess won't turn away a child in need."

"I think that's our best option." While life in an orphanage was not ideal, the bighearted owners gave the children in their care a nice place to live, plenty of food in their bellies and a whole lot of love. If the couple hired her, she'd be able to look out for Jasper and Ruby during their first days as orphans. In time, smiles and laughter would replace tears and sorrow, as they had for her after Mom and Pop Marshall had taken her in.

Callie inclined her head toward the area where the children's father had lost his life. "Do you need to tend to anything before we leave?"

"I saw to the most pressing matters. I'll come back as soon as I can to finish the job."

Since she saw no sign of smoke, he must have extinguished the fire. Without tools or a wagon, there would have been little more he could do. She'd get the details later. "We should get going. The sooner we get the children there, the better."

"You're right." He scanned the area. "I'm fairly certain we're alone now, but we don't want to encounter any…company en route."

They returned to the wagon. Jasper sat on the buckboard's seat between Chip and Callie, putting on a brave front that was at odds with his red-rimmed eyes and tear-streaked cheeks. Ruby sat in Callie's lap, trembling.

Jasper broke the lingering silence. "Where are you taking us?"

Chip answered. "To a place where some nice people will look after you."

"What kind of place?"

"It's called the Double T, and I think you'll like it." Chip sent the inquisitive boy a warm smile. "There will be plenty of other children to play with."

Jasper's brow furrowed. "Is it one of them orph'nages? Papa told me 'bout them. He said they're cold and dark and stinky."

Callie hastened to reassure the misguided boy. "The Double T is nothing like that. The buildings are big and blue, and there are lots of windows to let in the sunlight. Each child has a comfortable bed, a wardrobe full of clean clothes and plenty of delicious food to eat. Outside, there are horses and lots of cows. My brother, Isaac, works there. He teaches the children how to ride horses."

Jasper eyed her with suspicion. "Are you fibbing?"

"Not at all. It's a wonderful place. The boys live in Humpty Dumpty House and the girls in Miss Muffet House—for now anyhow. Mama Tess and Papa Spencer are adding Jack and Jill House, where the youngest children will live once it's opened. There is a large playroom on the first floor. Girls will live on the second and boys on the third."

He smiled. "I know them names! They're from Mother Goose."

"That's right." She sent him an encouraging smile. "What a bright boy you are."

The rest of the trip passed in a flurry of questions. Jasper's curiosity knew no bounds. Callie and Chip took turns telling him about every aspect of the Double T, from the cattle-ranching lessons Spencer gave the children to the impressive tree house in the massive oak behind the dormitories. She was surprised at Chip's familiarity with the orphanage, but then, according to her brother, he did make regular deliveries of wooden toys he'd created.

Chip turned off the main road in Shingle Springs, heading north. When they'd traveled about a mile, the Double T came into view.

Ruby had fallen asleep, but Jasper let out a whoop

that woke her. "It looks just like you said! I never seed so many cows."

Callie breathed a sigh of relief. They hadn't encountered any criminals along the way. Plus, she and Chip had succeeded in painting an accurate picture of the place and overcoming Jasper's hesitation. If all went well, the dear boy would find solace here.

Ruby rubbed her eyes, looked up at Callie and pouted. "Where's Papa?"

Oh, dear. The blond-haired darling hadn't grasped the sad truth after all.

Jasper rested a hand on his sister's arm and spoke with the assurance of a devoted big brother. "Papa went to heaven, Ruby, like Mama done, but it's all right. I'm gonna take good care of you." His boyish declaration melted Callie's heart.

Seemingly satisfied with her brother's explanation, Ruby clutched her doll tightly and nestled against Callie.

Chip brought the wagon to a halt in front of the main house. "You've got a right fine brother, Ruby." His compliment hit its mark, putting a smile on the young fellow's face.

Tess saw them and waved. The tall women left a group of older children working in the garden and crossed the yard. "Well, this is a surprise. One of the girls saw your wagon coming and told me a family had arrived, but I see that's not the case after all."

A surge of longing flowed through Callie. Her greatest wish was to have a family. The fact that she, Chip and the children had been mistaken for one was understandable. Jasper and Ruby, with their golden locks, did bear a resemblance to her, and the boy's eyes were the same sapphire-blue as Chip's.

Chip hopped from the wagon. "When I learned that Callie was coming this way, I offered her a ride. Along the way, we came across these children and discovered they'd been orphaned this very morning. We couldn't think of a better place to bring them."

Tess's hand flew to her throat. "The poor dears. All our beds are full, but we'll make do until you get the new ones built, Chip."

Callie glanced from Chip to Tess and back again. "Your next job is *here*? Why didn't you tell me?"

Chip shrugged. "It didn't come up."

She chuckled. "I'll have to remember that you're not the most forthcoming of gentlemen. All that aside, I'm glad you'll be making beds for these precious children." She turned to Tess. "This fine young man is Jasper, and the pretty girl in my lap is Ruby. Children, this nice lady is Mama Tess."

Jasper piped up. "She's real tall."

Tess nodded and spoke with her characteristic mix of efficiency and warmth. "That I am. Tall enough to help you down, Jasper." She lifted her arms, and he allowed the orphanage owner to assist him.

Chip had walked around the wagon. He reached for Ruby. "Come to me, princess."

Princess. Callie heaved a silent sigh. Could Chip have said anything sweeter? He would make all those children he planned to have a terrific father.

Ruby went willingly into Chip's arms. He shifted her onto his hip and offered his free hand to Callie—along with a knee-buckling smile. "Your turn."

An unexpected wave of shyness washed over her. "Thank you, but I've got it."

"I'm sure you do, but I'm here if you need me." The

rich timbre of his voice, coupled with his kindness, was her undoing. She didn't *need* his help, but she certainly *wanted* it.

"It *would* be easier if I had assistance." She took his hand. He clasped hers tightly as she navigated the sizable spaces from the wagon bed to the wheel's hub and from there to the ground below. Much to her delight, he didn't let go until several seconds after she'd completed her descent, giving her hand a squeeze—and her a wink—as he did. The handsome man possessed so much charm he was dangerous.

A slender young girl, around nine years old, sidled up to Tess. "I took the last of the gingersnaps out of the oven, Mama. What would you like me to do next?"

"I think these two youngsters might be eager to sample your baking, Lila. What do you say, Jasper? Would you and your sister like to go inside with my daughter and have a cookie?"

The boy cast a quizzical glance at Callie.

She nodded. "It's fine."

Uncertainty crinkled his brow. His gaze bounced between Callie and Chip. "You're not gonna go off and leave us, are you?"

Chip was quick to answer. "I have an errand to tend to, but I'll be back as soon as I can."

"What about you, Miss Callie? Ruby needs you." The boy put on a brave front, but clearly he was scared, too.

"I don't want to leave, but this isn't my home." Although she hoped it would be, she didn't know what her future held.

Tess faced Jasper, stooping to put herself on his level, and spoke in a reassuring voice. "Your new friends will be here for you. Mr. Chip is building furniture to fill the rooms in Jack and Jill House so we can invite more children like you to come and live with us, and Miss Callie is going to be working here, too."

"I am?" The words had slipped out before Callie could stop them. "But you haven't even interviewed me yet."

"That—" Tess straightened and waved a hand dismissively "—is entirely unnecessary. I've watched you when you visit your brother. Your love of the children is evident, and that's my top priority. I can teach you everything else you need to know."

"Thank you." She'd always wanted children to shower with love. Now she'd have them.

Chip set Ruby down, and the youngsters followed Lila inside. He looked at Callie, one eyebrow raised. "You didn't tell me you were coming here for a job interview. I thought you were just visiting your brother. And you said *I'm* not forthcoming?"

She ignored the teasing gleam in his eyes. The jovial man had a disturbing ability to weaken her defenses. She'd spent the past six months putting him and his endearing ways out of her mind. She responded with feigned detachment. "I wasn't sure I'd get the job, so I saw no reason to mention it."

Tess folded her arms and smiled. "I didn't realize you two were so well acquainted."

Callie rushed to answer, eager to dispel any false impressions. "We're not. Close, that is. I helped Chip with his orders a few times when he came into the Blair brothers' lumberyard, and we went to lunch once, but that's all."

"I see. Now, what can you tell me about the children?"

Chip quickly filled in Tess on how they'd come across

Jasper and Ruby and made the decision to bring them to the Double T.

"What did you find when you went in search of their father?" Tess asked Chip.

Callie had been wondering the same thing.

He cleared his throat. "It's, um, not a pleasant tale, nor one fit for a lady."

"Be that as it may," Tess countered, "since Spencer and I are taking the children in, I need to know what took place."

Chip rubbed the back of his neck. "When I got close enough to assess the situation, their father's wagon was fully engulfed in flames. The killers were nowhere to be seen. They must have ridden off, as Jasper said. Since I didn't know for sure or have any idea how many people were involved in the holdup, I approached cautiously. Jasper told us afterward that he'd seen two men and one woman, but all I saw were footprints. The trio took the horses and left the wagon's contents strewn all over the ground, evidence of a hasty search."

"What were they after?" Tess asked.

Callie blurted the answer. "Jewels."

He jerked his head toward her. "How did you know?"

"Jasper told me his father was on his way to Placerville to open a jewelry shop. If the crooks knew about that, it makes sense that's why they'd come after him."

He nodded. "Yes. I found a letter to that effect in his pocket from his new landlord."

"Was he still…in the wagon?" Callie dreaded the answer, but she had to know.

Chip shook his head. Tightness around his eyes and mouth showed his anger, but his voice was level. "I found Mr. Tate tied to the trunk of a tree a short distance from the wagon. Based on the number of cuts and bruises he'd sustained, it was clear that before they shot him, his killers roughed him up in an attempt to get him to tell them where to find the jewels."

Callie's eyes burned with unshed tears, but she refused to let them fall. She must remain focused on the children and their needs. Thanks to her new job, she'd be here to help them move beyond this tragedy and find happiness once again.

"I'm going to head up the hill now and see that Mr. Tate receives a proper burial. I'll stop by the sheriff's office afterward and report the crime to the deputy."

Tess took charge, as was her way. "I'd like you to ask Spencer to provide a couple of ranch hands. They can help with the task and ensure that you'd have backup if the murderers return to the scene of the crime. We'll have our workers keep a lookout for any suspicious activity here at the Double T, too. I wouldn't want anything to happen to the children."

"I'll talk with Spencer and get underway." Chip strode toward the barn.

Callie's chest tightened. "You don't really believe the children are in danger here, do you? It seems to me this would be the safest place possible."

Tess cast a watchful eye over the area before returning her attention to Callie. "I like to think that, but we can't be too careful. Now, about your job. Since you worked at Blair Brothers Lumber Company, I would like you to assist Chip."

"Me? Why?" No sooner were the words out of her mouth than Callie wished she could take them back. "Wouldn't a man be more suited for the position?"

Tess gave Callie's arm a reassuring pat. "I contacted

your previous employer and learned that you're a quick study and are quite knowledgeable about the lumber industry. Chip will be busy building the furniture, but he's sure to benefit by having someone close by who can hold things in place, hand him tools and help in other ways. You could do that and take care of Jasper and Ruby at the same time. They trust the two of you."

Although she would enjoy serving as Chip's assistant, spending so much time with him could make fighting her attraction difficult. "I'll do whatever you want, of course, but I had hoped to be working with more of the children."

"You will. When the furniture is built and Chip moves on to his next job, we can take in more children. You'll become one of the new group leaders. In the meantime, Spencer and I like to expose the children to different trades. We'll be sending some in to help in the woodshop, the word *help* being used loosely, especially with respect to the younger ones. You'll be responsible for seeing that they're kept out of harm's way—and Chip's, as well."

She could keep the children out of his way, but it wasn't them she was concerned about. Unless she wanted to set herself up for disappointment, she was the one who needed to keep her distance.

Chapter Two

Joyful shouts and bubbly laughter filled the air. The older girls at the orphanage congregated around the swings, while the older boys performed gymnastic stunts on three sets of parallel bars. Several younger children were engaged in a rousing game of follow the leader.

"Faster, Miss Callie. Faster," Jasper called from his end of the seesaw.

Callie stood behind Ruby, who sat on the end opposite her brother, and helped the little girl spring back up after Jasper had sent his sister's side down. "I'm going as fast as I can. Ruby isn't as big as you are."

"But I wanna go so fast that I bounce when I hit the bottom."

Callie smiled. "You're an adventurous one, Jasper. I have an idea. I'll give Ruby a ride." She reached for the little girl, who had clung to her ever since Tess's oldest daughter, Lila, had brought the children back outside. "Come here, sweetheart." Callie scooped Ruby into her arms, sat in front of the seat and T-shaped handle, with her legs to one side of the seat board, and held the little girl close.

The seesaws Callie had used as a girl had simple rope handles and had been made from roughly hewn white pine planks. The builder of this one had used Monterey pine, known for its strength and durability. Having been sanded until it was smooth, there was little likelihood of getting a splinter, as she had after riding the seesaw in a park near her parents' house in Chicago.

The memory of her father removing the sliver re-surfaced, causing tightness in her chest. Although he'd been gentle, his words had cut her to the core. *See that you're more careful after this, Caroline. I haven't time for such trivial matters. I've got more pressing business to attend to.*

As far back as she could remember, neither her mother nor her father had shown much interest in either of their children. As a result, she and Isaac had grown close. Her brother had been there for her back then, just as she was there for him now.

Although the war had been over for ten years, Isaac continued to deal with Soldier's Heart, an affliction many soldiers had developed, especially those who'd endured as many battles as he had. They experienced bouts of anxiety brought on by sudden loud noises, along with elevated heart rates. Aside from a limp, the result of an invading minié ball, her brother was as healthy as the horses he loved. But if his routine was upset or something startled him, he could become as skittish as a newborn colt. With her new job at the Double T, she could help him move beyond his painful memories and enjoy life again.

"Hold on, Jasper." Callie pushed her toes against the ground and bounced up, sending the boy dipping down a short distance.

He stated the obvious before she had an opportunity. "This won't work. You're too big."

"You're right." Even though she'd attempted to compensate for their size difference, the weights were uneven.

A tall young man of around thirteen crossed the yard and squatted beside Jasper. "Looks like you could use a partner."

The boy's eyes widened. "I thought orphans was little. You're almost all grown up."

"I'm not an orphan. My parents run the Double T. You met my mother earlier."

"Mama Tess is your mama?"

"She is. I'm Luke. Mama told me you're Jasper. Would you like to ride the seesaw with me and make your sister and Miss Callie go way up high?"

"Yes!"

Callie moved to the seat, putting Ruby and her everpresent doll in front of her. Luke took his place behind Jasper and shoved off with gusto, sending Callie and Ruby rushing down. Thanks to the wood chips spread under the seesaw, they had a soft landing. Callie used both feet to push against the ground as hard as she could. Ruby squealed as they shot upward.

Up and down they went, over and over again. Since Jasper and Ruby were having such a good time, Callie couldn't bring herself to put an end to their fun. Reality would return soon enough.

Chip's hearty laugh came from behind her. "What do we have here?"

At the sound of his rich, full voice, she experienced a rush of breathlessness that had nothing to do with her descent as Luke kicked off on the opposite side, and everything to do with the man who'd filled her thoughts ever since he'd left on his sorrowful errand. She'd missed his solid strength and reassuring presence.

"We're riding on a seesaw, Mr. Chip," Jasper said, as he and Luke started upward again.

"Would you mind letting me take your place, Luke? I'd like to get in on the fun."

"Not at all." Once stopped, Luke climbed off and headed to where the older boys continued their impressive feats on the parallel bars.

Chip positioned Jasper in front of him. "Let's see if we can make Miss Callie and Ruby bump a bit when they hit the ground."

"No! I wanna go bump." Jasper's mouth drooped.

Callie was eager to cheer him up. "Oh, you'll bump, Jasper. Ruby and I will see to that, won't we, sweetheart?"

Ruby nodded. "Don't be sad, Jaspy. We'll make you bounce weal hard."

"Yee-haw!" Chip hollered. "Let's have some fun then."

His enthusiasm was contagious. Before long both children were laughing, a welcome sound that warmed Callie's heart. There would be plenty of time for tears and cuddles, but showing the children that life would go on and they could still have fun was important, too.

Despite her best efforts, Callie couldn't send the seesaw upward with enough momentum to offset Chip's larger size and grant Jasper's wish. "We need to make a switch, Chip. I'll take Jasper, and you can take Ruby."

"That's a great idea. I don't know why I didn't think of it myself. I've got a lot on my mind, I suppose."

Understandable after his mournful task. "I'd like to hear about it. Later."

He and Jasper hopped off when they reached the bottom. Chip kept a firm grip on the handle and lowered the plank slowly until Callie and Ruby were resting on the ground. He covered the short distance between them and swept Ruby into his arms. The look he gave Callie, a mix of sorrow and determination, sent the message that he cared about the children as much as she did and would help ease their pain. "I talked with Tess, and there's to be a change in plans. When we're finished here, we can discuss it."

His serious tone didn't bode well. She hoped he hadn't balked at the idea of having her as his assistant because, despite her reservations, she wanted to spend time with the handsome, hardworking carpenter. As long as she reminded herself that he would finish the job in a few weeks and walk out of her life, everything would be fine. She could do that. Couldn't she?

By kicking off the ground as hard as he could while holding Ruby tightly, Chip managed to make Callie and Jasper hit the ground with a satisfying thump. Jasper's gleeful grin and Callie's musical laugh were his rewards.

Working with the cheerful young woman would present a challenge. Not only was she fun to be around, but she was also mighty nice to look at. The afternoon sun filtered through the trees, transforming her blond hair into a rich gold. Several strands had come loose from the thick braid swirled on top of her head, and they framed her lovely face.

Her radiant smile drew his attention to her pretty pink lips. Without warning, she pressed them together and raised a dainty eyebrow. Heat crept up his neck. She'd caught him staring at her. He would have to be content with surreptitious glances in the future.

Tess appeared a few minutes later, bringing their seesaw ride to an end. "Jasper and Ruby, I'd like you to come with me. I'm going to show you around the place."

Ruby tensed in Chip's arms but said nothing.

He summoned his most reassuring tone. "It's all right, princess. Mama Tess is a nice lady. She'll take good care of you."

"I wanna stay with you and Miss Callie." The tremor in the little girl's voice touched a chord. He could remember vividly the day he'd found himself alone in the world, bouncing around in the back of his father's prairie schooner, weak from the cholera that had claimed his last family member hours before. No one in the wagon train had cared about an orphaned boy likely to die.

But these children weren't alone. They would receive loving care at the Double T. "We'll still be here. You'll see us at supper."

Jasper hopped off the seesaw and rushed to his sister's side. "Don't worry, Ruby. I'm here with you."

Mollified, the little girl allowed Tess to take her by the hand. The caring woman offered Jasper her other one and headed for the playground, leaving Chip alone with Callie.

She stood beside him and watched with furrowed brow as the children got farther away. Ruby trudged alongside Tess, her tiny shoulders hunched as she hugged her doll tightly, but Jasper had a spring in his step. The energetic boy seemed to have Callie's positive outlook on life and wasn't ready to deal with his grief. Ruby, on the other hand, was understandably scared. Her fear brought out a protective instinct in Chip unlike anything he'd experienced before.

"The poor dears." Callie shook her head. "I know they'll be all right, but they'll have a difficult time ahead of them." She turned to him. "Were you able to give their father a proper burial and find out why those horrid people did that to him?"

He inclined his head toward two giggling girls skipping by with linked arms. "Let's go somewhere else, shall we?" He headed for Jack and Jill House, the largest of the three dormitories, beyond the two smaller ones. The impressive three-story clapboard building, recently completed, sat empty, awaiting furniture he'd been hired to build. He had a busy month ahead of him, but that was how he liked it.

Callie fell in step beside him. "Do you mind slowing down a bit? I can't keep up when you take off with that determined stride of yours." Although her tone was pleasant, he sensed an underlying edge.

"I cover ground when I've got work to do. I'll have to remember to take it easy when you're with me. I can't be leaving my assistant in the dust, can I?" He flashed her a grin.

She ground to a halt and stared at him in disbelief. "So, I *am* working with you?"

He stopped. "Yes. Tess told you that, didn't she?"

"She did, but you said the plans had changed. I thought…" She shook her head. "Never mind. It doesn't matter."

He'd built homes and furniture to suit the wives of many men through the years and had made an important discovery. If a woman said something didn't matter, that was rarely the case. "It obviously does, but I'm not sure what *it* is. Care to enlighten me?"

She took a sudden interest in her boots, clicking the heels of the tiny things together. "I thought you'd asked Tess to find you another assistant."

"Why would I? You know as much about lumber as most carpenters and have an impressive grasp of design. I'm looking forward to working with you."

He'd obviously said the right thing because Callie look up, beaming. "Thank you, Chip. I'll do my best to live up to your expectations."

Three resounding rings of a cast-iron bell sent a swarm of children their way. He'd learned during the many hours he'd spent at the Double T that Tess used the bell to convey messages to the children. Earning the right to swing the striker inside the large triangle was a privilege the orphans eagerly awaited. Three rings meant the end of playtime.

The boys scurried past them on their way to the barn, where their chores awaited them. The girls flocked to the kitchen on the bottom floor of Miss Muffet House, where they would help prepare supper.

"Let's get out of here before these young'uns run us over." Chip chuckled and put a hand on the small of Callie's back, steering her clear of the hubbub. Reluctant to release her, he kept his hand there as they walked. To his surprise, she didn't pull away. Interesting.

They reached Jack and Jill House, but he decided to take her to the woodshop on the far side of it instead. He opened the door for her. She stepped inside and inhaled deeply. "I love the smell of freshly cut lumber. Don't you?"

He fought a grin but lost the battle. "I like watching you enjoy it."

She gave his arm a playful swat. "Don't go making fun of me."

"I'm not. I like the way you embrace life." He wouldn't mind if she embraced him, too.

But The Plan didn't call for him to court a woman yet. From what he'd seen, the lovely Miss Caroline Hunt had potential, but if he gave in to his attraction so far ahead of schedule, he wouldn't accomplish his goals.

Callie's face fell. "Most days I have no trouble keeping a sunny outlook, but sometimes shadows cross our paths when we least expect them. I can't help thinking that the children's father drew his last breath this morning. Were you able to take care of everything?"

"Spencer's ranch hands helped me bury Mr. Tate at the cemetery in town." An image of the man's lifeless body rushed in, causing Chip's stomach to pitch, as it had earlier. He'd watched far too many cholera victims buried in the middle of the trail on the wagon train's trek to California—including the five from his family. He strode to the open window at the front of the wood-shop, placed his palms on the ledge and drew in several deep breaths of fresh air.

With a swish of her skirts, Callie was at his side, standing just to his left. She rested a hand on his upper arm and stood there, offering silent support.

Gradually, his nausea passed, and he became aware of the warmth radiating from her. He turned, putting her mere inches from him. She took his hands in hers and lifted compassion-filled eyes. "I'm sorry you had to go through that."

He was tempted to jerk his hands free, but the pull

was too strong. It had been years since someone had reached out to him and offered comfort. Like a weary traveler crossing the barren desert of Nevada, he drank in this unexpected outpouring of kindness. "I'm fine."

"You will be, I know, but in talking with Isaac, I learned that witnessing the aftereffects of such an atrocity can be difficult. But you did it, and I thank you for that. When the children are ready, they'll be able to visit their father's grave site and say their goodbyes."

"I just did what anyone else would have done, but I appreciate your kind words." He gave her hands a gentle squeeze.

She lowered her gaze to their clasped hands, pulled hers free and backed away. "I'm s-so sorry. I didn't realize what I was doing."

"I didn't mind." His admission surprised him as much as it did her.

She gave a nervous laugh, composed herself and continued as though nothing had happened, much to his relief. He didn't want to explore the reasons behind his confession.

"We couldn't talk earlier, but I've been battling curiosity ever since you told me about the letter you found. What else did you learn from it?"

"The children's father was George Tate. He was coming here from Marysville, where he worked in a jewelry shop. He was going to open his own, as Jasper said. It sickens me to think that he was brutally murdered less than five miles from his destination." He unfurled the fists he'd formed.

"It's tragic, but I take comfort in knowing that he spent his last days on earth looking forward to the fulfillment of a dream."

He scoffed. "How can you do that?"

"Do what?"

"Dismiss Mr. Tate's anguish. His final minutes must have been horrific."

Her features hardened, but her voice was calm, controlled. "I realize that, but focusing on the dark side of life does nothing but drag a person down into a pit of despondency and despair. I much prefer to look for the good in a situation."

"Sometimes there is nothing good." Sometimes people were so consumed by their own grief that they would leave a nine-year-old boy to battle a deadly disease on his own. But he'd shown them he was made of tougher stuff than they'd thought. He'd survived, and he would ensure that his family's legacy would live on in the children he would have one day.

Callie jerked her chin up. "The Good Book says that 'all things work together for good to them that love God.' I firmly believe that. Don't you?"

He wasn't in the mood for a theological debate, tired as he was after his harrowing task, but she deserved a response. "I believe God can bring good out of bad, but He doesn't promise that life will be easy." He had a hard time seeing how anything good could come out of losing his entire family inside of one week or Jasper and Rudy being robbed of their father.

Callie wandered over to his workbench, one of three in the spacious woodshop, where he'd set his toolboxes. She trailed a fingertip over the lids as she walked past each one. "No, but He does promise to be with us no matter what comes our way. That's a promise that fills me with hope."

Hope. Callie embodied it. He admired that, but her

rosy-hued outlook could keep her from accepting the harsh realities of life. And they were facing one now. As much as he'd like to spare her, he couldn't. "I'm afraid trouble could be coming our way."

"What do you mean?"

"In his letter, the landlord assured Mr. Tate that a safe would be installed before his arrival so he'd have a place to store the gemstones he was picking up in Sacramento City. The attempted robbery doesn't strike me as a random act. I think it was planned by someone who'd learned about the shipment."

She stopped and gave him her full attention. "You think it was premeditated, then?"

"I do." But there was more to it than that. "I'm not sure they got the jewels."

Her clear blue eyes bored into him. "Why? It seems to me they wouldn't have left until they did."

He disagreed. "Since his attackers beat him before taking his life, it makes sense they hadn't found what they were after and used force to get him to talk."

She challenged his supposition. "But why kill him if he hadn't revealed their whereabouts? Wouldn't they have kept him alive until he told them? I think it's more likely that he told them what they wanted to know, thinking they'd take the jewels and leave. They could have killed him so he couldn't report the report the theft or describe them. Since they didn't pursue us, I think they've probably left the area and are busy trying to sell the stones somewhere else."

He saw her point, but… "If he had the jewels, wouldn't he have given them up right away? I think it's more likely he didn't have them with him and that's why they did him in."

She placed her palms on his workbench, looked across it and studied him with narrowed eyes. Skepticism and concern waged a war in their depths. Concern won out. "If what you believe is true and he didn't tell them because he didn't have the jewels, where are they?"

"I don't know. Perhaps he entrusted them to Wells, Fargo and Company. I hope that's the case."

"Why?"

A simple question requiring an answer he was loath to put into words, but he must. "Mr. Tate's attackers were willing to resort to murder in order to get his gemstones, so I expect they won't stop looking until they find them. If they don't show up in an express delivery, I'm afraid his killers might come looking for the children and try to get information out of them."

He waited for Callie's reaction, expecting anger, shock or fear. Instead, she laughed.

"You can't be serious. They have no idea where the children are now since they took off when we showed up."

"I'm quite serious. It wouldn't take them long to find out, and once they did, they could try to find them."

"Why would they do that? They left the children behind so they wouldn't have to witness the...crime. That tells me they must have scruples."

Her positive outlook was admirable, but he dealt in facts, and those he'd collected had decided his course of action. "Given their history, it seems more likely they would stop at nothing to get what they want and wouldn't let the fact that Jasper and Ruby are children get in their way. We have to protect the youngsters, which is why Tess changed the plans. In most cases, she puts a new child in with the others right away to help them adjust as quickly as possible, but she wants us to keep a close watch over Jasper and Ruby. He and I will bed down on the third floor of Jack and Jill House, and Ruby will share your room on the second. I'll bring beds over from the bunkhouse to use tonight until I can get those we need done."

Callie sobered. "If Tess is concerned, she must believe the children are in danger."

"We don't know that for sure, but she agreed that taking precautionary measures would be wise."

"I understand why you're doing this, but I still think the murderers got the jewels. Even if they didn't and they came looking for the children, I believe they're safe here."

He wanted to believe that, too, but unlike Callie, he'd seen what Mr. Tate's attackers were capable of. The fatherless children were now in Chip's care, and he would do everything in his power to protect them.

But what if it wasn't enough?

Chapter Three

The dining hall was abuzz as scores of children sat at the long tables, carrying on animated conversations. Jasper was on Callie's left, his eyes roving over the scene. Although the room was large, it had a friendly feel, with paintings of characters from Mother Goose tales on the brightly colored walls. Older children wearing ankle-length white aprons and smiles carried in platters and bowls heaped with an assortment of mouthwatering dishes and set them on the tables.

Jasper's chin dropped. "I never seen so much food in one place before. And it smells real good."

That it did. Callie hadn't realized how hungry she was. Thankfully, no one could hear her rumbling stomach over the hubbub. "I'm sure it will taste good, too."

Ruby, seated on Callie's right, pointed. "Chicken."

"That's right, sweetheart. Fried chicken. Do you like it?"

The little girl nodded.

"She likes drumsticks," Jasper volunteered. "So do I."

Chip, seated on Jasper's other side, grinned, a playful gleam in his eye. "I do, too. I hope there's more than one left when it's our turn to pick. I wouldn't want to have to fight you for the last one."

The young fellow scowled at Chip. "Fighting is wrong. Papa says so." His face pinched with pain as reality rushed in. "He *said* so."

Callie sent a disapproving glance Chip's way and hastened to reassure Jasper. "Mr. Chip was teasing. He wouldn't take the last drumstick. He'd let you have it. But you don't have to worry. There's plenty of food."

"Miss Callie's right, Jasper. I was just having some fun with you, but it wasn't the right time. I'm sorry. Can you forgive me?"

The boy studied Chip intently, his forehead creased in concentration. A slow smile spread across Jasper's boyishly round face. "I'll forgive you—if you give me your drumstick, too."

Chip laughed. "Jasper, my boy, you drive a hard bargain, but if you think you can polish off two drumsticks, you can have mine."

Luke stopped behind the vacant spot next to Ruby. "Do you mind if I sit here?"

Callie smiled. "Not at all. We'd love your company, wouldn't we, Ruby?"

In answer, the little girl scooted closer to Callie.

"It's all right, sweetheart. This is Luke. Don't you remember? He's the one who rode on the seesaw with us."

Jasper chimed in. "I remember. He's not an orphan. He's Mama Tess and Papa Spencer's son."

"That's me, all right." Luke smiled, plunked himself down on the bench and leaned close to Ruby. "I know I'm big and scary, but I won't hurt you. I like girls. I have three sisters. I think one of them is your age. How old are you?"

"Th-this many." Ruby let go of the doll in her lap, raised a trembling hand and held up two fingers.

"Yep! That's how old Lucy is. She's the youngest. If you look over there, you can see her." He pointed to the head table, where Spencer and Tess sat with five children. "She's sitting next to Lila, the one who gave you the cookies. Do you remember her?"

Ruby glanced at the rest of the Abbott family and nodded.

"Who are them others?" Jasper asked.

"The older boy is Lewis. He just turned seven. The younger one, Lionel, is six. The other girl is Lorene. She'll be turning five next week. I can't wait. I'll get to eat chocolate cake two different times." He smacked his lips.

Jasper craned his neck to look at Luke. "How come?"

"Mama makes a cake just for us whenever there's a birthday in our family, but we'll have a party here in the dining hall, too, for all those who have birthdays in April. We do that on the first Saturday of every month."

Jasper held up his fingers, ticked off the months and looked up, his eyes wide. "All the orphans here get chocolate cake twelve times in one year?"

Luke nodded. "You will, too, if you're here that long."

"'Course I'll be here. I don't have nowhere else to go."

Callie's heart pinched. "You could get adopted and go live with a nice family who loves you."

A fierce scowl creased Jasper's brow. He folded his arms over his chest. "I don't want a new family. I just want my papa back."

The dear boy's reaction was understandable, given his circumstances, but his future could hold untold blessings, as hers had. "It's hard. I know. I lost my parents when I was young, too, but there are wonderful people out there who have hearts full of love, and they want to give it to special children like you and Ruby."

"I don't want no one else. You and Mr. Chip can take care of us." He gave a decisive nod.

Chip rested a hand on the grieving boy's shoulder. "We will be looking out for you. You can count on that."

Callie opened her mouth to speak, but Chip shook his head. He was right. Clarification could come later. The children needed reassurance now. "Yes. We'll be here."

Tess stood and clapped three times, bringing the chatter in the room to a close. "It's a special day here at the Double T. We've had two children join our happy family—Jasper Tate and his sister, Ruby. Welcome!"

Heads turned in their direction, and applause broke out. A few children even cheered. Jasper and Ruby went from stunned to smiling in a matter of seconds.

Luke leaned over and whispered, "I need to join my family now, but I'll see you all later." He left.

Once the room quieted, Tess continued. "As you can see, Jasper and Ruby, we're happy to have you here. Now, it's time for Papa Spencer to ask the blessing, so bow your heads and close your eyes."

Tess sat, and Spencer stood. "Lord, thank You for the food we're about to eat, for the many hands who helped make it and for each of the boys and girls here. I ask You to be with Jasper and Ruby. Thank You for bringing them to us. Please help them to feel at home here. It's in Your name I pray. Amen."

Callie opened her eyes to find Jasper blinking his. She leaned over. "What is it?"

"Papa Spencer was talking to God, wasn't he? About me and Ruby?"

She nodded.

"I never had anybody do that before, except for my papa."

"Mr. Chip and I have been praying for you, too."

"Really? Does God listen to you?"

Chip answered before she could. "Yes."

Jasper wiggled his mouth from side to side, stopped abruptly and jerked his head toward Callie. "Then He knows what those bad people did to Papa, don't He? And where we are now?"

"He does. Why?"

"Because He can still watch over me and Ruby, just like He did when we was with Papa."

It appeared the dear boy was scared, which made sense after what he'd gone through. "Of course He can, and He will, but I don't think you have anything to wor—"

"Here you go." Chip plopped a spoonful of mashed potatoes on his plate and shoved the bowl at her.

If she wasn't mistaken, he'd interrupted her on purpose. What did he have against letting the children know they were safe? She attempted to make eye contact with him, but he didn't look her way. He asked Jasper what he'd seen when Tess had given him and his sister a tour of the Double T, which prompted the talkative fellow to launch into a detailed description.

Fine. Chip might be able to ignore her now, but once they'd tucked the children in bed, she'd let him know what she thought about him cutting her off. He might believe Mr. Tate's murderers would come looking for Jasper and Ruby, but that didn't mean she agreed.

The meal passed quickly. Despite her opposing view, she was still drawn to Chip. For a man as regimented as he was, he certainly had a playful side, which the children seemed to bring out. He kept Jasper distracted with his stories throughout the meal and even managed to get a smile out of Ruby.

Tess stood. She clapped thrice, as she'd done before the meal, and the room grew quiet. "Children, I'm sure you'll want to see to the clean-up as quickly as you can tonight when you hear what special treat awaits you."

Excited murmurs swept through the room. Callie tapped Chip on the shoulder to get his attention and whispered over Jasper's head. "Do you know what's going on?"

A lopsided grin and a wink were her answers. She suppressed a stab of jealousy. Evidently, he was privy to information she wasn't. Just how much did he know about the workings at the Double T? And how had he come by his knowledge?

Once Tess had the youngsters' full attention, she continued. "You probably noticed our newest helpers who joined us for dinner. For those who don't know, Mr. Chip is a carpenter. He's going to be working here the next few weeks while he builds furniture for Jack and Jill House, and Miss Callie will be helping him."

The heads of several curious children turned toward them, and Callie smiled. She looked forward to getting to know everyone who called the Double T home.

Tess continued. "Some of you have been here longer than others and can remember when he built the seesaw, parallel bars and that wonderful tree house, his gift to all of you. And I'm sure you've seen the wooden toys he's made. Tonight we're going to discover another of his talents."

So Chip was the one behind the play equipment, was he? It appeared his generosity knew no bounds, which wasn't a surprise. Although he was focused on chasing after his goals, she'd heard numerous tales of good deeds he'd done up in Placerville. He'd added a room on a house for a young widow left with five children to raise on her own, fashioned a tiny coffin for a family who'd lost their infant son and repaired a roof for an injured miner's family—all with no cost to the recipients. It was a wonder the hardworking man had time for sleep.

Callie leaned forward, as eager as the children to find out what Chip was going to do.

Tess swept her gaze over the room, her smile evidence of how much delight she took in building the suspense. At last she spoke. "How many of you have heard of whittling?"

Hands shot up, some of them waving wildly. Jasper's was among them. As was Callie's.

"That's great. Many of you have seen the darling little figures Mr. Chip makes. Tonight he's going to do wood carving. He'll be creating something bigger and better than anything he's done before. And you get to watch him begin the sculpture."

A young boy raised his hand.

Tess called on him. "Yes, Freddie?"

"What's he going to make?"

She held up an index finger, leaned forward and grinned. "That, my dear boys and girls, is for you to figure out. The first one to guess correctly gets to ring the dinner bell tomorrow. Now, I'll excuse you. Once the clean-up is done, we'll gather on the bottom floor of Jack and Jill House, where we'll have benches set up."

One group of children began clearing the tables. The rest filed out in a noisy but orderly fashion. Jasper and Ruby watched the exodus, their brows furrowed. They had to be overwhelmed by all the changes in their lives. Callie had to admit she was feeling a bit unsettled herself. A new job could do that to a person. Her uneasiness had nothing to do with the handsome carpenter she'd be assisting. Or did it?

Chip stood. Callie rose, too, and planted Ruby on one hip. "You're a man of many talents. My brother told me you drop off toys here from time to time, but I didn't realize you'd built the playground equipment. No wonder you know so much about how things work around here. I've visited several times, and yet I have a lot to learn."

"I'm no expert, but I'd be happy to teach you what I know. All you have to do is ask." He sent her one of his most winsome smiles.

She chuckled. "All right. I'm asking. What happens next?"

"Very well. Now that Tess has excused the children, they'll complete their assigned chores under the supervision of their group leaders. Each of the groups has a name. Tess chose to use wildlife found in California for them. Whenever a new group forms, the children in it choose the name. You probably won't be surprised to hear that the first boys who lived here dubbed their groups the grizzlies, the cougars and the salamanders. The girls, on the other hand, went with quail, chipmunks and rabbits."

Jasper tugged on Chip's sleeve. "Mr. Chip."

"What is it, Jasper?"

"Can I be in the grizzlies?"

Chip leaned over, his hands on his knees. "You and I are going to be in a special group, just the two of us. And you—" he gave Jasper a playful tap on the tip of his nose "—get to pick the name."

"I do? Oh!" He scrunched his face in the cutest way

as he contemplated. A smile burst forth. "I know. We can be the bullfrogs. I used to hear them outside my window at night."

Chip grinned. "What do you think of that, Miss Callie? I'm sure you're fond of frogs."

"It's a fine name. I've seen some big bullfrogs up in Hangtown Creek. I even grabbed one once." Accidentally, when she'd mistaken it for a rock. She'd nearly shrieked her lungs out, but they didn't need to know that.

Jasper gazed at her with boyish admiration. "Really? How big was it?"

Chip's lips twitched, a telltale sign of his disbelief. "Yes, Miss Callie. Tell us. Just how big was this frog you befriended?"

Since she'd gotten Jasper's attention focused on something pleasant, she might as well finish the tale with a flourish. She suppressed a shudder at the memory of that dreadful experience, shifted a yawning Ruby to a more comfortable position and forged ahead.

"It was a spring day much like today, clear and warm, with not a cloud in the sky. Recent storms had filled the creek, and it was burbling over the rocks. I tossed stones in the creek just so I could hear the satisfying plops. I reached for a nearby stone, but I saw something else." She paused for dramatic effect.

"What was it?" Jasper asked.

A strangled sound from Chip stopped her. She recognized it for what it was—a cough covering a chortle. He was laughing. At her.

So be it. She wasn't going to let his amusement ruin Jasper's fun. "It was a big ol' bullfrog with bulging eyes. That fellow was *huge*. Why, he must have been as big as my hand. Or bigger." Definitely bigger. And very ugly.

Jasper trembled with excitement. "And you picked it up?"

"I sure did. He didn't like being disturbed, though, so he took a flying leap out of my hand." If she wasn't embellishing the tale for the boy's benefit, she might have mentioned that the slippery creature didn't have much choice, not when she'd flung him as fast and as far as possible. She could happily live the rest of her life without seeing another frog.

"Miss Callie is a brave woman, isn't she, Jasper? Now that she's finished her exciting tale, we should be going. I have to make sure everything's ready before the rest of the children arrive. How would you like a piggyback ride?" Upon receiving a nod, he hefted Jasper onto the bench and presented his back. The young fellow climbed up and wrapped his arms around Chip's neck. Chip galloped across the dining room, bringing forth peals of laughter.

Chip stopped at the doorway and turned. "The honorable knight and his trusty steed can't ride off and leave the pint-sized princess and her lovely lady's maid behind. It's our job to protect the ladies—and the realm."

There it was again—that edge of concern to his voice. Why was he so convinced that the children were in danger? And if he was, why had he cut her off earlier when she attempted to reassure Jasper? Those were questions she'd ask him as soon as she could get him alone, but with their two young chaperones present much of the time, opportunities to have Chip to herself could be few. Which could be a good thing. He might exasperate her on occasion, but his charisma and magnetic personality drew her to him.

Since she didn't know him as well as she'd thought,

she would be wise to keep her distance, for the time being anyhow. But there was nothing to stop her from inviting the attractive carpenter to have a cup of hot cocoa with her after they got the children in bed later that evening, was there? They did need to make plans, after all, and admiring him over the streaming beverage would be a nice way to end the day. If their time together led to her having sweet dreams, so much the better.

Carving with an audience wasn't something Chip had done very often. The few times he'd attempted it, he'd had a handful of adults looking on. Mindful of his need to concentrate, they'd remained silent. Carving with a group of curious children watching and calling out their guesses would test his ability to remain focused on his work, but he thrived on challenges.

He stood in the middle of the large space that would become the new playroom, with Tess by his side. She surveyed the setup. "Do you think this arrangement will work?"

"I do." The older boys, assisted by their group leaders, had carried in benches from the dining hall and arranged them in a U shape, three rows deep, with a sturdy table in the middle.

"Very well. Then I'll leave you to finalize your preparations." She headed out the door just as Callie walked in, with Ruby by her side.

Apprehension clamped a vise around Chip's chest. "Where's Jasper?"

Callie responded with a casual shrug. "Outside."

"Where?"

"I'm not sure exactly, but he's fine."

The vise squeezing Chip's chest tightened. "How do you know that, if he's not with you?"

"He's with Spencer and Luke. I believe they're capable of looking out for him, don't you?"

She didn't understand how important this was. He lowered his voice so Ruby, who was walking between the rows of benches, wouldn't hear them and become alarmed. "I know you don't think the children are in danger, but based on the facts, I believe they could be."

Her words were hushed but forceful. "If they are—and I'm not convinced that's the case—I see no need to alarm them."

"Neither do I."

"Really? Then why did you stop me at dinner when I tried to assure Jasper that they're safe here?"

How had she come to that conclusion? "I didn't—"

"Cut me off? Yes, you did. Jasper asked about the 'bad people' and was concerned that God wouldn't know where he and Ruby are and be able to watch over them. All I was going to say was that he didn't have anything to worry about, and you interrupted me."

"But there is cause for concern. Surely you can see that."

She huffed out a breath. "Of course I do. Life is fraught with dangers, but the children don't have to worry because we're here to see that they're safe, just as their father did and God does. The last thing they need right now is to sense any anxiety on our part. They need to feel safe and secure so they can deal with their grief. Surely *you* can see that."

"I'm not the enemy, Callie. I care about the children, too. I'm just trying to protect them, the same as you are.

It would be easier if we could work together on this. Can't we do that?"

He must have said what she wanted to hear because the tension in her lovely face eased. "That's what I want, too."

"Good. Then we're a team."

"Miss Callie?"

"What is it, sweetheart?" She sat on one of the benches and pulled Ruby into her lap.

"Where's Jaspy?"

"He's outside with Luke and his papa, but he'll be here soon."

"Where's our papa?"

Callie lifted sorrow-filled eyes to Chip. Her compassion knew no bounds. She shifted her gaze to the darling girl and spoke with such tenderness that his chest tightened. "Oh, sweetheart, he's gone, just like your mama. But Mr. Chip and I are here. Mama Tess and Papa Spencer, too. We'll take good care of you."

Ruby's chin quivered, and tears ran down her cheeks. "But I want my papa wight now."

"Of course you do. Losing a mama or a papa hurts in here." Callie placed a hand over Ruby's heart. "I know. Mine went away when I was a girl, too, but some nice people took me in. Someday, you'll have a new family, too, and they'll love you, but right now this is your home and we're your family."

Her sentiment was well-intentioned, but circumstances didn't create a family. You were born into one, and they loved you from the start. No matter what you did or how many mistakes you made, they were there for you, just as his had been there for him. Hoping for that same level of love and acceptance from someone else was foolhardy. He'd learned that lesson the hard way.

But Callie was right about one thing. The children would be well cared for. And they'd be safe. He would see to that.

"Let's dry your tears before the other children arrive." Callie pulled a handkerchief out of her sleeve, dabbed each of Ruby's cheeks and kissed them. "That's better, isn't it?"

The little girl nodded. "You're a nice lady."

Callie smiled. "And you're a lovely girl. Now, shall we see if Mr. Chip needs anything?" She held out a hand, and Ruby took it.

They slipped between the benches and joined him.

Ruby gazed up at him. "Do you need help, Mr. Chip?"

"As a matter of fact, I do. I could use someone to make sure I have all my tools lined up just right." He swept a hand to where he'd laid out his knives, chisels, gouges and the mallet. "All the handles need to be facing the edge of the table so I can grab them quickly. Could you tell me if any of them are backward?"

The adorable girl bobbed her head and started down the row, lifting her doll so she could *see*, too. He leaned against the bench, blocking Ruby's view of the final tools, reached behind his back and spun the wooden mallet around. She approached, and he stepped out of the way.

"Oh! This one's upside down."

"Why, look at that! You're right. Would you turn it around for me? It's not too heavy." And it wasn't sharp, as the other tools were.

Ruby righted the mallet and looked to him for approval.

He squatted, smoothed a strand of her blond hair behind her ear and cupped the side of her soft face in his work-roughened hand. "You did a great job, princess."

Callie sighed. He looked her way, and his breath caught. Minutes before she'd been irritated with him, but now her entire countenance shone with admiration. And it was directed at him. He wasn't sure what he'd done to bring about such a transformation. He hadn't changed his position on the need for safeguarding the children, but he would enjoy being in her good graces while it lasted.

She caught him staring at her and smiled. "You'll make a fine father one day, Chip."

So that was it, was it? She was pleased with the way he'd handled Ruby's offer of help. He hadn't done anything special, but Callie's approval meant a great deal to him.

Four rings of the dinner bell, the signal for a special event, brought the brief encounter to a close. She swept in to pick up Ruby and stood in one of the open corner areas between the benches. "We'll have a good view from here, sweetheart. I'm looking forward to watching Mr. Chip work, aren't you?"

Callie's enthusiasm eased the tension in Chip's shoulders.

A young boy about seven years old bounded in ahead of everyone else and plopped down in the middle of one the front row benches, facing Chip.

"You were fast."

"I ran," the boy said, breathless. "I wanted to get the best seat so I can see everything you do."

"You should be able to. What's your name, son?"

"Freddie. I got one of those animals you made. I wanna see how you do it."

"Ah, yes. You're the one who asked Mama Tess what I'll be making."

Callie walked down the row behind the lad and leaned close. "If you like working with wood, we can ask her to let you come help us one day. You'll learn a lot from Mr. Chip. He's very good."

Admiration *and* compliments? Was Callie sincere, or was she teasing him?

He had no time to ponder the question because the other children entered the large room and took their seats on the benches. Jasper squeezed in next to Luke. A group leader had to settle a minor scuffle as two young fellows vied for the same spot, but as soon as Tess stepped into the center and clapped, everyone quieted.

The tall woman smiled. "Thank you all for seeing to the after-dinner chores so quickly. Now you'll get to watch Mr. Chip make something special. He won't be able to finish it tonight, but he'll get as far as he can. I'm sure you'll have lots of questions, but he'll need to concentrate, so you'll have to save them until the end."

Freddie's eagerness to learn had overcome Chip's concerns about keeping the children quiet. "I remember having a hard time holding questions inside when I was a boy, so, if you're agreeable, they can ask their questions while I'm working."

"Very well." Tess turned her attention back to the children. "You may raise your hand to ask a question just as you will when you make a guess about what Mr. Chip's making, but wait for me to call on you before speaking."

Freddie's hand shot into the air.

Tess chuckled. "He hasn't even begun yet, Freddie. What do you want to know?"

"That chunk of wood on your table is really big, Mr. Chip. How can you make a little animal out of it?"

"This—" he patted the large round of white pine "—is for the statue I'll be carving. I use small pieces of wood and different tools when I whittle a toy."

Callie spoke up. "Would you be willing to show us, if it wouldn't take too long?"

"Sure. I could whip out a small figure in no time." And he knew just the one he'd make. He grabbed a scrap of white pine and his knife and set to work, sending chips flying.

"I have another request."

He paused and looked at Callie. "Yes?"

"If you could talk as you work, we'd all understand what you're doing."

Talk and carve at the same time? He'd never done that, but he could give it a try. "I'll do my best." He kept his hands moving as he explained the process. "I'm using a knife to remove all the wood that isn't part of the figure. That sounds simple, but that's really what it's about. I keep the image in mind and shave off everything that doesn't belong."

He continued, describing and demonstrating the four basic cuts as he worked. The children sat quietly with not a single hand going into the air. He was finished in no time. "Since Miss Callie asked me to make this little fellow, I'll give it to her, but I'm sure she'll pass it around so you can all see it." He handed her the creature.

She laughed. "Why, thank you, Mr. Chip. I'll think of you every time I look at this bullfrog."

One of the boys who'd been involved in the scuffle

piped up. "Why'd ya make a frog for her? Ladies don't like 'em."

Jasper rushed to her defense. "Miss Callie does. She even picks them up."

Chip hurried to take the focus off Callie. She was likely to bend his ear about his choice later. If he was correct, she'd had absolutely no intention of touching a frog that day and had mistaken it for a stone. He looked from Jasper to the other boy, who'd also spoken out of turn, and attempted a scowl, but he couldn't stifle his smile. "Gentlemen, I didn't see any hands go up, did I? I hope to soon, though, because I'm ready to start on the wood carving, and I look forward to hearing your guesses."

He began by tracing faint lines that wouldn't be visible to those on the benches and explained how they would be his guides. With his mallet in one hand, he tapped the handle of the chisel he held in the other. As before, he kept up a running dialogue.

A scant three minutes had passed when the first hand went up and Tess called for the guess. All he'd done so far was round off the top corners. "Is it a mountain?" a girl about Jasper's age asked.

"I'm afraid not."

He worked steadily but couldn't help stealing glances at Callie. Her interest rivaled Freddie's. She'd taken a seat on the end of a bench, with Ruby beside her, and was leaning forward, just as the curious boy was.

With Callie's lips parted like that, Chip thoughts wandered into dangerous territory, which wouldn't do. All it would take was one slip of the blade, and he could do irreparable damage. He dragged his gaze from her and returned his attention to the creation taking shape.

The guesses continued, none of them close. He'd been

hard at work for a good thirty minutes when another hand shot up, this one belonging to Luke's oldest sister. "It's going to be a cowboy sitting on a fence, isn't it?"

"You've come the closest so far, Lila. I'm impressed." Both Tess and her daughter beamed at his praise.

Another five minutes passed with not a single guess. He stopped and scanned the benches. With the children, their group leaders and a curious ranch hand or two, some sixty-five pairs of eyes were trained on him. The room was so quiet he could almost hear the children thinking.

He reached for a smaller gouge on the table behind him and turned back to his creation, stealing another look at Callie as he did. She smiled her encouragement and mouthed the words *keep going.* Her eagerness spurred him on.

As he began the telltale cuts that would reveal a key part of the sculpture, he anticipated more guesses coming soon. Sure enough, Freddie's wildly waving hand caught his eye. And was that Jasper with a hand raised, too?

Tess chuckled. "It appears we have a tie. I'd like you both to come up and tell me what you think it is." They joined her, taking turns whispering in her ear. She straightened and smiled. "We have two winners. I'll count to three, and you boys can say what it is together. One. Two. Three."

"Humpty Dumpty," they shouted in unison.

Callie began clapping, and the others joined in. Pride radiated from her, reminding him of Tess's response when he'd complimented her daughter earlier. He and Callie had only been caring for the children for several hours, and yet it was clear they'd already come to mean a great deal to her. She'd make a fine mother one day.

The Plan didn't call for him to find a wife to fill that role for three years yet, a fact he must keep in mind. But no harm could come from enjoying the company of his lovely assistant over the next few weeks, could it?

Chapter Four

Ruby sneezed.

"God bless you, sweetheart! Here. You can use my handkerchief, if you need to." Callie pulled the lace-edged square from her sleeve.

"I'm all wight. My nose just tickled." The little girl rubbed it with the back of her hand.

"Sawdust can do that, and there's plenty of it in here. Mr. Chip has been working very hard."

Callie looked around the large woodshop. Stacks of boards rested in neat piles. Some were waiting to be cut, others had been planed and a fair number were sanded and ready to be oiled before being assembled into bed frames.

Her gaze lingered on the handsome carpenter as he kept his saw busy—and his muscular biceps flexing. The steady rasp as he sliced through the pine planks kept time with the rapid beating of her heart. At the rate Chip was going, he'd have the first order of furniture for the new dormitory built in no time. She wasn't in any hurry. He was fun to be around, and he was so good with the children. She dragged her attention from him.

Jasper raced up to her on a stick horse. He'd whooped and hollered when Tess had dropped by with it the day before. He stroked the horse's cinnamon-colored yarn mane. "I know what I'm gonna name him. Gingersnap, 'cause he's the same color as one of them cookies we had after lunch. Do you like it?"

Callie smiled. "It's a fine name."

Chip paused, saw in hand. "I like it, too. You could call him Snap for short."

Jasper tilted his head. "Like a nickname?"

"That's right. Miss Callie has one. Her full name is Caroline."

Callie seized the opportunity to learn what his name was. "What is Chip short for? Christopher, Charles or something else?"

Chip shook his head. "None of those. My name is really Sebastian. The first carpenter I worked for when I was a boy of ten, a Scotsman, said it was too much of a mouthful for a laddie like me since I was no bigger than a wood chip. He called me Chip, and the name stuck."

"It suits you. Thanks for telling me. We're keeping you from your work, though." She held out a hand to Ruby. "We should find something else to do while Mr. Chip gets the next batch of boards cut. Let's see if Mr. Isaac has time to lead you around on the pony, shall we?"

The thumping of Jasper's stick horse on the wooden floorboards as he rode around the room came to an abrupt halt. "Mr. Chip don't need my help now. Can I go, too?"

"He *doesn't* need your help or ours just now, so I suppose you could join us." She leaned toward him, smiled and adopted a playful tone. "If you're interested in a riding lesson, that is."

"Yee-haw!" Jasper galloped over to them, one hand

holding the rope reins and the other swinging an imaginary lasso over his head. Ever since Jasper had seen the cattle on the day Chip and Callie brought him to the Double T, he'd been telling anyone willing to listen that he was going to be a cowboy when he grew up.

The room quieted. Chip stood with the saw hanging at his side and an exaggerated pout on his handsome face. "Are all my helpers going to abandon me?"

"Just for a short time. The children have spent the better part of three days in here with us. I understand why, but I thought some time outdoors would be good for them. Isaac mentioned that he would be free this afternoon and hinted rather strongly that he'd like to meet Jasper and Ruby."

"I see." Chip crossed the room in a few strides, wearing a smile. "And you're going to take your brother up on his offer and leave me here to slave away on my own, are you?" He heaved an exaggerated sigh. "Good help is so hard to come by."

Callie chuckled. "Since we really can't do much to help at this point, I figured you might appreciate having some time to yourself. Without distractions."

"Ah, but these are the best kind of distractions." He ruffled the children's blond heads. And winked at her.

Chip's impulsive gesture didn't mean anything. He was just being his usual engaging self, but even so, a shiver of delight raced up her spine.

His brow furrowed. "Are you cold?"

"Not at all." With him standing so close, she could smell the masculine mix of wood, linseed oil and sunshine that was Chip. Even better, she had a good excuse to look into his intriguing eyes, a far deeper blue than her own, with golden circles around the centers. Those eyes widened, and she realized she was staring. "You'll be fine without us for an hour or so, won't you?"

"No. I'll miss you something fierce, but I'll manage somehow."

She laughed and gave his arm a playful swat. "Oh, you."

Jasper gazed up at her, his brow furrowed. "Why did you hit him, Miss Callie?"

She'd momentarily forgotten about their young chaperones. "I didn't hit him. I just swatted him. Mr. Chip was teasing me, and I was teasing him back. That's all. But you're right. Hitting isn't a good thing. We should get on over to the corral. We'll see you when we return, Chip."

"You might see me sooner than that. I could use a break myself."

"We'd like that." She certainly would, more than he knew.

"Then I'll definitely join you." He flashed her a smile that held the promise of an enjoyable time to come. She had to force herself not to skip down the path.

Minutes later Callie stood outside the corral fence watching Isaac lead Ruby around on a pony. Callie's brother didn't let his war injury hold him back, but he still had trouble with loud noises or altercations of any kind between adults. He was fine with children, though, because, as he said, they posed no threat. He'd certainly overcome Ruby's hesitation in a hurry. The little girl was actually smiling.

Jasper waited beside Callie, his feet on the middle rung of the slat fence and his hands gripping the top one. "How long do I gotta wait for my turn?"

"Until Ruby's done. It won't be long now." Footfalls from behind caught her attention.

Tess approached them, with her hands behind her back and a smile on her face. "Since you want to be a cowboy one day, Jasper, you'll be needing one of these." She held out a small cowboy hat.

Jasper's eyes grew as round as wagon wheels. He took the hat and plopped it on his head.

Callie leaned close. "What do you say?"

He beamed at Tess. "Thank you."

"I'm glad you like it. The Double T is a good place for boys like you. Papa Spencer and his ranch hands can teach you everything there is to know about raising cattle."

Isaac led the pony up to the fence beside them. "This little lady had a nice ride. It's her brother's turn now."

"Yee-haw!" Jasper cringed and clamped a hand over his mouth.

Tess's forehead furrowed. "What's wrong?"

Callie rested a hand on the remorseful boy's shoulder. "He remembered that we're not supposed to make loud noises around horses. Isn't that right, Jasper?"

He bobbed his head.

Isaac passed Ruby to Callie and smiled at Jasper. "Sounds like you're well on your way to being a good cowboy then, but you need to learn how to ride a horse. Let's get you on the back of that pony, shall we?"

In no time, Jasper's lesson was underway. Ruby sat on a bale of hay near Callie playing with her beloved doll, giving Callie time alone with Tess.

Tess watched Isaac instructing Jasper. "I never of tire of seeing your brother sharing his love of horses with the little ones. He's come so far."

"I'm glad to hear it. Isaac witnessed carnage such as I can't begin to imagine. I look forward to the day he can break free from the shadows of the past and fully embrace the present."

Compassion shone from Tess's eyes. "Every person who arrives at the Double T has been wounded in some way and bears scars. While most of us eventually move beyond the traumas and tragedies that have come our way, some people have a harder time of it. The best we can do is love, support and encourage them, all the while praying that the Lord will work His healing."

A peal of childish laughter rang out, drawing Callie's eye. Isaac had said something that tickled Jasper. Tess was right. Isaac had made good progress at the Double T. One day he would be free of the mental anguish that plagued him, and she would rejoice. "I can't thank you enough for giving Isaac a job and a purpose."

"We're blessed to have him. I'm thankful he's brought you to us, as well. You're a wonderful addition to our happy family."

Tess excused herself and left, passing Chip, who was coming Callie's way.

He ambled up beside her, rested his folded arms on the top rung of the fence and watched Isaac and Jasper. "Our boy's doing well, isn't he?"

Our boy. The words sent a surge of longing through Callie. She could imagine the day when she had a husband like Chip and children like Jasper and Ruby. "He is. Just look at his grin."

"The hat's a nice touch. Another gift from Tess, I presume?"

"Yes. The caring woman has six children of her own and two dorms full, as well, but she makes time for all of them and knows just what will make each of them happy. If I'm blessed with children one day, I want to be that kind of mother."

"I'm sure you will."

His words warmed her, but she couldn't help thinking of the diagnosis that had destroyed her dream of bearing children of her own. If only something could be done to fix whatever had gone wrong inside her...

Chip turned to face her, leaning against the fence with one boot heel hooked on the lowest rung and his arms extended along the top one, a masculine stance that made him even more appealing. "If I recall correctly, you said Isaac looked forward to raising horses but is no longer able to ride himself, at least not without pain."

She smiled. "Your attentiveness speaks to your character, as does your tactfulness in not mentioning his limp or...the other thing he deals with."

"I have nothing but respect for the men who served. Many of them suffered—and are suffering still. You must be happy he's found a job he enjoys."

"Indeed, but what makes me happiest is that I located him. It took two years, but I did it."

Chip raised an eyebrow. "He didn't tell you where he was?"

"Because of his condition, he didn't want to be a burden, so he headed to California after the war. I'd get a postcard from him every now and then, each one from a different location here in the Gold Country, but that was all. I came west to search for him." She glanced at Isaac, smiled at the obvious delight on her brother's face and retuned her attention to Chip. "What he didn't know was that he could never be a burden. He's not just my brother. He's my only living relative. He's also a good friend."

"I can see why you were determined to find him. Nothing is as important as family."

"It must be so hard not to have any of yours left. When did you lose the last one?"

"When I was nine. We were headed West when cholera ripped through our wagon train, and we all took ill. The disease claimed all five of them in the space of one week."

"Oh, Chip, I'm so sorry. I wouldn't have brought it up if—" She followed his gaze, shocked to discover her hand resting on his arm. She pulled it away and hid it in the folds of her skirt. "F-forgive me."

"Please, don't feel badly. You had no way of knowing."

How kind of him to intentionally misinterpret her apology. "How did you survive?"

"I used this." He tapped his head. "People were saying the water had gone bad, and that's what caused the cholera. Once I was on my own, I noticed that the single men who sat around the campfire drinking coffee with Cookie hadn't gotten sick. I figured maybe something about boiling the water before drinking it made a difference, or maybe it was something in the coffee itself. I asked the old fellow if he'd bring me some in exchange for food from my family's supplies, which he did."

"I'm surprised you liked it. Most children don't care for the taste."

"I couldn't stand it." He shuddered at the memory. "Cookie put a pinch of salt in each pot to take out the bitterness, but it didn't do any good as far as I could tell. I added a good deal of sugar, and that helped me choke it down. I can't stomach coffee to this day, but according to Dr. Wright up in Placerville, it's probably what saved my life."

"Coffee? Really?"

"The sugar mostly. He'd read an article from a medical journal about a sugar treatment for cholera when he was in college. Seems I stumbled onto the cure myself. He said the boiled coffee probably helped, too. He boils his instruments because studies have shown fewer infections occur among the patients whose doctors employ that practice. Whatever it was, it worked."

"I'm glad. The Lord's used you to do a lot of good." Chip had no idea how much she knew about his philanthropic endeavors, so she wouldn't embarrass him by elaborating.

He shrugged. "I'm just doing my job."

And doing it well. He was not only hardworking and humble, but he was also ambitious. Many carpenters were content to spend their years framing houses, laying floors and putting on roofs. Not Chip. He'd begun as a carpenter but had gone on to become a joiner, too, enabling him to install a building's doors, windows and stairs. She'd learned over their memorable lunch that he'd arranged to spend several months working with a furniture maker three years ago, adding that skill to his repertoire.

What he'd neglected to tell her was that he would be heading up north for six months to work with a friend who specialized in sideboards and china cabinets. His farewell on his way out of town had come as a surprise. But he was here now, standing beside her and looking as winsome as ever. "Speaking of your job… I've been meaning to ask if the training you received up in Oregon was as beneficial as you'd hoped?"

Eagerness shone from his dark blue eyes. "Very much so. I'm eager to put everything I learned to work and complete the kitchen and dining room at my place. Once I do, I'll be able to move forward with The Plan."

"The Plan? What plan is that?"

"This one." He pulled a worn piece of paper out of his pocket and handed it to her.

She hesitated. "Are you sure you want me to see this?"

"Sure. It's just a list of goals I came up with when I turned eighteen. I've been ticking them off right on schedule ever since. Open it and see for yourself."

The pride in his voice piqued her curiosity. She unfolded the sheet and studied it. Chip had listed the year and his corresponding age down one side. Next to each of the twelve entries were two goals, which would take him all the way to age thirty. They began with "become a carpenter in my own right" and "purchase basic tools" and ended with "increase savings" and "have first child."

She looked up from the page. "So you're twenty-five and have already done everything you'd intended to up to this point?"

"I have. What do you think?" He'd resumed his casual pose, leaning against the fence, but the drumming his fingers against the top rail showed his eagerness to hear her answer.

"I'm impressed. In addition to learning joinery and furniture making, you've bought your quarter horse, Dusty, your workhorses and your wagon, along with a piece of property. You've also built your house, most of the furniture in it and a barn. As you said, all that's left is to complete those last two rooms, and you'll be ready to take the next steps."

"Correct. Now you know why I've been working so hard. The best is yet to come. I'll have the family I've dreamed of ever since I was nine."

That wouldn't happen for quite a while since The Plan didn't call for him to begin courting for three more years—after he'd added some unspecified amount to his savings in order to "ensure that my family is well provided for."

She cast a glance at Ruby. Assured that she was fine, Callie continued. "When I asked earlier how you survived, what I was really wanted to know was who took you in and how you fared with them."

"And I filled your ears with the tale of my remarkable recovery. Sorry about that." He gave her an apologetic smile.

"I'm glad you told me, but I am curious about the other."

He averted his gaze and drew circles on the ground with the toe of his boot. "I spent a few years with a carpenter once I reached California—the one who gave me the nickname. He taught me everything he knew, and I moved on. I found a few other woodworkers who were willing to take me in, and I gleaned what I could from them, too."

Clearly, there was more to his story, but she could understand why he wouldn't want to talk about it. "You've done remarkably well for someone who's been on his own for so long."

His head came up. He moistened his lips, which drew her attention to them. What would it be like to feel them against hers?

You have no business thinking about that, Callie. Get a hold of yourself.

"I can see why family is so important to you and understand why your upcoming goals are related to that, but I'm sure you realize they're different than the ones that came before."

"What do you mean?"

She chose her words carefully. "All of your goals to this point were, to a certain extent, under your control. A number of those coming up—find a woman to court, marry and have children with—aren't. You might find a lady you'd like to court, but she might not be interested in you." Although the possibility of a woman being able to resist Chip's many appealing characteristics seemed unlikely, it *could* happen.

He laughed. "Not that I'm vain or anything, but I don't think that will be a problem. I work hard, and I'm not bad looking."

Certainly not, but there was more to it. "Suppose the lady who captures your eye realizes what a wonderful man you are and marries you according to your plan. There's no guarantee children will come along according to schedule, is there? It seems to me the Lord would have a hand in that. Wouldn't you agree?"

All signs of amusement drained from his face. "You have a point, but He knows how much having a family of my own means to me. I see no need to alter The Plan. May I have it back, please?" He held out his hand, and she placed the paper in it.

Chip wasn't just regimented. He was resolute. "I didn't mean to upset you."

"I'm not upset." His curt response said otherwise. "I just thought you'd understand."

"I do. I'd like nothing better than for things to happen the way you want, but sometimes the Lord surprises us. You could meet a woman you fancy ahead of schedule. If that happened, you wouldn't want to miss out on the opportunity to have her in your life because she came along too soon, would you?"

"Mr. Chip! Miss Callie!" Jasper sat on the pony holding the reins while Isaac limped along beside him. "Can you see? I'm riding all on my own."

Chip spun toward the corral and smiled, once again his good-natured self. "You sure are. That's great."

Callie waved at Jasper. "You're doing so well."

Conversation turned to the children, to Chip's apparent relief. Not that she could fault him for avoiding her probing questions. She'd challenged his way of viewing the world. Due to the tragic loss he'd suffered years before, his need to exert control over his life made sense. She'd experienced the same compulsion after losing her parents, but in her case, it had been short-lived. She turned to the Lord and trusted Him to look out for her, as He always had. He provided the dearest couple to take her in. The Marshalls had lavished her with loving care, until they'd received their heavenly rewards. She hoped Chip could find peace in spite of his past, as she had.

Isaac helped Jasper off the pony and led it to the barn. The beaming boy strode over to Chip and Callie and slipped between the fence slats. He puffed out his chest. "I'm gonna be a good cowboy. Mr. Isaac said so."

"I'm sure you will," Chip said. "We should get back now. I had to use a plane while you were gone, so there are shavings to be picked up. I know just the young fellow to help with that."

"Yes! I can get more of 'em for my collection." He took off running.

"Whoa, there, Jasper! Let's walk like cowboys."

Jasper returned and gazed up at Chip. "How do we do that?"

"Like this." Chip hooked his thumbs in his pockets and demonstrated the loose-limbed, wide-legged swagger many associated with ranch hands. Callie couldn't take her eyes off him. He'd never looked as cute—or as appealing.

If only she didn't have that dreadful diagnosis to contend with. The trouble was that the longer she knew Chip, the more she liked him—and the more convinced she was that a woman like her would never interest him. He was set on having children of his own, and all indications were that she couldn't bear a child. Maybe someday she'd find a man willing to consider alternative ways of forming a family, but Chip wasn't that man. The sooner she accepted that, the better. To hold out false hope could only lead to heartache.

Chapter Five

When Tess had first suggested Callie as his helper, Chip questioned the idea. After only one week, he could see the wisdom behind Tess's plan. Callie worked as hard as he did, and she knew a great deal. He recalled the day he'd asked her for his jack plane, prepared to describe it so she could choose the right plane from the three different ones he'd brought with him. Before he could get the words out, she'd reached in his toolbox and pulled out the jack plane.

Callie looked up from her sanding to check on the children. Ruby, looking as sorrowful as ever, sat off by herself playing with her doll. Despite their attempts to draw her out, the little girl had retreated inside herself. Even exuberant Jasper could rarely bring about a smile.

Chip could relate. Once he'd recovered from the cholera enough to walk instead of bouncing around in the back of a wagon, he'd trudged along, keeping to himself and speaking only when spoken to. Not that anyone noticed. The disease had robbed nearly every family in the wagon train of at least one member, so a sullen boy was the least of their concerns.

He hefted another board onto his workbench, grabbed his crosscut saw and drew it across the grain of the pine with practiced ease. A breeze through the open windows sent the sawdust that coated the plank floor swirling. Memories of a windy spring day from his boyhood rushed in—his parents watching as their sons took turns trying to get a kite to soar, laughter as it swooped to earth, knocking his father's hat off, and joyful shouts as Jeremiah, the youngest, finally got the fickle thing airborne.

As he completed the cut, an idea formed. He had some wood that would make a suitable spine and cross spar. He had plenty of string, and Tess was sure to have some tissue paper that would make a kite sail. He put his saw away and went outside to his scrap pile behind the woodshop, where he located a small, thin board.

Jasper joined him. "What are you doing, Mr. Chip?"

He straightened, holding the strip of wood. "I'm going to build a kite. Have you ever flown one before?"

"No, but I seen one. A big boy made it go way high up. Can we do that?"

"We'll try."

Jasper raced inside ahead of Chip, his boots pounding on the wooden floor as he made straight for Callie. "Mr. Chip's gonna make a kite, and I'm gonna fly it."

Callie ceased her sanding. "A kite? That sounds like fun. Don't you think so, Ruby?"

The little girl sat cross-legged as she leaned against the wall several feet away, absorbed in her doll. She didn't even look up.

"Ruby!" Jasper clomped over to his sister, his fists jammed against his waist. "Didn't you hear us talking to you?"

Ever so slowly, she lifted her head, revealing tear-streaked cheeks. "Go 'way, Jaspy."

The boy's irritation evaporated. He dropped to the floor beside her and draped an arm across her shoulders and held her close. "I'm sorry you're sad, Ruby. Are you missing Papa?"

She nodded and mumbled something indiscernible.

Jasper glanced at Chip and returned his attention to his sister. "But he's a nice man."

A vise clamped down on Chip's chest. Ruby had accepted Callie, but apparently she hadn't warmed to him as much as he'd thought. He didn't have experience with little girls, but he had to try to overcome her hesitation.

He crossed the room and dropped to one knee. Ruby's eyes widened, and she drew even closer to Jasper. "I won't hurt you, princess. I'd like to help. What do you need?"

Her chin trembled. "I need my papa, but you didn't bwing him back."

The vise tightened. "I wanted to, believe me. I know how much it hurts to lose a papa. I lost mine when I wasn't much older than Jasper."

Her brow furrowed, and she studied him with narrowed eyes. "Did it make you cwy?"

"No."

Jasper tilted his head, one eyebrow raised. "Never? Not even one time?"

Since Chip couldn't squeeze any words past the lump lodged in his throat, he shook his head. He hadn't shed a single tear, but he had spent many a night reliving that agonizing week when he'd lost every member of his family. Once he woke from the heart-rending dreams, he would lay in the dark begging God to rid him of the tortuous memories. At first, the all-too-vivid images had invaded his sleep every night, but as the years passed, the nightmares had become less frequent. He hadn't been plagued by one in several months.

The inquisitive boy persisted. "What if you was to think about your papa and what happened to him? Would you cry then?"

"I don't think so." He didn't have any desire to find out.

A swish of skirts was followed by the gentle pressure of Callie's hand as she rested it on his shoulder. Her silent show of support helped chase away the shadows of the past.

"Some people don't cry when they lose a loved one, but some do," she said. "I lost my mama and papa when I was about Luke's age, and I soaked my pillow every night for two whole weeks. But I started feeling better after a while, and you will, too."

Jasper jutted out his chin. "I'm not crying. I'm being good and taking care of Ruby." He patted his sister's arm.

Callie's voice was soft and soothing. "You're a wonderful brother, but Ruby can still be sad. She might even feel like crying sometimes, and that's all right. Mr. Chip and I are here for you. If the sad feelings come and you'd like a grown-up to hold you, you can come to us."

Chip was quick to agree. "Miss Callie's right. You might need a hug every now and then, but sometimes you might want to have fun. Jasper wants to fly a kite. Would you like to do that, too, princess?"

Ruby peered at him through damp lashes. "I'm not a pwincess. I'm just a girl."

"A very special girl. And I think you would be a big help with the kite building. I'll need someone with small fingers to spread the glue, and I think yours are just the right size."

She held up her hand and looked from her splayed fingers to him. "Weally?"

"Sure. I'll show you." He grabbed a pair of his calipers and took turns measuring his fingers, Callie's, Jasper's and Ruby's.

His task complete, he turned to Ruby. "I have the proof now. Yours are the best fingers for the job."

Ruby produced the barest hint of a smile. The vise squeezing Chip's chest opened a little, and he drew in a deep breath scented with Callie's floral cologne, sawdust and hope.

A good hour later, Chip slipped his watch into his waistcoat pocket. Although he was falling behind schedule, the time had been well spent. Not only did they have a brightly colored kite completed, but Ruby had also actually helped build it. Better yet, she'd said a few words.

Jasper surveyed their creation. "Can we fly it now?"

"Not just yet. The glue has to dry first."

The impatient boy folded his arms and stuck out his lower lip in a pronounced pout. "I don't wanna wait."

Callie came to Chip's aid. "But waiting will give us time to do something else that's fun." Trust her to look for the positive.

Jasper was quick to challenge her. "What?"

"Well—" she looked around the room "—we could sweep. You like doing that, don't you?"

He shook his head. "Not now. There aren't any curls."

Chip smiled. He'd called shavings the same thing when he was young. "You're right, but we can fix that. I'll teach Miss Callie how to use my jack plane, and then there will be plenty of curls."

Callie spun to face him, her pretty pink lips parted. "Really? I thought you wanted me to continue with the sanding."

"You can do that, too, but you've been at it for days. I figured you'd welcome a change." And he'd welcome the opportunity to teach her.

Chip placed a board from the scrap pile on one of the two student workbenches and stuck a steel bench dog into a hole at each end to hold the board in place. Callie stood close by, listening intently as he explained how to make sure the plane was properly adjusted, while Jasper watched from a safe distance. Ruby plunked herself down several feet away, absorbed in her doll.

Once Callie had mastered setting the steel edge of the plane iron so just the right amount of blade protruded for the job, Chip demonstrated how to use the tool. "It's important to keep the plane level. If it's not, you could remove more at the ends of the stroke than you do in the middle."

He held out the plane to her. "Go ahead and give it a try."

"I'll do my best." With tool in hand, she approached the board—at an angle. The plane skipped and stuttered as she guided it along the face of the board, leaving the surface rippled. She extended her lower lip and blew out a puff of air, fluttering the stray hairs that framed her lovely face, a cute gesture that had him hiding his smile. "You make it look so easy, but it's harder than I thought. Oh, well. I'll get it soon enough. You'll see."

"What you're experiencing is called chatter. It's common with beginners, but with practice, you'll smooth out your strokes." He'd give her the opportunity to make some corrections herself, and then he'd offer some suggestions.

She made two more attempts, her efforts yielding the same result, and turned to him. Her sigh of resignation was followed by a chuckle. "Evidently, I'm doing something wrong. Would you please tell me what it is?"

Her eagerness to learn was impressive, as was her willingness to admit when she needed help. "You're holding the plane level from side to side, which is important, but you have to keep it level front to back, too. I could show you, if you'd like."

"By all means." She held out the plane.

"You keep it, and I'll guide your hands. If that's all right with you," he quickly added.

Several seconds passed before she sent him one of her warm smiles, enabling him to breathe again.

"Please show me." She took her place beside the workbench, rested the plane on the board's face and awaited instruction.

"Go ahead and grip the knob and tote, er, rear handle."

She did so. "Like this?"

"Actually, I find it helps to hold the tote with three fingers and extend the index finger alongside the frog, like so."

Jasper scoffed. "That's not a frog."

"Not a real frog, no, but this angled part of the plane the blade rests against—" Chip pointed to it "—is called that."

"Why?" Jasper asked.

"I don't know. It just is."

Callie chuckled. "Probably because a man named it. A frog-loving man. Or boy." She smiled at Jasper.

Chip whispered in her ear. "I gather you're not fond of them yourself."

She smirked and whispered back, "Whatever gave you that idea?"

"Don't worry. Your secret's safe with me." He proceeded with the lesson, preventing a retort. "Two more things that will help are to put more pressure on the knob and to skew the plane so your hands are in a more natural position. Go ahead and hold it, and I'll show you."

She faced the workbench and grasped the tool in her hands. He adjusted her grip on the tote and the angle of the plane on the board. "That feels more natural, doesn't it?"

She nodded. "I suppose so."

"I'm going to place my hands over yours now and guide them so you can feel what it's like to make a smooth pass over the surface." He stepped close and reached around her. Unlike his callused hands, hers were soft and smooth and delightfully feminine. And she smelled nice, like spring. *Focus, Evans, or you'll make a mess of the cut.*

Although three or four passes would have sufficed, he stretched the lesson as long as he could. It had been ages since he'd enjoyed having a woman so close. He relished the feel of Callie's hands beneath his and her hair tickling his cheek as they moved the plane.

She glanced over her shoulder. "I think I have it now. If you don't mind, I'd like to try it on my own again."

He forced himself to step away and watched her work. She was a quick learner, producing gossamer-thin shavings the full width of the blade. Jasper crept closer, his eyes on the growing pile of them. Chip scooped up some and dropped them in the boy's outstretched hands.

"Thanks, Mr. Chip. I'm gonna see which one is the longest, and then I'll crunch them up. I love that sound."

So did he, along with the steady *zvish zvish* of the

plane as Callie scraped it over the face of the board. But it was time to move her from practice to actual planing.

Chip positioned a seventy-four-inch-long piece of pine on his workbench between two iron bench dogs, holding it snuggly in place. If only his feet were as securely planted, but after being so close to Callie, his world was a bit off-kilter. Not that he minded.

She set to work, and he returned to his sawing. He'd be glad to have that task behind him so he could assemble the bed frames and get started on the wardrobes.

They'd been at it some time when Ruby padded over to him, standing well away from the work area, as he'd taught her. "I think the gwue is dry, Mr. Chip."

No doubt she'd learn to say all her words correctly before long, but he'd enjoy her cute way of talking while it lasted. "Is it now? Well, that's a good thing, because I could use a break. What about you, Miss Callie?"

"Just a minute. I've almost got this board done. I'd like to finish."

"Let's watch, shall we, princess?" Ruby didn't shy away from him, so he picked her up and moved to where they could see Callie in action.

Callie's confidence had grown. She moved the plane over the board with impressive skill for one who'd only been doing so for such a short time. Seeing her engrossed in a job that brought him such satisfaction filled him with pride. He'd learned when he met her during her days working at the Blair brothers' lumberyard that she shared his love of wood. That contented smile as she ran a hand over the smooth surface showed she enjoyed woodworking, too.

She turned to him, her eyes alight. "I think it's nearly done. Do you want to check?"

"Sure." He set Ruby down, got his straight edge and moved it over the board. "It looks good, all except for this one high spot. I'll mark it, and you can take it off." He pulled a pencil out of his apron, outlined the raised area and filled it in with some scribbles.

Callie set to work and, in no time, completed the task. "I can see why you like working with wood. It's such fun."

He chuckled. "You might not say that when you've been standing over a workbench for hours, but I agree. Just wait until we assemble that first piece and you can see it all come together."

"I look forward to that."

Jasper left his pile of shavings, joined them and gazed up at Chip, wearing a scowl. "I been waiting and waiting. Can we fly the kite now?"

"Yes."

"Yee-haw!" The boy galloped around the shop on a make-believe horse.

"I'll get the kite." Callie picked it up from the third workbench and grinned. "I've never flown one before, so this will be fun. Let's go." She took hold of Jasper's hand, dashed out of the room and skipped down the path toward the field with childlike glee.

Chip followed with Ruby in his arms, eagerness putting a spring in his step. Callie wasn't the woman for him, having come into his life a full three years before he was ready to establish a courtship, and Jasper and Ruby weren't his children, but when he was with the three of them, he could envision the future he'd had in mind when created The Plan. If the family God gave him brought him even half as much joy, he'd be a happy man.

Before that could happen, though, he had to finish

his house and increase his savings. Unlike his father, he wouldn't start a family before he could adequately provide for them. If his pa had waited, he would have been better able to provide for his wife and sons and wouldn't have been as likely to fall prey to the promises of a better life out in California. And Chip wouldn't have lost them all.

The Plan was there for a reason. He couldn't forget that, no matter how much he enjoyed Callie's company.

Callie's first week at the Double T hadn't gone the way she'd expected, but it had turned out to be a blessing. The Lord had entrusted her with the care of two precious children, given her the job of her dreams and arranged for her to work alongside a talented carpenter with a heart of gold.

She stood next to Chip in a field well away from the buildings and trees as he squatted in front of the children and explained what was involved in flying a kite. He dealt patiently with Jasper's endless questions and managed to coax a few words out of reticent Ruby.

Since Chip hadn't grabbed his hat, the wind riffled his thick brown hair. She fought the urge to run her fingers through it. As she'd anticipated, working alongside the handsome man was a distraction. The plane had stuttered over the board on her first pass, echoing the stuttering of her heart.

As if him watching her work wasn't challenging enough, he'd reached around her, placing his large, work-roughened hands over hers and sending a shiver shimmying up her spine. Since he hadn't mentioned her reaction, she hoped he hadn't noticed. As hard as she tried to fight her attraction, she couldn't.

Chip straightened and continued his instructions to the children. "Before we try to get the kite in the air, we have to find out which direction the wind's coming from. The first one to figure it out gets to hold the kite as we attempt to send it sailing."

Jasper piped up with a question posthaste. "How can we tell?"

"Like this." Chip wet the tip of a finger and held it up. "The side that feels cool is the one the wind's coming from."

Jasper stuck a finger in his mouth, pulled it out with a pop and stuck it in the air. He turned it this way and that, frowned and folded his arms. "That don't work."

"I have another idea." Chip plucked a few blades of California bunch grass from a clump nearby. "If you let the pieces of grass go, they should fly off in the opposite direction that the wind's coming from. Why don't you try it with me?"

Both children yanked generous handfuls of grass. Ruby flung hers in the air, and they drifted to the ground.

Jasper held out his hand at his side as Chip did and released the grass slowly. The pieces fluttered toward the hills at the eastern edge of the field. The eager boy smiled and pointed to the west. "The wind is coming from there."

Chip nodded. "Sure is. Since you guessed correctly, you can stand with your back to the wind, hold the kite by its bridle the way I showed you, let out a little line and see if it will take off."

The eager boy grabbed the kite as instructed, promptly let it go and grimaced when it fell to the ground. "It don't work."

"Not that way, it doesn't." Chip lips twitched, but he

didn't laugh. Callie admired his restraint. "I have an idea. You hold it here at the bottom, like this." He positioned Jasper's hand at the lowest point of the diamond. "I'll take the spool of string and walk a few feet back, and we'll try again."

Once Chip was in position, he instructed Jasper to hold the kite as high as he could. "Now we have to wait for a gust to come along. When it does, I'll tell you to let go, so listen carefully."

A stiff breeze buffeted Callie.

"Let go!"

Jasper obliged, and Chip managed to get the kite aloft. It swooped wildly and came crashing to the ground.

Ruby rushed over. "It's not broke, is it?"

Chip grabbed the colorful kite and inspected it. "That was a close call, but it appears to be fine. We'll try again, but it's your turn to hold it, princess."

Moments later, the two of them were in place. The wind picked up, Ruby released the kite, Chip fed out line and the kite rose into the cloudless sky.

Jasper thumped his sister on the back, his eyes shining with brotherly pride. "You done it, Ruby! It's flying."

The little girl shielded her eyes from the sun and watched the kite ascend. "It's high up."

"And getting higher." Callie scooped Ruby into her arms, balanced the girl on one hip and watched as Chip let out the line, causing the kite to climb rapidly.

Jasper gazed at Chip with admiration. "You're a real good kite flyer, Mr. Chip. Could you show me how to get it up higher?"

"Sure." Chip dropped to one knee. "Stand in front of me and hold on to the line."

Ruby whispered in Callie's ear.

"Of course you can have a turn, sweetheart, right after Jasper."

Chip invited Ruby over a few minutes later. Callie sat on a knoll and watched. He took his time with each of the children, patiently answering Jasper's many questions and offering softly spoken reassurances to Ruby. She said little, but she did look at him with glowing eyes when he paid her compliments, which he often did. What a wonderful father he would be.

Callie smiled at the memory of the pride shining from Chip's deep blue eyes when he'd handed her the well-worn sheet with his yearly goals written on it in his bold script. The Plan had served him well, but he could be setting himself up for disappointment.

Love and children didn't come along according to schedule, at least not from what her two friends she'd come west with had told her. Becky hadn't expected to fall in love with James O'Brien when she'd begun caring for his ailing mother, and yet she had. Now she had a home of her own, two adorable children and a thriving bakery business. Jessie certainly hadn't thought that her boss and make-believe beau, Flynt Kavanaugh, would become her real-life husband, but they were married now and busy establishing their own engineering firm.

Chip left the children gripping the string together and sauntered over to Callie. "It's your turn to fly the kite."

She took the hand he offered, and he pulled her to her feet. They stood inches apart, their hands still linked. His was warm and strong, his grip firm but gentle. She glanced up at him, hoping for a smile. Instead, his serious side had reappeared. His gaze swept over her face, coming to rest on…her mouth?

Was it possible Chip wanted to kiss her? What would

she do if he tried? Part of her wondered what it would feel like to have his lips pressed to hers, but the more sensible part—

"Don't you wanna fly it, Miss Callie?"

Jasper's question shattered the moment, which was for the best. Chip wasn't ready to court anyone. The trouble was that the more time she spent with him, the more she found herself drawn to him.

She slipped her hand from Chip's and produced what she hoped resembled a carefree smile. "Of course I do, Jasper."

In no time, she held the string in one hand and the reel in the other. The smooth cotton line passed easily between her fingers as she let out more. The kite bobbed high above.

"Careful that you don't feed too much too fast, or it could begin to loop."

No sooner had Chip finished speaking than the kite spun and began to dive. "It's going to crash! What do I do?"

"Let go of the line and take a few steps toward the kite." He grasped her elbow and ushered her forward. "There. That should do it."

"It is pretty high. Maybe I should reel it in a bit."

"I think it will be fine now."

The kite might, but being so close to Chip made concentration difficult. "Then perhaps I should turn it back over to the children. You'd like that, wouldn't you, Jasper?"

"Yep!" He relieved her of the spool and string.

The dinner bell rang twice, signaling the end of the school day. Children poured out of the schoolhouse, which Spencer and Tess had built to accommodate all the children at the Double T. Boys and girls descended on the playground. A lone figure ran toward them.

Freddie arrived breathless but beaming. He pushed out his request between gulps of air. "I saw…your kite. Can I…fly it?"

Chip's serious side took over. "Do you have permission to be here?"

The boy nodded. "Mama Tess said to come over and ask if I could help in the woodshop when you're done flying the kite. I've been hankering to help ever since you carved that Humpty Dumpty. Can I?"

A smile replaced Chip's stern expression. "If Mama Tess said it's all right, then it's fine with me. But first, Jasper, you'll give Freddie a turn, won't you?"

"Yep. Me and him will have fun."

Ruby had grown bored and found a spot nearby to hold an imaginary tea party with her beloved doll as her guest. Callie sat in the grass, close enough to watch the children, but far enough away to give the children a feeling of freedom. After their week spent indoors with constant supervision, they deserved some time to themselves.

Chip dropped down beside Callie. "I can't believe you'd never flown a kite before."

"Isaac and I didn't have a lot of freedom as children." That was an understatement.

"Strict parents?"

"Strict governess." She mentally kicked herself. The words had come out before she could stop them.

"I see."

How could he? She'd kept that part of her life to herself. "It's not what you think."

He gave her one of those lopsided smiles she found irresistible. "And what do I think?"

"I'm not a spoiled little rich girl. My father did well for himself, but he worked hard for his money." Too hard. He was consumed with expanding his business.

"Why the frown?"

She drew in a deep breath and forced herself to relax on the exhale. "I have a good life."

"But it wasn't always that way, was it?"

My, but he was perceptive. "Perhaps not, but the Lord provided. After our parents were ki—" No, she refused to dwell on that dark day. "After we lost our parents, a kindly couple took me in. Mom and Pop Marshall hadn't been able to have children of their own, and they doted on me. Isaac had already headed off to fight, but I spent six years with them. They were the best years of my life."

"Why did you leave?"

"I lost them both shortly after I turned eighteen. They left their cottage to the church so the congregation could make a parsonage out of it. I received enough to pay for my train fare to California and tide me over until I could find a job, so that's when I came in search of Isaac."

Chip scanned the area, checking on the children. Satisfied that they were all right, he continued. "And now you're working here with your brother. I'm glad you two have each other."

The wistfulness in his voice tugged at her heart. "I'm sorry you don't have anyone left, but you do have friends."

She reached for his hand, intending to give it a squeeze, but pulled hers back. Such a gesture could be seen as forward, and she didn't want give him the impression that she was harboring notions of anything more than friendship. Which she wasn't.

The thought of having a man like Chip in her life was appealing, but he'd made it clear he wasn't ready to welcome a woman into his heart. And there was the pesky matter of his desire to have children of his own that would keep him from considering her as someone he could court anyhow.

Chip studied her. "You have a way of finding something positive in even the bleakest of circumstances. I don't know how you do it."

She shrugged. "I suppose it's become a habit."

"You weren't always this way?"

"Dealing with the loss of one's parents has a way of changing a person. Wouldn't you agree?"

Something behind her drew his attention. He cupped his hands around his mouth. "Boys, come back this way."

Callie spun around. Jasper and Freddie were in plain sight. "They're fine. You worry too much."

"I'm being careful, and you should, too. George Tate's murderers are still out there."

"I know that, but it's been a week, and we've seen no sign on them. They've probably moved on."

Chip released a drawn-out sigh. "I didn't want to tell you, but one of Spencer's men spotted a stranger on the property. He went to investigate, but the fellow jumped on a horse and got away before the ranch hand reached him."

"How does he know the man was a stranger if he didn't get a good look at him? It could have been a neighboring rancher looking for a lost cow or something."

"The man was in the trees at the edge of the clearing over yonder." Chip pointed to the stand of oaks beyond the boys.

"Oh. Then I can see why you called them back, but

I still don't think it's wise to let the children know your suspicions. Jasper might be able to handle that information, but poor Ruby is upset enough as it is."

"We'll keep the concerns to ourselves for the time being, but we must be vigilant, Callie, for the children's sake. If anything were to happen to them, I'd never forgive myself."

Concern creased his brow. She reached up and ran her fingertips over the furrows. "Please, don't torment yourself. I'm sure they'll be fine."

He caught her hand in his and looked so deeply into her eyes that he was likely to see the effect he had on her. "I hope you're right, but promise me you'll be careful."

With him gazing at her like that, the danger she faced wasn't from nonexistent villains. It was from Chip himself. How was she to remain immune to his charms? And did she even want to?

Chapter Six

"Hurry up, Freddie," Jasper pleaded. "I wanna play on the seesaw again."

The young boy kept his focus on the board he was sanding. "I have to go slow so I don't ruin the board."

Callie leaned toward Chip, who was standing at his workbench, and spoke softly. "As if he could. That young fellow is as careful as you are. He'll make a fine carpenter one day." Freddie had come in every day for the past week as soon as the dinner bell signaled the end of classes.

Chip crunched the last bit of a peppermint and spoke beside her ear, his breath warm on her cheek. "You've done a wonderful job with him, and your patience with Jasper is admirable. There's no end to his questions, is there?"

She faced forward. Although the temptation to turn was great, doing so would put her so mere inches from Chip and his mint-scented mouth. She had a hard enough time not looking at his well-formed lips as it was. "He's a curious fellow, but he doesn't share Freddie's love of woodworking. I can't begin to count the number of times I've reminded Jasper to use long strokes and go with the grain. Your idea of having him work on the insides of the boards that will form the bed frames was wise. Since they won't show, he can't do any real harm. Besides, Freddie isn't satisfied to leave any of Jasper's uneven places. Doing so goes against his grain."

Chip chuckled. "Well said."

Callie took two steps back, putting distance between them, a necessity if she was to regain control of her wayward thoughts. "I'll pry Freddie away as soon as I can and take the children outside for a while."

"In the meantime, I have an idea that might get Jasper more interested in the job."

Leave it to Chip to come up with something. He had a real knack for knowing what Jasper would like. "What's that?"

The door to the woodshop opened, and Lila ran inside. "Miss Callie, Mama wants you to come to the house right away and bring Ruby with you."

"Do you know why?"

Tess's daughter shrugged. "She didn't tell me."

That was odd. "Please tell her we'll be right over."

Callie watched the slender girl race out the door and turned to Chip. "I wonder what that's about. You don't happen to know, do you?"

"Tess didn't say anything to me."

"Well, I'll find out soon enough." She crossed the room and held out a hand to Ruby. "Come with me, sweetheart. Mama Tess wants to see us."

The little girl stared at Callie's hand but made no move to take it. "I don't want to go."

"We have to. Please, take my hand."

Ruby shook her head.

"I'll have to carry you, then." Callie scooped the little girl into her arms, propped her on one hip and took off.

They'd made it past Jack and Jill House and were in front of Humpty Dumpty House when Ruby hollered—right in Callie's ear. "My baby!"

"I know how much you love your dolly, but I don't have time to go back for her."

"Pwease!"

The little girl's wobbly chin gave Callie pause. Surely another minute or two wouldn't make a difference. She turned and had taken all of five steps when Lila's voice stopped her.

"Miss Callie, where are you going? Mama's waiting."

Callie wheeled around. "We forgot something, but we'll get it later."

Tears streamed down Ruby's cheeks. The precious girl would just have to do without her doll for a few minutes. She buried her face in Callie's shoulder, soaking the calico.

Lila led them into the Abbotts' entryway. "I'll let Mama know you're here."

The girl slipped inside a room on the right, leaving Callie alone with Ruby. Several pairs of small shoes and a few toys littered the floor, signs of a house where children were welcome. A very large lady's hat sat on a wide shelf overhead.

Lila returned moments later with Tess right behind her. The young girl excused herself and disappeared into the dining room on the left. The table had eight place settings ready. Most nights the Abbotts ate in the dining hall with everyone else at the Double T, but Fridays were reserved for their family dinner.

"Thank you for coming so quickly, Callie."

"Is everything all right?"

Tess glanced at Ruby, who was still glued to Callie's

shoulder. The concern in Tess's eyes caused Callie to clutch Ruby even more tightly. "There's a woman inside who has come to inquire about adoption. She's looking for a young girl with blond hair like her own. I brought in two girls, but she wanted to see another."

Callie inhaled sharply. "You wouldn't separate siblings, would you?"

"It's not my practice, but I'd like you to meet the woman and tell me what you think."

"All right, but…" What else could she say? Tess was in charge.

"Good." Tess gave Callie's arm a reassuring pat and ran a hand over Ruby's curly locks.

Callie followed Tess into her parlor, a room decorated in slate blue with burgundy accents, the very colors of Tess's dress. A blond-haired woman with shifty eyes and a too-wide smile perched on an armless chair. She stared at Callie, or, more accurately, the crestfallen girl clinging to her.

Ruby wouldn't make a good impression in her current state, but that was for the best. Callie couldn't bear the thought of losing the precious girl. That day might come, but Ruby hadn't even had an opportunity to grieve her loss and adjust to her current situation. She needed time, not a new family.

Tess sat on a floral settee and patted the spot beside her, which Callie took. "Callie, this is Mrs. Mary Smith. Mrs. Smith, this is Miss Caroline Hunt, one of our esteemed group leaders, and one of her charges."

Callie squeezed a greeting through a throat that had grown tight. "Good afternoon."

"Likewise, my dear." Mrs. Smith's endearment, delivered in a syrupy tone, didn't sit well with Callie.

"Mrs. Smith has given me some information about her situation." Tess retrieved a tablet from a side table and perused her notes. "She and her husband, John, are new to the area. They've been married six years but have yet to be blessed with a child of their own, so they're eager to adopt. She has her heart set on two children. She'd prefer that they be fair-haired, as she and her husband are." Tess turned to the woman. "Did I cover everything, Mrs. Smith?"

"Those are the basics, yes, but you didn't mention how I've longed to be a mother and how happy I am that my husband has finally agreed to provide a home for two unfortunate orphans. Like many men, he had his heart set on having children of his own, but my John is a gem. He's put my happiness before his own, and I'm grateful for that."

Callie's heart stuttered. Mrs. Smith had put into words what Callie had often thought. It was a rare man who could set aside his desire to father children of his own and welcome an adopted child into his home and his heart instead. It appeared Mr. Smith didn't have any choice, since he and his wife were already married. Chip did.

Tess tapped her pencil against the tablet. "I'm curious why your husband didn't join us."

Mrs. Smith blinked several times, her chin trembling. She pulled a handkerchief from her reticule and dabbed at her eyes, although not a single tear had fallen. If Callie wasn't mistaken, Mrs. Smith was putting on an act.

"Forgive me. It's just that I've waited so long for this day." The silk-clad woman slipped the lacy square into her handbag and closed it with a snap. "John was called away on business, but he suggested I come myself so I could find out what's involved if we decide to take a child into our home. Asking to see the children today was my idea. I had to know if you had any who'd be a good fit for our family, and it appears you do." Her voice lost its wistful tone, becoming strong, sure and...demanding. "I'd appreciate it, Miss Hunt, if you would have the girl turn around so I can get a good look at her."

Callie dreaded subjecting Ruby to the pushy woman's scrutiny. Mrs. Smith was sure to consider the adorable girl a fine choice. "I need you to look at the lady."

Ruby shook her head.

"I'm sorry, sweetheart, but you must. Just for a moment." Callie pried Ruby's arms from around her neck and turned her to face Mrs. Smith. "You'll have to excuse her. The poor dear has had a difficult morning." She'd had a rough two weeks, but Callie wasn't about to give this woman any more information than necessary.

Mrs. Smith had the decency to observe Ruby from where she sat. Although Callie appreciated that, the glint of excitement in the woman's eyes concerned her. "My, but you're a pretty girl. Just look at those flaxen curls."

Ruby lifted her chin, took one look at Mrs. Smith and burrowed into Callie's shoulder once again. The little girl trembled. "I want to go back to Jaspy now. Pwease, Miss Callie."

The inquisitive woman arched an eyebrow. "Jaspy? And who might that be?"

"Her brother," Tess said, much to Callie's relief. She would have had a hard time being polite.

The woman was up to something. Callie was sure of it. She'd heard of people who took in orphans and treated them as servants—or worse. If that was the case, though, she would be looking for older children capable of doing chores, wouldn't she?

The woman leaned forward, making no effort to hide her interest. "She has a brother, does she? That's wonderful. How old is the boy? And is he blond, too?"

Callie's suspicions intensified. It took every ounce of restraint she possessed to keep from running out of the room and taking Ruby as far from this cold, calculating woman as possible.

Tess glanced from Callie to Mrs. Smith. "He's several years older, and his hair is darker."

Hope rushed in. Tess felt the uncertainty, too. She must, for she'd stretched the truth. Although Jasper had just turned five and Ruby was still two, which was three years difference and could technically be referred to as several, her birthday was the following week. Not only that, but Jasper's hair wasn't that much darker than Ruby's— a shade or two at most. Anyone who saw him would say he was blond.

Mrs. Smith smiled, but it appeared forced. "Would it be possible to see him?"

Ruby tensed. Callie rubbed her back, murmured words of comfort and waited for Tess's reply.

Tess shook her head. "I'm afraid today's not a good day. He's in the middle of a project, but if you would like to schedule an appointment for a return visit with your husband, I could see to it that the young fellow is available then."

"I'm not sure when John is expected to return, but I'd like to know what we'd need to do to get the children we've been longing for."

Callie held her breath. Surely Tess wouldn't consider letting this woman take Jasper or Ruby.

Tess jotted a note. "My husband, Spencer, and I work hard to ensure that a child will be a good fit for a family. Because of that, we request that a couple visit the Double T three times prior to releasing a child into their care."

"Three times?" Mrs. Smith exclaimed and then quickly softened her tone. "That seems a bit excessive."

"Perhaps, but that's our practice. The first time, a couple answers a series of written questions, meets a number of children and finds a potential match. The second time, they spend an afternoon with the child here at the Double T. Afterward, we interview the couple and the child separately to see if they want to proceed. If so, we arrange for the child to spend a day at the couple's home, with a group leader present, of course."

Mrs. Smith narrowed her eyes. "Are you saying that you would allow a child to override the desires of a prospective couple?"

"We consider what a child has to say, but Spencer and I make the final decision. Our highest priority is seeing that a child is welcomed into a warm, loving home."

The more Callie heard, the more her respect for Spencer and Tess grew. No wonder the children at the Double T were so happy. They didn't have to worry about being placed into homes where they would be mistreated.

"What about the third visit to the Double T?" Mrs. Smith asked. "You didn't cover that."

Tess smiled. "That's what we call the Day of Celebration, when the other children and staff gather with the child and his or her new parents for a party and joyous sendoff."

Callie smiled. "That's beautiful."

"It is, but I doubt John would agree to such a lengthy process." Mrs. Smith gave a dejected sigh. "I'll tell him what you said, though. For now, I'll bid you good day and be on my way."

She stood, cast a lingering glance at Ruby and left.

Tess gave a dry laugh. "That was…interesting. I doubt she'll darken our door again."

"I hope not." Callie debated how much more to say.

"I've interviewed many prospective parents over the years. Many of them question me, but I got the distinct impression Mrs. Smith was far too interested in our newest additions." She inclined her head toward Ruby, who hadn't shown her face since her pitiful plea.

"You noticed that, too? I thought it was just me."

"I'm going to have one of the ranch hands follow her and see what's going on." Tess jumped to her feet. "I'll leave you to see yourself out." With a swish of her skirts, she was gone.

Callie stood. "It's all right now, Ruby. It's just you and me. The lady left. Have you seen her before?"

The little girl lifted her head and sniffled. "Can we go back now?"

"We sure can." Callie wouldn't press Ruby for answers in her present state. Besides, the word of a soon-to-be three-year-old wouldn't carry much weight with the authorities.

Laughter poured from the open door as they reached the woodshop minutes later. Callie stepped inside and set Ruby down. The little girl darted across the room, grabbed her doll and hurried back over. She clung to Callie's skirts.

"Do it again, Mr. Chip," Freddie pleaded.

"Do what?" Callie asked.

Jasper raced over to her, a red bandana hanging loosely around his neck. Freddie wore a matching one, and Chip sported a larger blue version. "We're teaching Freddie how to walk like a cowboy. Mr. Chip was showing him, but it's my turn now." He clomped around the room with a loose-legged gait while Freddie followed, imitating Jasper.

Chip grinned as he watched the boys for a moment. "We had a great time while you were gone. And speaking of that, what did Tess want?"

"I'll tell you later." She inclined her head toward Ruby, who watched the boys with downcast eyes and a drooping mouth.

He spoke in hushed tones. "Is she all right? Do I need to do anything?"

"Just keep on being your entertaining self. We could use some cheering up."

His gaze bored into her, but she had nothing to hide. He'd been right all along. The children were in danger.

He flashed her a smile, but the tightness around his eyes remained. "I know just the thing. Boys, let's show Miss Callie what else we practiced while she was gone."

Jasper and Freddie took their places, one at each of the two student workbenches, where boards had been anchored in place.

"Guess what we're gonna do," Jasper said.

"Some more planing?" she asked.

"Yep, but we're cowboy carpenters, and we do it cowboy-style." Jasper pulled up his folded bandana, tugging the flat edge of the triangle over his nose.

Freddie spoke, his voice slightly muffled due to the colorful bandana covering the lower half of his face. "It was Mr. Chip's idea. He told us cowboys build things, too, like fences and troughs for the cows to drink out of and such."

None of which would require any planing. Not that

she would mention that. Chip had found a way to interest Jasper in woodworking, and it was working. Jasper had the plane in hand and was gliding it over the board with as much care as Freddie.

"The bandanas keep the sawdust out of the cowboy carpenters' mouths," Jasper added. "And the dust on the trail when they're on a cattle drive, too. Mr. Chip said so."

"That Mr. Chip is a clever fellow. He knows a lot of things, and he's usually right."

Chip let loose with a bark of laughter. "I don't know what I did to convince you, but it tickles a man's ears to have a lovely lady singing his praises."

Did he realize what he'd said? She wasn't lovely, but she rather liked hearing him say so, all the same.

Now to forget about the unpleasant scene in Tess's parlor for the time being and join in the fun. Callie pried Ruby's hand from her skirts and took hold of it. "I reckon these here hardworking cowpokes will be getting hungry, sweetheart. We womenfolk can rustle up some make-believe grub. I'm thinking a big pot of beans and some cornbread will do."

Chip leaned close and whispered in her ear. "Sounds good, but what I'm looking forward to is our nightly cup of hot cocoa and talking with you."

The warmth in his voice filled her with anticipation. If only she didn't have such shocking news to share. She'd much rather spend the time enjoying his company.

"What else do cowboy carpenters build, Mr. Chip?" Jasper yawned. Sleep would claim him soon.

Normally, Jasper's endless questions didn't bother Chip, but he was eager to find out what Callie had to tell him. It must be serious because she'd been unusually quiet ever since she'd returned from her time with Tess—except for reprimanding Jasper when he'd run ahead of them as they headed toward Miss Muffet House for dinner. It wasn't like Callie to speak so sharply to one of the children.

Chip tugged the blanket up to Jasper's chin, just the way the inquisitive boy liked it. "Papa Spencer's ranch hands helped build the second bunkhouse."

In the waning light streaming through the window, Jasper's blond hair appeared darker than usual. "Did they make their beds, too?"

"I built those." He'd met Spencer and Tess years ago and done a number of jobs for the Double T. If he hadn't been out of town the past six months learning all he could from his talented friend up in Oregon, he would have helped build Jack and Jill House for the Abbotts, too. He'd recommended some of his carpenter friends for that job, but Spencer and Tess had saved the furniture-building for him.

"This time you got lots of helpers making the beds, and I'm one of them," Jasper said with pride. "I'm a good cowboy carpenter."

"That you are, son."

Jasper stared at Chip with eyes as big and round as a wagon wheel window. "I'm not your son."

"No." He wasn't, but the word had slipped out before Chip could stop it. "You'll make some man a fine son one day, though."

"You mean when Ruby and me get adopted, don't you?"

"Yes." The word tasted bitter. "Now, it's time for you to get some sleep."

"Aren't you gonna tell me a cowboy story first, like you always do?"

"By all means." Chip concocted a tale about a runaway bull, a rancher who had a way with a rope and a successful recovery. "And his friends cheered for him when he led the ornery fellow back into the corral. The end. Good night, pardner." He kissed Jasper on the forehead, pulled the door to their room closed and descended the two flights of stairs in record time.

The rich scent of cocoa greeted him as he entered the large playroom. Callie sat at a small round table with two steaming mugs in front of her. She pushed one toward him. A foamy white peak floated on top of the dark brown beverage.

He grinned. "Compliments this afternoon and whipping cream tonight? What did I do to deserve all this?"

She smiled, but it didn't reach her eyes. "You've been working hard."

"So have you. Because of your help, the job's going to be done ahead of schedule."

"Then you can go back to Placerville, build those last pieces of furniture for your house and check another item off your list. You must be looking forward to that."

Normally, the thought of moving to the next step in The Plan sent a surge of excitement though him, but doing so would mean leaving the Double T, the children and Callie. He'd grown accustomed to having her working alongside him, hearing her cheery laugh and inhaling the flowery perfume she wore. "It will be nice to have the house finished."

She picked up her mug, blew on her cocoa and took a sip. A blob of whipping cream clung to her upper lip. She removed the foamy white smudge with a quick swipe of her tongue, a gesture that had him thinking of things far sweeter than cocoa—chocolate-flavored kisses.

"Mmm." She cradled the mug in her hands. "A warm drink before bed is so soothing, isn't it? I could use its calming effects after today."

He enjoyed the cocoa, but the best part of their nightly ritual was having Callie all to himself for a few minutes. At last, he could find out what had brought about the change in her. "What did Tess want?"

"A woman had come to inquire about adopting two children, a boy and girl, and Tess wanted my opinion. Something about the woman made me uneasy. Tess felt the same way. Mrs. Smith was far too interested in Jasper and Ruby. I can't help thinking she could be one of those horrid people who left them fatherless."

"What gives you that idea?"

"She was insistent that the children be blond, like her."

"It makes sense she'd want children who resemble her. Wouldn't you?" Level-headed Callie wasn't one to jump to conclusions, but perhaps her feelings for the children had clouded her judgment.

"I would, but there was more. Ruby took one look at her and began shaking. I think she recognized the woman."

"Wouldn't she have said something if she did?"

Callie took two more sips of cocoa. He got the impression she was giving herself time to come up with a stronger argument. "I asked her, but perhaps she was too scared to say anything. You know how withdrawn she is."

"Are you sure you're not letting your feelings color your perceptions? It's no secret that you're fond of the children." Fond was an understatement. He was fairly certain she loved them.

She bristled. "You are, too, which is why I thought you'd take my concerns seriously. You're the one who's been telling me the danger they could be in."

He chose his words carefully. The last thing he wanted to do was upset her further. "I think the threat is real, but I have a hard time believing that one of the killers would come to the Double T and ask to see the children. In my experience, criminals operate in the shadows."

"Maybe that's exactly why she did it, because we wouldn't suspect a woman who came to adopt a child. What if everything she said was part of a ploy? Take the names she used for instance—John and Mary Smith. They're so common."

"They are, which is why it's quite possible her name really is Mary Smith."

"Fine." She set down her mug with such force that the cocoa threatened to slosh over the rim. "Maybe it is, but she referred to her *supposed* husband as a *gem*. I find that odd. Don't you?"

The hairs on the back of his neck jumped to attention. "I can't believe the woman would have the audacity to show up like that, but from what you've said, it sounds like she might have. If that's the case, the children could be in even more danger than I thought."

The color drained from Callie's face. She pressed her hands to her pale cheeks. "Ruby and I were sitting not six feet from that woman. It sickens me to think that we let her get away."

Chip reached across the tiny table and took her hands in his. "There's nothing you could have done. We have no proof. Just suspicions."

"I was so quick to dismiss your concerns. I wanted to believe the children would be fine, but now... Oh, Chip,

what can we do? I would never forgive myself if anything happened to them."

"We'll keep on doing what we've been doing—
watching over them and praying the Lord keeps them
safe."

A piercing cry came from above.

Callie yanked her hands free. "Ruby!"

Chapter Seven

Callie bolted up the stairs to the second floor. Chip's footfalls thudded right behind her as she ran down the hallway to the room she and Ruby shared.

She reached for the door handle, but Chip stopped her. "Someone could be inside. I'll go first."

He opened the door a crack, looked in the room and heaved an audible sigh. "It's all right. There's no one here but Ruby."

Callie shoved past him, burst into the room, sat on the bed and pulled the sobbing girl into her arms. "It's all right, sweetheart. We're here."

Chip rested a hand on Callie's back. "I'm going to check on Jasper. I'll be right back."

Ruby clung to Callie, her tiny body shaking. Callie rubbed the girl's back, rocked her and murmured words of comfort.

In no time, Chip was back, holding Jasper in his arms. Chip inclined his head toward Ruby. "How is she?"

"She's beginning to settle down. I think she had a bad dream. Has she had them before, Jasper?"

"I don't think so. Least, I don't remember any times."

Callie spoke softly beside Ruby's ear. "Are you doing better now?"

Ruby lifted her head and looked at Callie, her tear-streaked face just visible in the low light. "I dweamed the b-bad lady—" she drew in a shuddering breath "—comed to get me."

Chip sat Jasper on the bed beside Callie and kneeled next to her. "What bad lady, princess?"

"The one at Mama Tess's house. She was with the bad men who took Papa away."

Callie's gaze met Chip's. A look of understanding passed between them. Ruby had just confirmed their suspicions. Not only did those who had killed Mr. Tate know his children were living at the Double T, but the murderous trio was also bold enough to send a member of their team to investigate. If they would risk exposing the woman's identity, they must not have found the jewels and believed the children had information on their whereabouts. Even worse, they appeared to be intent on doing whatever it took to get it out of them.

Well, those horrid people weren't about to get anywhere near Jasper and Ruby, not if Callie could help it. She would do whatever it took to keep the children safe. Chip would do the same, as would Spencer, Tess and every single person who worked at the Double T.

Jasper used the sleeve of his nightshirt to wipe his sister's tears. "I won't let the bad lady get you. I'm a cowboy carpenter now, and I'll hit her over the head with one of Mr. Chip's hammers if she comes back here."

Chip placed a hand on Jasper's shoulder. "I know you want to help, pardner, but there are lots of grown-ups at the Double T who will take very good care of you. You're safe here. Now, it's time to get you back upstairs."

Jasper gave Ruby a hug and followed Chip out of the room.

It took Callie a good half hour to get Ruby settled down again, at which point she hurried down the stairs and entered the playroom. "Oh, Chip, I—"

She came to an abrupt stop. They weren't alone. He was helping a ranch hand set up a cot just inside the front door of the huge room. Another cot sat by the back door.

The men finished, the ranch hand left and Chip joined her. "I spoke with Spencer and Tess. He's arranged for two of his men to sleep here, and they'll be armed. No one will be able to get past them."

"That's good." Disturbing, but good. She'd hoped to keep the children from knowing the danger they were in, but they were well aware of it now. The best thing she and Chip could do would be to assure Jasper and Ruby that no harm would come to them. Having bodyguards in place overnight should do that.

"Tess said the ranch hand she'd sent to follow the woman couldn't find her. He rode down the road toward town, but her footprints ended abruptly. Apparently, one of her accomplices had a horse waiting for her."

Callie stepped outside, rested her hand on the porch railing and scanned the area, with Chip at her side. Everything appeared peaceful. The children were all inside. Even the animals were settling down for the night. The squeak of the weather vane on top of the barn as it shifted direction slightly and the rustle of leaves as a gentle breeze blew were the only sounds. "It makes me sick to think that those awful people are out there somewhere. They need to be caught."

"I agree. So does Spencer. He's going to have a deputy come out and talk with us in the morning. You and

Tess can give him a description of the woman, and Jasper can give them some information about the men. He got a good look at them the day we found them and filled my ear with his recollections after I took him back up to our room."

"I'm not surprised. He's bright and observant. We should have talked with him about the abduction earlier... like you suggested. I wanted so much to believe that those awful people posed no threat to the children, but I was wrong."

Chip leaned back against the railing of the wrap-around porch and crossed his arms and his ankles, a masculine pose she found quite appealing. She couldn't make out his face in the waning light, but his tone was kind. "Bringing it up earlier wouldn't have made that much difference. Until the woman showed up here and Ruby confirmed her identity, we had no way of knowing for sure that the children were in danger."

"It's kind of you to make excuses for me, but I should have listened to you. The sheriff and his deputies would have had more accurate descriptions to go on."

"They will now, and I trust they'll find the culprits. It's obvious they're still in the area and have no plans to leave."

Callie rubbed her arms and willed herself not to think, not to feel.

Chip straightened and draped an arm around her shoulders, a comforting gesture that meant a great deal to her. "You're cold. We should go back inside."

"I'm fine. It's just that I know what it's like to live with that kind of fear."

He dropped his hands to his sides. "What do you mean?"

"I, um, have a similar story. My parents were held at gunpoint during a robbery, and—" Memories assailed her, dark, bleak and terrifying in their intensity. Masked intruders. Gunshots. Splintering wood. Retreating footsteps. Eerie silence.

Her throat constricted, and she struggled to draw a breath, but her throat was too tight. She swayed and clutched Chip's arm.

"Here. Let's take a seat." Chip wrapped an arm around her waist, guided her to the steps and helped her lower herself onto the top one.

She fought the urge to lean against his shoulder. "Th-thank you. I'll be all right. I just need a minute."

He sat beside her, saying nothing but offering his comforting presence. Mere inches separated them. His warmth seeped into her, melting the ice-cold fingers of fear that had slipped past her defenses, bringing with them the sense of hopelessness that she'd kept at bay ever since that dreadful day when she was twelve. She'd clawed her way back from the depths of despair and vowed never to go there again. She wasn't about to return now.

If she recited the events as quickly as possible, she would reach the joyful conclusion before the pain of reliving that horrid day could consume her. "My father refused to open the safe and give the robbers what they wanted. He and Mother paid for his greed with their lives. I managed to crawl under a table during the scuffle. The cloth over it hid me from view, so I was spared. Mom and Pop Marshall arrived a short time later and took me to their house. They were such a blessing." She sighed. "Not a day goes by that I don't miss them."

Chip placed a hand on either side of her face. They

were the callused hands of a hardworking man with a kind heart, but his caress was gentle.

"I'm sorry for all you went through, Callie." He leaned toward her.

Was he going to kiss her? Anticipation swirled in her chest. She slid her eyes closed and waited for his mouth to claim hers.

He tilted her head down, pressed his lips to…her forehead? Clearly, he had no feelings for her. That was the kind of kiss he gave Ruby.

"I understand now why you wanted to spare the children any pain."

She did her best to sound cheery. "I'm sure they'll be fine. They have so many people looking out for them."

"What about you? This is sure to have dredged up—"

"Don't worry about me. I put all that behind me." She didn't like cutting him off, but spending time in the past did no good. They needed to look to the future.

She'd thought Chip might have been considering the possibility of having her as part of his someday, but she'd obviously misread things. Well, so be it. She didn't need a man to be happy. Her new position at the Double T gave her what she'd hoped for—a place to belong and children to love.

Chip would only be working there a few more weeks. She could ignore her growing feelings for him and keep things professional that long. Couldn't she?

"I know it's hard, Jasper, but anything you can remember might help."

Chip sat on a bench opposite the sheriff's deputy, with Jasper at his side. Breakfast had been served an hour ago, so the dining hall was empty, but the scent of bacon lingered. "Did your papa tell you where he put the jewels after he picked them up down in Sacramento City?"

"He said he hid them."

The deputy leaned forward. "That's good. Did he tell you where?"

Jasper shook his head. "I wanted him to draw a treasure map, but he said he didn't need to 'cause everything was stored in here." He tapped his head.

"That's it? He didn't say anything else?" Frustration furrowed the deputy's brow.

"No! I told you everything. Can I go now? Mr. Chip is gonna show me some tricks on the parallel bars."

Chip rested a hand on Jasper's shoulder. "You've done a fine job. If you'll wait by the door, I'll have a quick word with the deputy. Then we can have our fun."

Jasper stomped across the room and stood with his arms folded, scowling. Chip could understand Jasper's irritation. He'd endured ten minutes of questioning. Sitting still that long wasn't easy for Jasper, even when he was talking about something he liked. Having to stay put all that time while dredging up memories of the darkest day in his life was more than any child should have to bear.

The deputy stood, and Chip did the same. "I'm sorry Jasper couldn't be of more help, but he's told you everything he'd told me—and then some." The deputy's prodding had led to Jasper recalling what his father had said regarding the jewel's hiding place, not that the information was of much use.

"His descriptions will be useful, but if he happens to recall the whereabouts of the jewels, let me know right away. Once we have them and spread the news, we can eliminate the threat to the children."

Chip gave the deputy his assurances and saw him off. Jasper grabbed Chip's hand and tugged. "Come on."

"Let's see if Miss Callie and Ruby want to join us."

The eager fellow scoffed. "Girls don't play on the bars."

"No, but your sister might like to swing." With the other children tending to their Saturday morning chores under their group leaders' direction, the playground was empty. Since it would be just the four of them, perhaps Ruby would feel comfortable enough to enjoy the time outdoors. She'd been shy before her nightmare, but that morning she'd clung to Callie and begged her not to go to breakfast. They'd taken her anyway, but the slip of a girl hadn't eaten more than two bites. She'd kept her head down and jumped whenever there was a loud noise.

Chip and Jasper entered the woodshop. Chip spoke with Callie, who was hard at work doing some planing. Ruby sat in the corner clutching her doll and staring into the distance, a blank expression on her face.

Chip squatted before Ruby. "How would you like to go outside, princess? Miss Callie said she'll take you for a ride on the swing."

Ruby slowly turned and focused on him, her lower lip trembling. "But the b-bad people could be out there."

"I looked all around, and I didn't see anyone. You'll be safe. I'll make sure of that."

"The bad lady comed here alweady. She could come back."

"Miss Callie and I will be there, and so will Jasper, won't you, pardner?"

Jasper plopped down beside his sister and pulled her close. "Mr. Chip is big and brave. He won't let nobody hurt you, and neither will I. I'm a cowboy, and cowboys are tough." He tugged on his much-loved cowboy hat.

Callie set the plane down and joined them. "I know what we need. A dog. I'm sure Mama Tess would let us borrow theirs if I asked. She said Woof has always been a good watchdog. If a stranger were to come anywhere near us, he would bark."

Woof was hard of hearing and moved slowly, but if having him there would calm Ruby's fears, Chip would get the old fellow.

Jasper embraced the idea with his characteristic enthusiasm. "Woof is real nice. Luke said he fell in a hole when he was little like me, and Woof barked and barked so Mama Tess could find him. We'll be safe with Woof there. So, we can go now, can't we?"

Ruby stared at Callie for several seconds and nodded. "I'll go, if Woofie is there."

"Great." Chip stood. "I'll go get him and meet you in the playground."

Callie lifted her lovely lips in a smile, but it lacked its usual warmth. She'd seemed distant all morning. She was probably concerned about Ruby.

Minutes later, Chip strode across the playground with the trusty dog ambling along beside him, tail wagging. When Tess heard why they wanted Woof's company, she'd been happy to send him. She'd given Chip two good ideas, as well. As soon as he could get Callie by herself, he'd see what she thought of them.

"Mr. Chip, you're back! And you got Woof." Jasper loped over to them sporting a grin. He dropped to his knees and wrapped his arms around the friendly dog's neck. "Howdy, fellow."

Callie sat on one of the swings with Ruby in her lap. Callie looked their way, but Ruby's focus was on her doll.

Jasper stood, beckoned to Chip and headed for the three sets of parallel bars. "C'mon. Teach me all the big boys' tricks."

He led Jasper to the lowest set of bars. "I'll show you some of them, but you're not old enough to do everything they do. We'll start at the beginning. Grab the bars with your hands even, jump up and hold yourself in position with your shoulders strong."

Jasper practiced until he could hang in place with the correct form. "I wanna do something else."

"Try shifting your weight from side to side while lifting up your hands, one at a time, like this." Chip grabbed the highest set of bars and demonstrated. "Think of the pendulum on a clock. That's what it's like."

Jasper raised himself into position and mimicked Chip's motion. "Tick-tock. Tick-tock. Tick-tock." He said the words in a singsong voice as he swung to and fro. "Can you see me, Miss Callie? I'm doing it."

"Yes, you are. You're a quick learner with an excellent teacher."

Callie's compliment eased some of the tension in Chip's shoulders. Perhaps he was right and her aloofness earlier had nothing to do with him.

When Jasper had mastered that skill, Chip taught him how to travel forward and backward down the bars. They moved on to an *L* hold. The energetic boy's arms trembled, but he kept at it until he could lift his legs and hold them parallel with the bars.

"You've done very well, pardner, but you need to take a break, or you could find it hard to move later."

Jasper hopped down and looked up at Chip. "Can you do fancy tricks like the big boys?"

"Some, yes." He'd spent many a recess on the parallel bars.

"Show me. Please."

"Sure." He didn't need to be asked twice.

Callie set Ruby down, took her hand and headed for the bars, with Woof walking along behind them. The wood chips beneath the play equipment crunched under their feet. "Ruby and I would like to see what you're doing, too."

"Since I have such an eager audience, I'll do my very best." He mounted the bars, straightened his arms and completed a series of basic lifts, followed by walks. A quick glance at Callie showed her attention riveted on him.

"Mr. Chip is real strong." Jasper's voice held the awe Chip had experienced when he'd watched the older boys years ago.

"He is, but I already knew that. All you have to do is watch him saw a board. His muscles are so—" Callie inhaled sharply, cutting herself off at a most inopportune moment.

"So what?" Jasper's question echoed the one Chip wanted to ask.

"So, um—" she cleared her throat and lowered her voice "—well developed."

She watched him when he worked, did she? And apparently she appreciated what she saw. All the more reason to show her what he could do.

He launched into a routine that included every exercise he'd ever learned—swings, rolls, handstands and more. With practiced ease, he executed each swiftly and crisply, just the way he'd been taught. His last feat included a trio of full extension swings, releases and underarm catches with a backward somersault into his dismount.

Jasper cheered, Ruby clapped and Callie stared at him, her lovely mouth agape.

"That was incredible, Chip. I've never seen anything like it. You were moving so quickly, and yet you looked so graceful. How did you learn all that?"

"The older boys taught me when I was in school, but I enjoy the doing all the exercises and have continued to practice." He'd built a set of parallel bars at his place for that reason. One day he would have sons of his own and teach them all he knew.

"I'm quite impressed. You have so many talents. Every time I walk past Humpty Dumpty House and see the sculpture you carved sitting in its place of honor on the porch, I stop and admire it. The woodshop, the furniture, this playground equipment you built—" she swept a hand toward it "—showcase your many skills. It seems there's nothing you can't do with wood. Your house must be a work of art."

Normally, his heart would slow its rapid beating fairly quickly after exerting himself, but with Callie gushing the way she was, it continued to race. "Thanks. I do my best, but so do you. I've never known a woman as interested in woodworking as you are. *You've* impressed *me*."

She gave an airy laugh. "You don't have to flatter me just because I paid you a compliment."

Not *a* compliment, but compliment*s*. She'd given him one right after the other. He'd store them up to revisit later, but for now he had to convince her of his sincerity. "I meant what I said. You could be a fine carpenter."

"Thank you. Since you appreciate my interest and don't find it odd, I wondered…" She caught her lower lip between her teeth, drawing his attention to her supple, kissable lips.

She realized where his gaze was focused and lowered hers, focusing on his mouth. Could it be that she wanted him to kiss her? If only their two little chaperones weren't there.

The moment stretched, filling Chip with a sense of certainty. One day, he would kiss her. The sooner, the better.

She took a step back and slowly raised her head until she was looking into his eyes once again. "As I was saying, I wondered if you'd be willing to let one of the older girls here at the Double T come and help us sometimes. Tess said the girl expressed an interest after your carving demonstration and has continued to ask if she could come over when Freddie does. She's fourteen, so I'm sure she would be of help."

"A girl wants to learn? Wonderful. I'll tell Tess to send her over this afternoon."

Callie gripped his upper arm. "Thank you. I know it will mean a great deal to her. A girl is rarely given an opportunity like that. But you're not like other men. You appreciate people for who they are. Like me and Isaac."

Jasper shoved his way between them. "How long are you two gonna talk? Ruby and me want to play. Don't you, Ruby?"

The little girl nodded.

"She can't do the bars, and she don't really like swinging."

"If she *doesn't* like swinging," Callie said, "perhaps we can think of something else."

She was so good with the children. He could picture her standing in front of his house with a flock of youngsters around her, smiling at them as she was at Jasper now. She stared at the sky and tapped her cheek with a fingertip, giving Chip an opportunity to admire her captivating profile. She'd make a fine wife, too. For the right man. He wasn't ready for that. He had things to do first, but a man could dream, couldn't he?

He could have admired Callie a lot longer, but she snapped her fingers and turned away. "I know just the thing. Stay here with Mr. Chip, and I'll be right back."

Jasper watched her head to the garden shed. "What's she gonna do?"

"I don't know, but whatever it is, I'm sure you and Ruby will like it." He hoped she would, anyhow, but she was as withdrawn as ever. He scooped her into his arms. "Do you have any idea what Miss Callie is up to, princess?"

Ruby clutched her doll and said nothing, shaking her head instead.

Callie returned shortly with her hands behind her back and a sunny smile on her face. "Who wants to see what I have?"

Jasper hopped from one foot to the other, his hand waving in the air. "I do! I do!"

"And how about you, princess? Would you like to see what I brought with me?"

She nodded.

"I want to hear you say it. Go ahead. Ask me what I have in my hands." Callie's persistence was admirable, but getting Ruby to say an entire sentence was a challenge.

Ruby stared at Callie for the longest time, but Callie

stared right back, smiling her encouragement. At length, Ruby relented. "What are you hiding?"

"Jump ropes." Callie held out her hands, from which four ropes dangled. "I haven't used one of these since I was a girl, but I used to love skipping rope. Have you ever done it?"

The reticent girl started to shake her head again, but stopped. "No."

"I haven't, either," Jasper said, "but I wanna try."

"Let's do it, then." Callie passed out the ropes, giving short ones to the children and a nice long one to Chip. She grinned at him. "I'm sure you're a champion rope jumper, aren't you?"

He chuckled. "As a matter of fact, I held the record for jumping the most times without missing when I was a schoolboy."

"Then perhaps you'll show the rest of us what to do. I was often the first one to get tangled in my rope, so I could use a few pointers."

"I find that hard to believe, but I'd be happy to teach Jasper and Ruby what to do."

The next half hour was one of the happiest Chip had ever spent. Jasper took to skipping rope with ease, which was no surprise. He called it lariat jumping and did it with his cowboy hat firmly in place. What did surprise Chip was seeing how much Ruby enjoyed the experience. She left her doll sitting on a nearby bench *watching* the proceedings and tried over and over again to get the rhythm down, giggling with glee the entire time. Why the activity had captivated her, he didn't know, but he was glad it had.

As he suspected, Callie had intentionally downp'
her skill. She challenged him to see who could ju

longest without missing and gave him a good-natured pat on the back when he outlasted her by a full forty-two revolutions. She raced Jasper up and down the playground while they skipped rope with loping strides. What Chip enjoyed most was helping Callie turn a rope while Ruby skipped it. The little girl had only been able to manage a successful jump or two while practicing on her own, but with their help, she got all the way to fifteen. The pride on her face rivaled the surge of pride in his chest.

Callie stood by his side watching the children play. Ruby had picked up her rope again and was studying Jasper, who had taken on the role of teacher.

"You gotta be ready to jump when the rope gets in front of your feet. Watch me."

The tenacious girl tried again and mastered the feat, jumping over the rope six times in a row. "I did it!"

Callie clapped her hands together with a loud smack. "Yes, you did, sweetheart. I'm so proud of—"

Ruby looked their way and shrieked. She raced over to them and buried her face in Callie's skirts, muttering something about a bad man.

Chip wheeled around, spotted the new ranch hand headed their way and heaved a sigh of relief. "It's all right, princess. That's Mr. Hardy. He works for Papa Spencer."

Ruby didn't budge. Callie picked up the terrified girl and held her close.

The stocky fellow lifted one shoulder in a sympathetic shrug and addressed Chip. "I didn't mean to startle the young'un. Spencer wanted me to tell you that he would have time to show young Jasper how to throw a lasso tomorrow, if you're agreeable."

Jasper bounded over. "Please say yes, Mr. Chip. I gotta learn so I can be a good cowboy."

"Yes."

"Yee-haw!" Jasper twirled his rope over his head as though it was a lasso.

Making the enthusiastic boy happy was easy. Figuring out what to do for Ruby required more effort. They'd gotten a glimpse of the carefree girl she must have been before tragedy struck, like a beautiful carving emerging from a nondescript piece of wood, but she'd hidden herself away again.

His message delivered, Hardy left. Callie coaxed Ruby into skipping rope with Jasper by promising that she and Woof would keep a look out for any "bad men."

Callie watched the children, who had moved several feet away. She lowered her voice. "I wish I knew what to do for Ruby, but I'm at a loss. Ever since that woman showed up, she's been even more fearful of others than before. I don't know how she'll handle the attention a week from now when everyone is wishing her a happy birthday at the monthly party."

She'd given him the perfect opening. "I think we should take the children somewhere else next Saturday so she can enjoy a quiet celebration. Somewhere she feels safe."

"What a great idea. I know just the place. My friend Becky and her husband, James, own an apple orchard in Diamond Springs. The trees would be in bloom now. I'll write and ask her if we could pay them a visit that day."

"It was Tess's idea, actually, but I agreed. She had another suggestion. She thinks that if Mr. and Mrs. Smith do show up, we should let them meet with Jasper. could use him to pass on information, setting up a tra

Callie's eyes went wide, and she cut him off. "I can't believe Tess would suggest such a thing. If that woman dares to come back with her husband—if he actually is her husband—we need to send for the sheriff's deputy, not let the couple spend time with Jasper."

He held up his hands, palms forward. "Whoa there. You didn't let me finish. We don't have any solid evidence. A judge isn't going to take the word of a five-year-old. If we lure the criminals to a specific spot and catch them searching for the jewels, that changes things."

She eyed him warily. "And you're willing to use Jasper to reveal the location?"

"He'll be fine. They're not going to try anything out in the open. You and I would be right there with him."

"But he's sure to recognize them and say something."

He'd said the same thing to Tess, but she believed Jasper was up to the task. Taking her years of experience with children into account, Chip had to agree. "We'll prepare him ahead of time. He's a bright boy. If we tell him we need his help catching the bad guys, he'll be more than happy to cooperate."

"It might not come to that since we're not even sure they'll come back." Callie's voice took on an edge. "I hope they don't."

"The deputy is fairly certain they will. He contacted the jewel supplier down in Sacramento City. Mr. Tate's order was substantial. If the crooks are set on getting the gems, we believe they'll show up again to see what information they can get out of Jasper."

Her lovely brow furrowed. "And if he tells them what they want to know, then what?"

"They would head for the location, and we'd follow them."

She inhaled sharply. "You'd go? I thought the deputy would see to it."

"Of course I'd go. He would need a posse, and I'd be part of it."

"But—" She shook her head.

"What is it?"

"You could get hurt."

"I've got a gun, and I know how to use it."

She stepped so close that he could inhale her flowery scent. "I'm sure you do, but promise me you won't take any unnecessary risks."

Her pleading tone broke through his defenses. It had been years since anyone had cared about him the way she did. He chuckled in an effort to lighten the mood. It was either that or pull her into his arms and kiss her soundly, but this wasn't the time or the place. "I'll be careful. After all, I wouldn't want to deprive you of my company."

A slow smile bloomed on those tempting lips of hers. "I'm glad to hear that, because I've gotten used to having you around."

He liked having her around, too. Very much. The trouble was that The Plan didn't call for him to begin courting a woman for another three years. Although he'd considered making an adjustment to it, he couldn't. To do so could endanger the safety and security of the family he planned to have, and that he couldn't do.

Chapter Eight

"The apple trees in bloom are a sight to behold, aren't they?" Callie threw her arms open wide and turned in a slow circle, inhaling the rich perfume of the blossoms overhead.

"They're nice, but I've seen things I like better." Chip leaned against a low branch, sporting a knee-weakening grin and looking right at her.

She scooped a fluffy pink flower from the ground, pulled off a petal and watched it float to the ground. A game that had been played by some of her doe-eyed schoolmates came to mind. *He loves me. He loves me not.*

Chip didn't love her, of course. Such a thought was pure silliness, but his heavy-lidded gaze left no doubt he found her attractive.

Girlish chatter drew Callie's attention. Ruby sat on a blanket in the shade of the canopy of blooms serving tea to her doll in acorn cups and looking more serene than she had since they'd found the children. The light breeze riffled the girl's honey-colored curls. Bringing the children to the O'Briens' orchard had been a good idea.

Jasper galloped up to them and reined in his imaginary steed. "Whoa there, Snap." He pretended to dismount and sauntered over, walking with his wide cowboy stride. "Can we play hide-and-seek?"

"I don't think that's a good—"

"Sure," Chip said. "I'll be the seeker. You can find your own hiding place, and Miss Callie can help Ruby."

It wasn't like Chip to cut her off. She turned, putting her back to Jasper, and whispered, "I'm sure the children are safe here, but letting Jasper out of our sight doesn't seem wise."

"He won't be."

"But if you're the seeker, your eyes will be closed while you count and he hides."

"They'll *appear* to be closed." He winked.

"Oh! Of course."

"You can trust me, Callie."

She did trust him. It was herself she didn't trust. The more time she spent with him, the harder it was to keep her distance. That morning as they'd bounced along the rutted road on their way from the Double T up the hill to Diamond Springs, her mind had wandered places it had no right going. Sitting on the bench seat with Ruby in her lap and Jasper wedged between her and Chip had fueled her dream of having a family. She'd imagined what it would be like to have a husband she adored and children as dear to her as these two.

Jasper huffed his impatience. "Why are you talking so much? I wanna play."

"We're done talking, pardner. First we need to set some boundaries. You have to stay in this part of the orchard, where the flowers are pink. No going where they're white. Do you understand?"

"Yes."

"Get ready to hide, then, because I'm going to start counting. When I reach one hundred, I'll come looking for you." Chip covered his eyes with his hands, but he used his fingers instead of the heels, which would allow him to peek through the gaps.

"Come on, sweetheart. Let's find a good spot." Callie held out a hand to Ruby. The little girl stared at it for several seconds but took it and followed without protest.

They played six rounds of the game, taking turns being *it*. Jasper enjoyed himself immensely, and so did Ruby. She shouted with glee when she discovered his hiding place during the final round.

"I found you, Jaspy!" Ruby took off running, her short legs pumping as she attempted to beat her brother back to the base.

They touched the tree at the same time. Chip celebrated their tie by giving the children piggyback rides.

Becky wove her way to them through the trees and stood beside Callie. "I'm happy to see that you're all enjoying yourselves, especially the birthday girl."

"I appreciate you letting us come for a visit. Ruby's the happiest I've ever seen her."

"You're looking rather exhilarated yourself. That wouldn't have to do with the presence of a certain carpenter, would it?" Becky inclined her head toward Chip, who galloped through the trees with Jasper on his back urging his *horse* to go faster.

"I enjoy his company. As you can see, he's quite good with the children."

"Speaking of the children, I'd like to take them inside to help me frost Ruby's cake. My little Mariela would love the company."

"Certainly. I'll round them up and come with you."

Becky placed a hand on Callie's arm to stop her. "We'll be fine. You and Chip spend all your time with them, so I'm offering you a short break. Just the two of you. The way he's looking at you tells me he would appreciate having you to himself for a few minutes. I hope you make the most of the opportunity."

Callie's mouth gaped. She quickly closed it. "If I didn't know better, I'd say you were encouraging me to, well, flirt."

"By no means would I suggest you trifle with him. Just be your warm-hearted, convivial self and welcome the opportunities that might arise." Becky smiled. "Now, we'll be off."

Jasper went willingly, as did Ruby when Callie told her she'd get to show her doll to Becky's two-year-old daughter. That left Callie alone with Chip—and her vivid imagination. Thanks to her friend's none-too-subtle hints, she envisioned a romantic scene.

"Everything worked out, just like I said it would, didn't it?"

Chip's question jerked her back to the present. When had he moved so close? "What? Yes. The children had a good time. I enjoyed seeing Ruby have so much fun."

"Did you? Have fun, that is?" He speared a hand through his hair, leaving the thick brown locks tousled.

She reached up and smoothed them, realized what she'd done and quickly lowered her arm. "I'm sorry. I've gotten so used to taming Jasper's unruly curls that I forgot what I was doing."

He flashed her one of his most disarming grins yet. "I have that effect on women."

While she enjoyed seeing him give his lighthearted side free rein, his playfulness made it difficult to imagine their time together being anything out of the ordinary. "You're so good with the children."

"And you're good at changing the subject. Why is that?" His countenance changed and his voice became low and intimate. "I got the impression you enjoyed my company."

"I do, but…" The swift change of his demeanor from teasing to tender robbed her of the ability to think.

He brushed the back of his hand over her cheek. "I enjoy yours, too. We make a good team, don't we?"

She couldn't speak, either, so she nodded.

"You're an amazing woman, Callie. You're bright, talented and…beautiful."

His gaze swept over her face, slowly and thoroughly, as though he was committing every detail to memory. She used the opportunity to study him—the lines around his eyes resulting from many smiles and laughs, his angular jaw and his mouth, which was moving toward hers.

Chip was going to kiss her!

She tilted her head and waited breathlessly, with her heart slamming against her corset. Her knees wobbled so that she placed her hands on his broad chest to steady herself.

He cupped her face in his hands. She closed her eyes and felt the gentle pressure of his lips on hers, a sensation so delightful that a soft moan escaped her. He pulled her closer, and the kiss grew into something far greater than anything she'd ever dreamed. She slid her arms around his trim waist, held on tightly and gave way to the joy that filled her.

All too soon, he brought the incredible experience to an end. He trailed his hands down her neck, rested them on her shoulders and grinned. "I've been wanting to do that for a long time."

"You have?" What a silly thing to say. Not that she could have come up with anything better in her fuzzy-headed state.

"Spending time with you has made me question things."

Was that good or bad? "Such as?"

A shadow crossed his face, but his ready smile returned quickly. "I've realized how eager I am to find someone, settle down and build a family with her."

That wasn't the answer she'd expected. Had Chip been reevaluating The Plan? Had he been considering courting her, perhaps? The possibility put a smile on her face. "I've had similar thoughts. Being around the children makes me long to be part of a family again."

"I agree. I look at Jasper and Ruby and wonder what it would be like to have a child of my own. One day I will."

The doctor's diagnosis flashed through her mind. No matter how much she'd enjoyed Chip's kiss, she couldn't forget that his primary goal was to have a family with children who looked like him and would carry on his family's legacy. "We should probably be going. Jasper won't take too kindly to us keeping him waiting. It might be Ruby's birthday cake, but he's more excited about digging into a slice of it than she is."

"Who needs dessert after a kiss like that?" He winked. "But I suppose you're right."

Letting go of him was difficult. Who knew when they'd be able to share a moment like this again? Or if they ever would. She couldn't keep her diagnosis a secret forever, not if he was entertaining the idea of having her

as his sweetheart. Once he knew about her condition…
She sighed and headed to the O'Briens' house.

The birthday party was a success. Ruby loved the doll dress Callie had made and the tiny bed Chip had built. Becky's chocolate cake was delicious. James had two slices, as did Chip. Jasper wolfed down his piece, but Ruby took her time.

James set his fork on his plate and stood. "I wonder. Are there any children who would like to play in the tree house out front?"

"Me!" Jasper jumped up from the bench and raced to the door.

Chip hopped up and joined him. "Whoa, pardner. We need to wait for the others."

James reached for the baby boy in Becky's arms and nodded at her plate, where a piece of cake she'd barely touched sat. "We'll leave you two lovely ladies in peace. I'm sure you have plenty to talk about."

"Thank you." Becky handed their son to James and smiled. "I'll miss you, of course, but I appreciate the opportunity to have Callie all to myself for a few minutes. It's a very altruistic gesture, but then you're known for them," she said with a smile.

James chuckled. "It's self-serving really. I'd like Chip to take a look at the construction and tell me ways I could improve the design."

"I know he's a talented carpenter, but you did a fine job." Becky turned to Chip. "My brilliant husband added real glass windows, safety rails around the porch and a lift that operates on an elaborate pulley system."

Chip took Ruby by the hand. "Come on, princess. Let's go. I'm looking forward to getting ideas for the tree house at the Double T."

Callie smiled at the way the two men were so eager to compliment each other. She hadn't realized how humble Chip was. The more she learned about him, the more she liked him.

James balanced little Billy on one hip, offered his free hand to Mariela and followed the others out. The house grew so quiet that Callie could hear the ticking of the clock on the mantel over the rock-faced fireplace.

Becky sighed. "I love my children dearly, but it's nice to hear myself think every now and then. I'm sure you understand. I'd imagine silence is rare at an orphanage."

"It is, but I don't mind. Well, there are times when Jasper's endless questions get to be a bit much." Callie chuckled.

"You love the children, don't you?"

"Very much."

"And Chip? Do you love him, too?"

The question took her aback. "No! I care about him, but— Why are you smiling?"

Becky patted Callie's arm. "I saw your face when the two of you came in. It was evident you took my suggestion and allowed things to happen."

Callie picked up her fork and sank it into the cake. She lifted the bite to her mouth and savored the rich chocolate flavor. "You're such a good baker."

"And you're prevaricating."

"I see you still like using big words."

Becky shook her head and chuckled. "You've avoided answering twice. You must love him very much. Now that we've established that, what are you going to do about it?"

"I didn't say I love him. I care for him, yes, but that's all. He's wonderful with the children, he's fun to be around and he works hard." She frowned. "Too hard, in fact."

"What do you mean?"

Callie rested her fork on her plate and told Becky about The Plan and Chip's strict adherence to it.

"So he won't even consider courting a woman for another three years?"

"After we ki—" Callie cleared her throat in an attempt to cover her slip. "After we talked, he did say that he's eager to establish a family."

Becky smiled. "A kiss does have a way of making a person reevaluate things. James and I have had some of our best conversations after sharing one." She paused. "Your eyes are as big as pie crusts. I didn't mean to shock you."

"It's all right." Her friend was happily married, so it made sense that talk of kisses came more easily to her.

Yes. Becky *was* married. And she'd worked as a nurse. It made sense she'd know about medical matters. "May I ask you a question? It's…personal."

"Certainly."

Callie summoned her courage. Although she wasn't what anyone would consider a shy person, certain topics were delicate and not something a lady would discuss. Her mother had drilled that into her. But if she wanted to know, she had to ask, whether it made her uncomfortable or not.

"While we were on the train heading west, I told you and Jessie about the day the horse kicked me in the stomach when I was six and how I forced myself to learn to ride in spite of my fears. There's more to the story. The doctor said my injuries could have left me…" The words lodged in her throat. Why was saying them out loud so difficult?

She drew in a deep breath and pushed out the sentence on her exhale. "He said I won't be able to bear children."

"I'm so sorry." Becky squeezed Callie's hand and spoke in a soothing tone. "It must have been extremely difficult to hear such news."

Difficult, no. Confusing, yes. She'd been too young and in too much pain to fully comprehend everything at the time, but she'd heard snippets of a conversation between her mother and the doctor years later. Something about irreparable damage and consequences.

"I'm not one to question a medical professional," Becky said, "but how he could know for sure?"

The same question had gone through Callie's mind countless times. "He suspected it after the accident but confirmed it when I was older and failed to experience, um...you know."

"Monthly reminders of your womanhood?"

Leave it to Becky to know how to put it delicately. She had such a way with words. "Exactly. He said that was a sure indication, but what if there's something that could be done? Some new surgery or procedure that could make a difference? There have been advancements made in so many areas recently."

Becky ate her last bite of cake and heaved a contented sigh. "Of all the things I bake, chocolate cake is one of my favorites. This one turned out quite moist and flavorful. I'll have to remember what I did so I can replicate it."

"Now who's *prevaricating*? You think I'm being unrealistic, don't you?"

"I have no way of knowing what advancements might have been made, but you could always visit a doctor to discuss your situation. I can recommend one." Becky looked at Callie with compassion in her warm brown eyes. "What I do know is that the Lord has a plan for you. If He wants you to experience the joys of motherhood, He'll make it happen. The Lord doesn't always answer our prayers in the ways we expect. There are other ways to become a mother."

"I know, but not everyone is willing to explore the alternatives."

"Are you talking about Chip?"

"I'm just speaking hypothetically." She didn't know what Chip thought about adoption, but she'd embraced the idea of adoption years ago, after Mom and Pop Marshall had taken her in and shown her what a loving family looked like. The orphans at the Double T dreamed of being taken in by loving families. Jasper and Ruby had captured her heart. Surely other children would, too, should she find herself in a position to become a mother to some of them one day.

But Chip's situation was different. He'd loved his family dearly and wanted to carry on their legacy, so the possibility of him considering adoption was so slim as to be nonexistent. As hard as it was to accept, all she could hope for was to relive the memory of the wonderful day they'd just had. There could be no more kisses. Chip was her friend, and that was all he could ever be.

The sky to the west was ablaze with color when Chip pulled his team to a stop in front of the Double T's massive barn that evening, a fitting ending for a ripsnorter of a day. Callie had welcomed his kiss. And what an amazing kiss it had been. Just thinking about it made him smile.

Hardy crossed the dusty yard, rousing Chip from his reverie. "I can take care of things from here if you'd like. I'm sure the young'uns are tuckered out after their busy day."

"If you'll park the wagon and put the horses in their stalls, that would be great. I'll come back and groom the team after I get this cowpoke tucked in." Chip reached for Jasper and helped him down.

"I could help you, Mr. Chip."

"As much as I appreciate the offer, pardner, I think you're going to be asleep as soon as your head hits the pillow." And he could spend a few minutes with Callie. Alone.

"I'm not tired." Jasper yawned.

Chip stifled a laugh. "Looks to me like you are. You can help me tomorrow instead."

"You mean it? Nobody's ever let me groom a horse before, not even Mr. Isaac."

"He doesn't know what a big helper you are yet, but I do."

Callie scooted to the edge of the wagon's bench seat. "May I hand the birthday girl to you, Chip? She's about ready to nod off."

"Certainly. Come here, princess." He took Ruby in his arms.

She rested her head on his shoulder. Her soft curls brushed his cheek. "I want my bed."

"We'll have you there in two shakes."

"Not that bed. The new one you made for my baby." Ruby patted the pink cheek of her rubber-headed doll. "She's sweepy."

"Is she now? We'll get you upstairs first, and I'll come right back down and get her bed."

The four of them entered Jack and Jill house. Callie led the way. Jasper trooped after her. Her footsteps were light, but he clomped across the wooden floor in his new cowboy boots. Chip followed with Ruby in his arms.

Callie stopped at the first floor landing to allow them to catch up. She pointed to Ruby and spoke softly. "Is she asleep?"

"Almost."

"If you'll wait here, I'll get her covers turned down." She set off down the hall, pushed open the door to the room she shared with Ruby and gasped.

Concern sent Chip hurrying toward Callie, but Jasper flew past him.

"No!" She closed the door with a bang, rousing Ruby. "D-don't go in there."

"What's wrong?" Jasper got the words out before Chip could.

The color had drained from Callie's face and her breath came in rapid bursts, as though she'd run a foot race. Whatever she'd seen had rattled her. "It's a bit of a mess in there, that's all. I, um, need to straighten a few things."

"You didn't clean your room?" Jasper shoved the door open, and his mouth fell open. "Oh, no. This looks bad. Real bad."

Chip turned Ruby's face into his chest and stepped behind Jasper. The sight sent a surge of white-hot anger surging through him. Someone had ransacked the place!

The wardrobe doors gaped. The contents were strewn around the room, covered in fuzzy brownish gray fluff. It looked like…horsehair? A quick glance confirmed his suspicions. The vandal—or vandals—had sliced open the mattresses and rummaged inside them.

Retreating footfalls clomped down the hallway.

"Jasper! Stop!" He couldn't let the lad go upstairs alone, but he couldn't leave Callie, either.

"Go ahead. I'll take Ruby."

He relinquished the whimpering girl. "I won't be long."

"We'll be fine."

He gave her what he hoped was an encouraging look and rushed after Jasper. That boy needed to learn to do what he was told.

The scene in Chip and Jasper's room resembled the one downstairs. The culprit had to be connected to Mr. Tate's murder. Whoever he was, he was certainly thorough.

Jasper rammed his hands against his hips. "The bad people messed up our room, too. Why?"

"They must have been looking for something."

"But we don't got any treasure. Just clothes and stuff. And my hat. I'm glad I had it with me." He patted the brim of his prized possession.

"You're right. But your papa did have something they might want."

Jasper's brow creased. "You mean the jewels you was asking me about, don't you?"

"Are you sure you don't know where he put them?"

"No. I told you. He hid 'em."

No matter how many times they asked Jasper, his answer was the same. That would work in their favor if the couple came back and questioned him. Preparing Jasper for the ploy couldn't be put off any longer because it appeared the killers were intent upon getting their hands on the jewels by whatever means possible.

"So you did. We need to get back to Miss Callie and

Ruby right away." They couldn't reach them soon enough to suit him. It appeared whoever had done the deed was gone, but Chip wouldn't feel safe until he'd canvassed the entire building.

He bounded down the stairs with Jasper right behind him, looked into the bedroom Callie and Ruby occupied and froze. They were nowhere in sight. "Callie!"

She stepped through the doorway of the adjoining room. "We're fine. Since these beds are finished, I thought Ruby and I would move in here."

"Good." He drew a breath in an attempt to slow his racing heart and closed the distance between them. "I'm going to leave Jasper with you while I make sure we don't have any unexpected visitors."

Her eyes widened but she managed to sound calm, an admirable feat after the shock they'd experienced. "I understand. I'll see to things here."

He completed his investigation as quickly as possible and returned to Callie and the children. She sat on a new mattress that had arrived in yesterday's shipment and cradled Ruby in her lap. The little girl had drawn herself into a ball.

Jasper sat beside them with his knees to his chest, looking more on edge than Chip had ever seen him. "Did you find the bad guys?"

"No. There's no one here but us."

"Someone *was* here and messed everything up. Wh-what if he comes back?" Jasper swiped a tear away.

Chip gritted his teeth. His fisted hands hung at his side. Tess would have to supervise the visit if the couple did return because if he laid eyes on them, he would have to fight the urge to wrestle them to the ground, tie them up and tell them exactly what he thought of their reprehensible acts. What kind of people would commit such heinous crimes?

Callie planted a kiss on top of Jasper's head. "We'll take good care of you. Mr. Chip and I will be with you all day, and the ranch hands will be on guard at night while we're asleep."

Jasper's lower lip protruded. "Where will Mr. Chip and I sleep? These are the only beds that aren't all torn apart."

"I have a great idea, pardner."

"What?"

"You and I can use bedrolls like real cowboys do. We can even bring in saddles for our pillows."

"Yee-haw! Can we keep our boots on, too? Mr. Hardy said he does when he sleeps on a cattle drive."

"Sure." Anything to take Jasper's mind off the intruder. "I'm going to help Miss Callie get this room ready first, and then we'll get our *camp* set up—after I get the bed for Ruby's doll, that is."

Callie waved them away. "You go ahead. We'll be fine."

"Will I see you later tonight?" They had plenty to talk about.

She tucked her lower lip between her teeth and gazed at the ceiling. Was she thinking about the kiss they'd shared? He certainly was. She nodded. "I'll be there."

Chip wasted no time gathering the items needed to bed down "cowboy style," as Jasper called it. Sleeping on the floor wasn't something Chip enjoyed. It brought back memories of nights spent sleeping under a wagon on the trail west and in barns when he was working for various carpenters while finishing his education. The day he'd turned eighteen and written The Plan, he'd vowed to spend every night from there on out in a bed.

But tonight was an exception. He'd gotten Jasper's focus on something other than the possibility of the intruders returning by suggesting the campout, so he would do his part.

Chip stretched out on his bedroll, rested his head on his saddle and crossed his arms and boot-clad feet. "It's time for us to head to the land of Nod, pardner."

"Mr. Chip, what do you and Miss Callie talk about when you go back downstairs?"

"What do you think?"

Jasper yawned. "Grown-up stuff."

"That's right."

"Do you kiss her good-night like you do me and Ruby?"

He would if he could. "A gentleman doesn't kiss a lady unless she makes it clear his kiss would be welcome." Which Callie clearly had.

"Do you want to marry her?"

"What makes you think that?"

"'Cause you look at her the way Papa Spencer looks at Mama Tess."

Did he? "I can't talk to her until you're asleep, so how about closing your eyes and listening while I tell you a story?"

Chip concocted a tale about a cowboy who loved chocolate cake and ate so much of it that it made him very sleepy. Not the best one he'd come up with, but his mind was on other things. Sweet things such as Callie and that kiss. That was a heap better than thinking about the unrelenting threat to the children from their father's murderers.

Jasper succumbed to sleep not long after Chip finished his story. He crept out of the room and padded down the hall, careful not to wake either of the children. Now to see how Callie had fared after their unnerving experience.

He found her sitting on the front steps of Jack and Jill House with her elbows on her knees and her chin in her hands, staring into the distance. She didn't stir until he sat beside her.

"Oh, there you are. I was miles away."

Standing in an apple orchard underneath the fragrant flowers perhaps? That's where his thoughts continued to roam. "I can see why. The here and now has its challenges. I saw Spencer while I was getting the saddles. He hadn't heard about the break in, but he'll ask around and see if any of his men saw something. Tess heard us talking and came out. She said not to deal with the cleanup tonight. She'll have someone take care of that tomorrow. Their primary concern is the children."

"I can't believe the lengths those awful people will go to in order to get their hands on the jewels." Her voice brightened. "At least the children are safe. I know they were shaken up by this, but they'll be all right—in time."

"About that. I feel certain the couple will come back for another meeting with Tess since they didn't find the jewels in our rooms, but I don't think having Jasper talk with them if they do is such a good idea after all. I'd have a hard time looking them in the face myself after all they've done, so I can't ask that of him."

She didn't answer right away. He waited, listening to the sounds of the night—horses moving about in the corral, frogs croaking in the nearby fields, ranch hands laughing over at the bunkhouse.

When she finally spoke, determination added force to her words. "If we let others cause us to cower, they've won the battle. We can't sit by and let fear cripple us. We must face it head on with faith, courage and hope."

"You might be able to do that, but I'm not sure Jasper can." Not everyone had Callie's ability to remain positive, even in the midst of trying situations.

"I feel certain he can, once he understands how his participation could help us catch the bad people who took his father from him. We must try, anyhow. I'll talk with him, explain everything and assure him that I'd be there, too. I've already seen the woman and didn't let on that I doubted her story, so she wouldn't suspect me."

If anyone could make this work, it was Callie, but... "I'm not willing to put you or Jasper in harm's way. These people are dangerous."

"I appreciate your concern, but what choice do we have? If we don't lure them out and put an end to this, they'll keep right on terrorizing the children."

The need to protect them burned within him with such intensity it threatened to consume him. He couldn't let anything happen to them. He wouldn't.

But Callie was right. Fighting an unseen foe was a losing battle. They had to take control. "I see your point, but if you do this, I'll be nearby ready to do whatever it takes to see that you and Jasper are safe."

She placed a hand on his arm. "I know you care about the children as much as I do and won't let any harm come to us. That's why I'm willing to do this."

Her faith in him fueled his desire to be the kind of man she could trust, but doubts gnawed at him. He cared for Jasper and Ruby, and his feelings for Callie were growing with each passing day, but he wasn't ready for others to rely on him yet. In order to provide the stability and security a wife deserved and children craved, he must follow The Plan. That's why he'd put it in place. He must stick to it, even if it meant distancing himself from Callie. "I look out for my friends."

"I know, and I appreciate that." She slid her hand down until it rested on top of his.

As much as he longed to twine his fingers with hers, he couldn't give her the wrong impression. The kiss had been wonderful. He had no regrets, but he mustn't give way to the attraction between them, no matter how much he might want to.

Chapter Nine

Footsteps on the porch of Miss Muffet House put Callie on alert. Three days had passed without incident, but she remained vigilant.

Chip entered the dining hall, and she released the breath she hadn't realized she'd been holding. "Good morning."

He hung his hat on a hook by the door, settled Jasper and Ruby on one of the benches and pulled Callie off to the side. "I do believe it is. We had a quiet night, and no one's seen any intruders skulking around this morning."

"I still can't believe someone walked right on to the property and no one noticed. How could that have happened?"

"The mystery's been solved. It turns out one of the older children saw someone slip inside Jack and Jill House that day. Apparently she thought it was just a ranch hand, so she didn't say anything—until she overheard her group leader telling another one about the break-in."

"I won't rest easy until all three of Mr. Tate's murderers are caught." She clutched the notes for the short talk she would be delivering in a few minutes. "I've found myself hoping the couple will show up soon so we can enact the plan and put an end to this ordeal. Living on tenterhooks is taxing. I've found myself quite distracted, which made preparing this morning's devotion difficult. I hope I don't make a fool of myself in front of everyone."

She'd been honored when Tess asked her to lead them in their daily worship, but now that the time was at hand, her chest tightened. Normally the scent of bacon made her eager to dive into her breakfast, but she wasn't sure she'd be able to eat a thing.

Chip sent her an encouraging smile. "You'll do a wonderful job, Callie. Just be your delightful self." He winked and took a seat beside Jasper and Ruby.

His compliments gave her hope that she'd misread things. Perhaps the cooling on his part since the night they returned and found their rooms ransacked was due to the tension they were under and nothing else. She'd placed her hand on his, thinking he might welcome the opportunity to hold it, but he'd pulled his away, which was puzzling. He had kissed her earlier that day, after all.

The arrival of the children drew her attention to the task awaiting her. She glanced at her notes one more time. Tess had asked her not to rely on them too heavily, but having them handy gave Callie a measure of comfort. She'd knew what she intended to say and wasn't a shy person, but speaking in front of a large number of people had been known to make her mind go blank.

When everyone was seated, children and group leaders alike, Tess stood and clapped. The room quieted. "It's lovely to see your smiling faces this morning. We're going to start this lovely spring day with a devotion from Miss Callie. I'm sure you'll enjoy it."

Callie stood and took her place at the front of the room. She clutched her sheet of notes in a trembling hand. "Mama Tess asked me talk to you about 1 John 3:18. It says—" she read from the paper "—'My little children, let us not love in word, neither in tongue; but in deed and in truth.'"

She looked up, saw all those pairs of eyes trained on her and froze. After several painfully long moments of silence, a hand shot up.

"Yes, Freddie?"

"What does that mean? We aren't supposed to say nice things to somebody? That doesn't seem right."

Bless the dear boy. He'd given her an idea. She abandoned her carefully prepared and oft-rehearsed script. "I'm going to tell a story about two boys. We'll call them Howard and Stanley. Suppose they were playing on the parallel bars and Howard picked on Stanley. Their group leader would ask Howard to apologize to Stanley, wouldn't he?"

Freddie nodded, as did several others.

"That would be showing love with words, which is a good thing, but there's more to it. Suppose Howard *said* he was sorry, but as soon as the group leader looked away, Howard turned to Stanley and did this." She stuck her thumbs in her ears, waggled her fingers and smirked.

The children burst out laughing.

She waited until they'd quieted and continued. "What I did might seem funny, but Stanley wouldn't think Howard was really sorry, would he? No. Stanley would know Howard's words weren't true because what he did was different than what he said."

Her gaze landed on Chip. He sent her an encouraging smile. She was struck by the fact that his words and actions were in alignment—but hers weren't.

Somehow, despite her realization, she managed to corral her thoughts and complete the devotion. She took her place between Jasper and Ruby and prepared to enjoy her breakfast after all. The tightness in her chest had eased, but her mind was whirling. Although she'd hoped her relationship with Chip could grow into something even more special than it already was, she hadn't been entirely honest with him—or herself. He'd made it clear he wanted children of his own. Unless something could be done to repair the damage she'd suffered, she wouldn't be able to bear any. She couldn't, in good conscience, encourage him. Not until she got some answers to her questions, anyhow.

Over a plate of crispy bacon, scrambled eggs and fried potatoes, she sought the help she needed. *Lord, please prepare me to face the truth, whatever that may be, to say what needs to be said and to do whatever I have to do. I trust You to provide the openings.*

Before Callie knew it, the meal was over. As soon as the tables were cleared, the school-aged children trooped after their teachers, followed by the younger children with their group leaders.

Jasper hopped up. "What are we gonna do today?"

A voice came from behind her. "You and Ruby could have a riding lesson. If that's all right with Mr. Chip and Miss Callie, of course. I have an opening right now."

Callie whipped around to find Isaac standing just inside the doorway. "What a good idea. I can take you and give Mr. Chip some time to himself." She glanced at him. "You don't mind, do you?"

Chip folded his arms and heaved an exaggerated sigh.

"It won't be easy, but I suppose I could do without my hardworking helpers for a little while."

Ruby peered up at Chip. "I'm not a helper. I just play with my baby."

"You may help if you'd like, princess. I'll be assembling the beds for another room today, and I could use someone to hand me the nails. Would you do that for me?"

She nodded, setting her curls bobbing.

He smiled. "Good."

They all left the dining hall together. Jasper walked alongside Isaac, slowing his steps to accommodate Isaac's limp and peppering him with questions. Callie reached for Ruby's hand, but she didn't take it.

"Jaspy can go first. I'm going to help Mr. Chip now."

"Very well." Seeing the precious girl take an interest in something other than her doll was encouraging.

Chip and Ruby headed to the woodshop. He scooped her up, placed her on his shoulders and gave her a bouncy zigzagged ride, which resulted in girlish giggles. The sight warmed Callie's heart. One day, the good Lord willing, she'd have a family with a devoted husband who doted on his children the way Chip doted on Jasper and Ruby.

But they weren't his children, and that's what he had his heart set on. Nothing would change unless he revised The Plan and entertained the possibility of adoption. Dare she hope he would?

Jasper's chatter came to a stop when he and Isaac neared the corral, drawing Callie's attention. The young cowboy-in-training soaked in every instruction Isaac gave him, one of them being to respect a horse's need for quiet. She wasn't sure if Isaac was thinking about the animal's needs or his own, but his eager pupil complied.

Her brother limped alongside Jasper as he walked his mount around the corral. They came to a stop nearby.

"You've got that down, Jasper. You're ready to move on to a trot. With my bum leg—" he patted it "—I can't keep up, so Hardy is going to help. I'll explain what you'll be doing, and he'll take you around."

"Really?" Jasper said softly. "That's gonna be fun."

Isaac went over the steps, with Jasper listening intently. Hardy took over, and Isaac joined Callie at the fence. "That boy is a born horseman. I wish all my students were as attentive and eager to learn."

"You do such a fine job with them. I love that you've found a purpose here. You're happier than I've seen you in a long time."

"Me, happy?" He chuckled. "I don't know about that, but I am doing better. You, on the other hand, are so happy you're almost glowing with it. Must be all the time you're spending with Chip."

"I enjoy his company, but it's the children who have put a smile on my face."

"Others might believe you, but I'm your brother. I know you, sis. You're smitten."

Arguing with Isaac would do no good. "Ruby's doing better today. She asked to help Chip. She's in there right now handing him nails."

"Changing the subject doesn't work on me. You know that." He pinned her with one of those probing gazes he was famous for. "So, tell me. Why are you afraid to admit you have feelings for him?"

She fought the urge to look away. "He's not ready to settle down, and even if he was, I don't think I'm some-one he'd be interested in."

Isaac barked out a laugh. "What nonsense. That man

can't take his eyes off you. It's a good thing I think so highly of him, or I'd be concerned."

Was Chip as attracted to her as she was to him? If so, perhaps he would be willing to alter his plans. She'd find out soon enough because he was headed their way, with Ruby skipping at his side and looking more at peace than ever before.

They reached the corral, and Isaac greeted them. "Are you ready to ride again, Ruby?"

She looked up at Isaac and responded without hesitation. "Yes."

"Well, then, let's get started."

Chip leaned on the top rail and watched as Isaac lifted Ruby onto the pony's back. "Our little butterfly has emerged from her cocoon."

"It's wonderful to see, isn't it? Your patience and kindness have played a big part in that. You're good with all the children."

"Seeing those two out there—" he swept a hand toward the corral, where Hardy jogged along Jasper and Isaac led Ruby "—makes me more eager than ever to achieve my goals so I can start my own family."

As hard as it was say the words, she had to know. "I can understand that. I find myself wondering what it would be like to give the children a home. Have you ever thought about adoption?"

Chip spun to face her and leaned back against the fence. "I know it's an option for some, but it's not one I've considered. I want to carry on my family's legacy."

Her chest grew tight, but she forced out a response. "I see."

"I don't mean to discount your experience. Adoption

can be a blessing in a case such as yours, but it's not for everyone."

He hadn't exactly slammed the door on the idea, but he'd come close. Even so, she felt compelled to stick her foot in the gap. "No, but it my case it worked out well. Mom and Pop Marshall were the ones who helped me overcome my fear of horses."

"I didn't know you were afraid of them. What brought that about?"

She'd prayed for an opening, and the Lord had provided one. Now she just had to say the words. "When I was young, I was a lot like Jasper. I liked adventure and thought riding a horse would be one. I convinced Father to let me learn when I was six. All went well until the horse got spooked and threw me. I tried to roll out of the way, but I got kicked."

Chip snapped to attention. "I'm so sorry. How bad was it?"

"I was laid up for several weeks. Apparently, there were a few critical days at the beginning that sent Mother and Father to their knees." She couldn't remember them since she'd been given hefty doses of laudanum for the pain, but it was nice to think that her parents had taken an interest in her. Sadly, they'd resorted to their usual busy ways soon after she'd recovered and left her care to Nanny Jean.

"They must have been beside themselves with worry. Caring for Jasper and Ruby these past weeks has shown me how hard it is to see a child hurting or scared. I can't imagine how I'd feel if they were fighting for their lives."

She knew exactly how he felt. The thought of either of the children being harmed was more than she could bear. "I don't know how it affected them, since they rarely spoke of it afterward." Except for that cold, wet winter's day shortly before the robbery, when the doctor arrived to examine her and confirmed his earlier diagnosis.

"Perhaps it was too painful to dwell on and they wanted to put it behind them."

She doubted that. Her mother had seemed quite distressed over the fact that few suitors would consider a *damaged* woman. Sadly, it appeared she'd been right. Since Chip was bent on having children of his own, he wouldn't be interested in her.

Or would he? If what Isaac said was true and Chip was attracted to her, he might be willing to modify his dream. After all, people had been known to do all manner of things for those they cared about. There was one way to find out. She could tell him the rest of the story, and see if that made a difference. "I'd like to think that, but—"

"Miss Callie!"

She wheeled around to see one of the group leaders headed their way. The young woman arrived, winded from dashing across the yard. "Tess asked me to get you and Jasper. There's a couple here that wants to meet him."

"Is the woman blond?"

"Yes."

Callie's skin turned to gooseflesh. They'd come. She glanced at Chip. The stricken look on his face must mirror her own. "Very well. Please tell her we'll be along shortly."

The messenger left, and Callie gripped the fence railing. "I felt certain they'd return, but now that they have, I dread subjecting Jasper to this."

"Don't do it." Chip's firm tone brooked no argument.

She rested a hand on his arm. Tension radiated from

him. "I know how you feel, but if we're to get the evidence needed to convict them, we must."

He covered her hand with his own. "If anything were to happen to you or Jasper..."

"I appreciate your concern, but what I need right now is for you to trust me. And to pray."

"If you insist on doing this, I'm not letting you go in there alone."

"It's all right. Spencer will be there. Tess will see to that." She'd feel better with a man present. Preferably a man with a gun.

Minutes later Callie entered the Abbotts' parlor with Jasper at her side. They'd rehearsed the plan one more time, and he was as prepared as he could be. He strode in with his usual confident air, cowboy hat in hand.

If only she was as self-possessed as Jasper. She'd been twelve years old when she found herself in her family's parlor with her parents' cold-hearted killers, and she'd crumbled. He was only five, and yet he'd chosen to face the very people who'd taken his father's life. She couldn't be more proud of him—or more concerned about him.

Lord, I love this dear boy so much. Please protect him. And, if it's Your will, let this turn out the way we planned.

Tess took charge, exhibiting her characteristic mix of competence and compassion as she interacted with the couple, appearing to put them at ease with friendly conversation. Her performance set the tone, with Spencer following his wife's lead. He even managed to produce an easy laugh at something Mrs. Smith said.

The scheming woman carried the couple's end of the conversation, with her supposed husband doing little more than answering direct questions. Mr. Smith's smiles were forced, and his gaze darted to Jasper far too often for Callie's liking. Thankfully, she wasn't expected to say much because she would have a hard time keeping the revulsion she felt out of her voice.

Jasper, seated beside Callie on one of the settees, was the shining star and took the attention coming his way in stride. He didn't even flinch when the woman squatted in front of him, pinched his cheek and declared him a "handsome little fellow."

Mrs. Smith—or whoever she was—returned to her seat, adjusted her silk skirts and spoke in a syrupy sweet voice. "It's lovely to meet Jasper, but I expected to see his precious sister, too. John and I are eager to get to know both of them better, aren't we, dear?"

The slender man, blond like the woman, nodded dutifully, but a bitter taste filled Callie's mouth.

Tess responded with a polite smile. "That won't be possible, I'm afraid. Jasper's sister isn't feeling like herself today."

That was true. Ruby had blossomed. Watching her reach out to Chip the way she had that morning was a rare but welcome sight. His response had warmed Callie's heart. He might say he had no desire to adopt, but he was wonderful with Jasper and Ruby. He always had a ready smile, word of encouragement or playful jest for Freddie and the other children at the Double T, too.

Mrs. Smith sighed. "I'm sorry to hear that. I'd so looked forward to seeing the precious little thing again, but we'll be patient, won't we, dear?" She glanced at her husband.

"Yes, of course. We're more than happy to talk with this young man." He nodded at Jasper and smiled, if one could call that pinch-lipped attempt a smile. Clearly, the woman was more adept at acting.

Mrs. Smith patted the man's knee. "Do forgive my husband's eagerness. I told him we would have to complete the paperwork first, but I wondered, Mrs. Abbott, if you and your husband might be willing to bend your rules a bit? Since John and I are in agreement that these children would make a wonderful addition to our family, might you allow us to visit with them today, combining two visits into one? John must go out of town on business again soon, so our time is limited."

Tess hesitated. "We rarely make exceptions to our policy, but if you'll give us a moment, my husband and I will discuss your request."

They stood in the entryway just outside the door, effectively blocking the only exit. Tess and Spencer cast glances at the couple and whispered. No doubt, they had plenty to say about the imposters, for Callie was certain that's what they were.

Mr. Smith hadn't even met Ruby, and yet the couple was willing to adopt her. Didn't the Smiths realize most prospective parents would want to see the child first?

Callie fought the urge to take Jasper and flee, but he sat there as placid as could be, turning his cowboy hat around and around in his hands. He'd been unwilling to leave it on one of the pegs in the entryway.

"Would you please come here for a minute, Callie?" Tess asked. "Spencer and I would like to know your thoughts."

Callie joined them, and Tess whispered, "We thought if we left them alone with Jasper a minute, they might question him. We'll pretend to be having a discussion ourselves, but keep your ears tuned to theirs."

The three of them carried on a hushed conversation, with Spencer and Tess apparently disagreeing about altering the policy and doing their best to enlist Callie's support. She wasn't expected to say much, enabling her to listen to the conversation in the parlor. Since she was facing the room, she could surreptitiously watch the interaction inside, too.

Mrs. Smith nodded toward Jasper's hat. "Are you a cowboy?"

He looked up and beamed. "Not yet, but I'm gonna be. Mr. Chip taught me how to walk like a cowboy, and Mr. Isaac's been teaching me to ride."

"Was your father a cowboy?"

"No. Papa worked in a jewelry store up in Marysville, but he was getting ready to open his own up in Placerville before he…went away." Jasper had taken the opening the couple had given him and done a wonderful job of working in his father's profession, previous location and destination. The coaching she and Chip had done paid off.

Mr. and Mrs. Smith exchanged a telling glance.

The man's eyes glinted with ill-disguised greed. "That sounds interesting. Did he make the jewelry himself?"

"Yep. And he was real good at it. He was gonna make a whole bunch for his new store. The jewels he got were all sparkly. He let me hold 'em."

Mr. Smith leaned forward. "Where are they now?"

"He said he hid 'em, but I don't know where. He was with us all the time—except for when Ruby's doll fell off the wagon and got hurt."

They pressed Jasper for more information and heard the tale of how Mr. Tate had slipped out to the barn behind the Railroad House hotel to reattach the doll's rubber head to her cloth body—out of sight of his heart-broken daughter. After hearing the story for herself, Callie had taken a look at the repair. The stitching was evidently the work of a novice, but it showed how much Mr. Tate had loved his daughter.

Mr. Smith's tone grew more insistent. "Where did this happen?"

Callie held her breath. Jasper had trouble remembering the name and generally required a bit of coaxing. Would he recall it this time?

Jasper blew out a breath, fluttering his lips in the process. "I can't remember. It's not Placerville, but it has a *ville* in it."

Her heart sank. If Jasper couldn't think of it, their plan could be foiled.

Mr. Smith scowled, but his wife smiled. "Clarksville, perhaps?"

Jasper brightened. "Yep. That's it."

Tess chose that moment to bring her feigned discussion with Spencer and Callie to a close. "Let's pray they've gotten what they came for and leave."

The three reentered the room, and Tess took charge. "I'm sorry to keep you waiting. I've managed to persuade my husband to forgo our usual policies and allow you to complete the forms and spend time with Jasper today. If you'll follow me, I'll get you set up at the dining table. It should only take half an hour or so."

Mr. and Mrs. Smith stood, and she sent Tess such a sugary smile that Callie's teeth hurt. "We're sorry to have troubled you, Mrs. Abbott, but John and I have decided that with all the traveling he's been doing lately, it wouldn't be wise for us to pursue adoption at this time. We'll return once his situation changes."

The couple left, and Callie whooshed out a breath. "That was interesting. Now what?"

Tess held up a finger. "We wait just a moment."

Jasper sidled up to Callie. "How did I do?"

She pulled him into a hug. "You were great!"

Footfalls thundered down the stairs, and, to Callie's surprise, Hardy appeared. "They headed west, just like you predicted, Spencer."

"Fine. Alert the others. We've got some criminals to catch."

Jasper burst into the woodshop and raced over to Chip. "The bad people came, and they took off. You gotta go after them."

Before Chip could reply, Callie appeared and leaned against the door frame. Her face was drawn and her breath ragged. "The couple took the bait, and they're headed west. Spencer's rounding up the posse as we speak."

A jolt of energy surged through Chip. He shot out a rapid-fire response. "Good. We can catch them now."

He yanked off his apron and tossed it on his workbench. He pulled his holster and Colt from the high shelf overhead, strapped them on and strode to the door.

Callie jumped in front of him, blocking his way. She rested a hand on his biceps and gazed at him with concern and deep affection, sending his heart rate soaring even higher. "I don't want anything to happen to you. Please be careful."

"I will."

"I'm counting on it." She went up on her tiptoes, brushed her lips across his cheek and disappeared inside the woodshop.

Callie had kissed him!

As much as he would have liked to pull her into his arms and hold her close, he had a job to do. He dashed to the barnyard. Isaac handed him the reins to one of his workhorses, already saddled and ready to go. In no time, Chip was in the saddle and filling in the other men on the plan he and Spencer had developed.

Isaac peered up at Chip. "I'd like to help, but with this leg, I wouldn't be much use. And then there's the other." He scuffed the dirt with the toe of his boot.

Although he'd been an excellent marksman, Isaac, with his aversion to sudden loud noises, lacked the qualifications for a posse member. "I'm counting on you to keep watch over Callie and the children while I'm gone."

Her brother glanced in the direction of Jack and Jill House, where Callie and the children were safe and secure. "I won't let anyone get near them."

Hardy, who had cut short Ruby's lesson to act as lookout earlier, drew alongside Chip. "Do you really think the couple will search the barn in broad daylight? Seems to me they'd wait for nightfall."

"They might, but if they think we just discovered the whereabouts of the jewels, too, they'll be out to beat us to them."

"So where are they?" Hardy asked.

Chip shrugged. "We don't know. I sent some telegrams to Placerville soon after we found Jasper and Ruby, but not a single shipment bound for their father has shown up. The deputy took some men down to the barn in Clarksville and performed an extensive search a few days back, but it didn't turn up anything, either."

"Quite a mystery, isn't it?"

"One that may never be solved, I'm afraid. The best I can figure is that Mr. Tate realized he was being followed and tossed the jewels out somewhere along the way, intending to go back and get them later."

Hardy's horse whickered. He leaned over to rub the gelding's neck. "Easy, fellow. We'll be on our way shortly."

Not soon enough for Chip. He watched as two more hands saddled their horses.

"Sad to think of the jewels going missing, isn't it?" Hardy asked. "They could have provided a good future for the young'uns."

Chip smiled. "I'm sure they'll have a good one. Spencer and Tess will see to that." As would the Lord.

"You could always find yourself a gal and take them in yourself."

"I could." If that was The Plan, which it wasn't. In order to have the family he'd been preparing for, he couldn't veer from it, even though a golden-haired beauty had him wondering what it would be like if that was an option.

At last, all the horses were saddled. Chip, Spencer, Hardy and three other hands rode out. Spencer had sent someone to town to alert the deputy, who would catch up to them.

The posse set off at last. With Clarksville ten miles away over rocky terrain, the ride would take a while. They would have been wiser to go into Shingle Springs and head down the main road than take off cross-country, but Chip hadn't wanted to add any distance to their trek.

The ride became even more of an adventure as they neared Clarksville, with rock walls to jump and flocks of grazing sheep to avoid. They would definitely return on the immigrant road, preferably with Mr. Tate's three killers in tow.

When they reached the edge of town, Chip had everyone circle up. "Here's what we're going to do. We'll gather in front of the Railroad House, leave our horses there and steal around back. I'll go into the barn first, with Spencer and Hardy right behind me. The rest of you will watch the rear entrance in case any of the killers make a run for it. Only two of them showed up at the Double T, but it's likely the third member of their trio was waiting for them."

Spencer chimed in. "In case you haven't heard, one of them is a woman. She was wearing a blue silk dress with white lace. She and her accomplice both have blond hair."

"We're not going to wait for the deputy?" Hardy asked.

"If we do that," Chip said, "it could be too late. We'll tie up the hoodlums and wait for him. Everyone ready?"

The men nodded and followed him to the hotel, where they dismounted and sneaked around back. Ignoring the sound of blood rushing in his ears, Chip darted across the yard and pressed himself to the side of the barn. He motioned for the others to join him. Spencer and one ranch hand came from the corner of the hotel closest to the barn, Hardy and the other two hands from the far end. They moved into their assigned positions.

Chip drew his breath—and his Colt—and crept toward the open doors. He listened for anything unusual, but all he could hear were the sounds of horses shifting in their stalls.

Had the trio inside realized he and the other men were there? Were the killers going to rush out with guns blazing? Would he be injured—or worse?

Summoning every ounce of courage he possessed, Chip slipped into the barn with his weapon at the ready. He stared into the vast expanse with his heart hammering against his ribs.

A quick glance around sent his breath out of him in a noisy puff. He spoke through gritted teeth. "It can't be!"

The murderers were no longer there, but they had been. The barn was a shambles, with tools, tack and feed strewn everywhere.

Spencer stood beside Chip, his revolver aimed into the expanse. "Looks like we just missed them."

Hardy joined them. "It appears they heard us and made their escape." He pointed to the back doors, which were ajar.

Chip raced the length of the barn, dodging shovels, pitchforks and all manner of other things. He slipped through the opening and found the remaining ranch hands staring into the distance, where a trio rode away. Blue skirts flapped around the legs of one of them. He shoved his gun into his holster with more force than necessary.

Hardy reached Chip, followed the others' gazes and produced a sliding whistle of disappointment. "That's tough."

"I can't believe they got away. We were so close."

Hardy slapped Chip on the back. "Don't worry. We'll get them next time."

The good Lord willing, there wouldn't be a next time. "At least we have proof of who they are and what they look like now. That should help the sheriff catch them."

"You sound like Miss Callie. She's always looking on the bright side."

Callie. Chip's shoulders drooped. How was he going to face her after failing to bring this ordeal to an end?

Chapter Ten

How much longer would the posse be gone? It would be time for supper soon.

Callie sat between Jasper and Ruby on a bench at the edge of the playground and did her best to focus on the story he was telling, but her thoughts were in Clarksville with a kind, caring and very courageous carpenter. Although she'd lifted up more prayers that day than she had in the past month, she added another. *Please, Lord, protect Chip and the others*.

"Miss Callie?" Jasper tapped her on the shoulder. "You weren't listening, were you?"

"I'm sorry. What did I miss?"

"The end, and that's the best part. Cowboy Bob caught the cattle rustlers, and everyone was safe."

"That's good." Surely Chip and those with him had been as successful. Since Jasper and Ruby would no longer be in danger, she and Chip wouldn't need to protect the children from a trio of ruthless killers. They could focus on the furniture they had yet to finish. That certainly seemed to be Chip's focus. Ever since that delightful kiss they'd shared, he'd been distant, preoccupied.

Of course he had. He was a man of action, and yet he'd been forced to watch and wait. But not anymore. Now that Mr. Tate's murderers were caught, Chip would be able to complete his job at the Double T, return to his place and tackle the next tasks in that precious plan of his—a plan that didn't allow for someone like her.

The sound of hooves on hard-packed earth made Callie shoot to her feet. "They're back! Let's go." She scooped Ruby into her arms and took off after Jasper, who sprinted toward the barnyard.

"Be careful around the horses, Jasper."

He raced toward the men busy dismounting but slowed when he neared them, much to Callie's relief. The brave boy had been as eager for Chip's return as she had. The only thing that had kept Jasper from asking her repeatedly when Chip would return was a gentle reminder that the questions could upset Ruby. Ever the protective older brother, he'd exercised remarkable restraint, but, like Callie, he'd scanned the area every few minutes for signs of the posse.

At long last they were here, and the killers were in jail where they belonged. She couldn't wait to congratulate the men on their part in capturing the trio.

"Mr. Chip!" Jasper wove his way to Chip's side, with Callie right behind.

Chip turned and smiled at them, but the smile was forced. Had something gone wrong? Had someone been hurt? He didn't appear to be, but perhaps one of the other men was.

A quick scan revealed a group of men as fit as ever but moving slowly and methodically, each wearing the unmistakable cloak of defeat. She took a step back, swallowed and managed to summon a pleasant tone. "We're glad to see you. Ruby and Jasper have missed you. So have I."

Perhaps she shouldn't have added that, but it was true. She'd spent the past several hours thinking of little else but him, his safety and how devastated she would have been if something had happened to him. Ever since she'd met Chip, she'd found him a delightful companion, but he'd become so much more than that over the past weeks. Working alongside him had revealed one endearing trait after another.

Chip's eyebrows rose at her admission, but he quickly turned away, focused on removing the saddle from his tired and dusty mount. All the horses looked equally spent, and the men appeared just as weary and disheveled. Their discouragement was palpable. If she wasn't careful, she could fall prey to its pull.

He hefted the saddle into his arms and spoke softly. "They got away."

She kept her voice low, too. "I surmised as much, but you'll get them next time."

Jasper shoved his way between them. "Can I help you brush your horse?"

"Sure thing, pardner."

Chip's consideration warmed Callie's heart. Even though he was battling fatigue and frustration, he'd set aside his needs for Jasper's sake.

Ruby watched them as they headed to the barn. "Mr. Chip is nice."

"That he is, sweetheart. While he and Jasper tend to the horse, you and I could have a make-believe tea party. Would you like that?" If she kept busy, she wouldn't have time to dwell on the posse's failed attempt to capture the killers and could keep up a cheery front. She mustn't give Ruby any reason to suspect what had taken place that afternoon—and what hadn't. If she knew the bad people had returned to the Double T and were still on the loose, she might retreat again.

The dinner bell rang once, calling everyone in for supper, and yet Chip and Jasper hadn't returned. Callie coaxed Ruby to leave her acorn teacups behind with a promise of another tea party the next day. Hand in hand, they made their way to Miss Muffet House and entered the dining hall.

Chip and Jasper were already seated. Callie and Ruby took their places. As much as Callie longed to know what had transpired down in Clarksville, her questions would have to wait.

At long last, dinner and the post-meal playtime were over and they could take the children up to bed. A good half hour passed before Ruby succumbed to sleep's call and Callie was free to join Chip downstairs.

She reached the bottom floor of Jack and Jill House, but there was no sign of Chip. No doubt he was having a hard time getting Jasper settled. The inquisitive boy was sure to have plenty of questions. She'd answered all those she could after the men set out, but he'd want to know everything that had happened after the posse rode off. So did she.

Before Callie could talk herself out of it, she climbed the two flights of stairs and marched down the hall, past the room that had been vandalized, to the room Chip and Jasper now shared. She stood outside the door with a fisted hand raised but dropped it to her side.

No sound came from within, which was odd. She would have expected to hear voices. If Jasper was already asleep and she rapped on the door, she might wake him.

Chip wouldn't thank her for that. She'd just have to wait until he showed up downstairs.

She returned to the large playroom. Empty, as before. Could Chip be waiting for her outside?

The sound of male voices drifted through the open window, close enough to distinguish who they belonged to but not near enough to make out the words. Chip was talking with Spencer.

Apparently, Chip hadn't waited for her. The realization stung.

The need to know what had taken place sent her outdoors. The men stood under a large oak tree that shaded a corner of the corral by day. With the sun setting, they were in shadow, making it impossible for her to make out Chip's expression. His sagging posture and flat voice spoke for him. He felt like he'd failed. Well, she could do something about that.

She ambled over to the men. Spencer saw her first and inclined his head toward her. Chip's shoulders rose and fell, as though he'd heaved a sigh. He said something to Spencer, turned and trudged toward her.

They met halfway. A shaft of light made his dark brown hair gleam, but there was no light in his eyes.

She kept her voice bright. "It's a lovely evening, isn't it? Not too warm. And look at the colors in the sky tonight."

He glanced at the wispy clouds streaked with pinks, oranges and purples but quickly lowered his gaze, focusing on a spot somewhere behind her. "It won't work, Callie."

"What do you mean?"

"You can't ignore the truth. The killers are still on the loose, thanks to me."

Chip was taking full responsibility for something out of his control. "They're out there somewhere, but that's not your fault."

He scoffed. "It's my job to protect you and the children. I take that responsibility seriously."

"I know you do. That's why it hurts me to see you blaming yourself." She closed the distance between them, rested her hands on his broad chest and peered up at him. "You've done a wonderful job, and you'll keep right on doing it until those horrid people are caught. I know that, and so do Jasper and Ruby. We trust you."

He stared at her for several seconds. And then, without warning, he pulled her into arms, pressing her cheek against the broad expanse of his chest. "I won't let you down again. You have my word."

The intensity of his vow sent a surge of warmth through her. Chip cared about her. He might not say it, but his actions proved it. Although Mr. Tate's killers were still at large, she and the children had a fierce protector. The thought evoked a sense of peace in the midst of the uncertainty.

Emboldened by Chip's embrace, she slid her hands down his sides and wrapped them around his waist. He tensed. She lifted her face to him, searching for reassurance. Instead, he placed his hands on her shoulders and took a step back. Her arms fell to her sides, feeling as heavy as her heart. He didn't care for her after all.

No! That wasn't true. A gentleman like Chip didn't dally with a lady's emotions. His kiss proved he cared. Something was keeping him from giving way to his feelings, and she knew just what that was. *The Plan.* She'd come along too soon. If she bided her time, perhaps he would alter that plan and—

"They left before we got there."

His statement brought her musing to an abrupt end. She said nothing, waiting for him to continue, which he did, speaking in a dull, lifeless tone.

"I don't know what tipped them off. Perhaps one of them was watching for us. They hadn't wasted any time, though. Mrs. Tong's barn had been turned upside down. We gave chase, but they went through several fields filled with goats. There were so many tracks that we couldn't make theirs out and lost the trail. We returned to the Railroad House and put things to right for Mrs. Tong. She fed us lunch in the hotel's dining hall, and we came back here."

"Since they didn't find the jewels, what will they do now?"

"The deputy thinks they figured out it was a trap, hightailed it and—" He clamped his mouth shut.

"And realized we don't have them, either, and will leave us alone, right?" The possibility, albeit unlikely, gave her hope.

"That's not likely." His voice had an edge to it. "They'll think we found them and come looking for them. Again."

Her brow furrowed. "But they've already searched our rooms."

"Our rooms, yes, but not the woodshop. If they've been watching us, as Spencer and I suspect, they know that's where we spend most of our time, so it makes sense they'll search it. He's going to have a ranch hand sleep there, too."

Her hope faded. "So nothing's changed? The children are still in danger?"

"Yes, but so are you and I. If they think we've found the jewels, everyone at the Double T is at risk. And *I* brought this on them." He removed his hat and speared a hand through his hair, leaving it rumpled.

"Not you. *We.* I agreed that bringing Jasper and Ruby here was a good idea. We got into this together, and we'll see things through together. We're a team, Chip." At least that's how she saw it. If only he did, too.

He blew out a breath. "I'm sorry for speaking so sharply. Today was…frustrating. I wanted to return with good news, but I couldn't. And now we're back to waiting and worrying. We don't even know what will happen next or when it will take place. It's impossible to plan for something like that."

"I'm sure everything will be fine. Now that the sheriff has a description, he can send out wanted posters. The killers will be caught, and we can have fun completing the furniture." She didn't want to think about what would happen after that. Things could change. They would change.

"We'll finish the job, but we'll need to be more vigilant than ever. I can't abide the thought of those money-grubbing murderers harming you, the children or anyone else." Footfalls on hard-packed earth announced the arrival of the ranch hands on night duty. "Since they're here, I'm going up. It's been a long day, and I'm exhausted. I'll see you in the morning."

He strode toward Jack and Jill House, leaving her alone and confused. If he cared about her, as she suspected, why was he forgoing their nightly ritual? He'd been tired before, but he'd still passed a pleasant half hour with her. She needed him and his reassuring presence, but apparently he didn't need her.

Unable to think of sleeping yet, Callie wandered over to the swings. She clutched the chains on the nearest one, walked back as far as she could, jumped on the seat and enjoyed the gentle breeze as she glided to and fro. With all the children in their rooms, she had the playground to herself. Her petticoats flapped about her ankles, but since she faced away from the buildings and the sun had set, propriety wasn't a concern.

The swish of skirts caused her to turn. Tess joined Callie and took a seat on the swing beside hers. "Lila saw someone from her bedroom window, and I came to investigate. We can't be too careful these days, what with Mr. Tate's killers still out there somewhere."

Callie dragged her feet to bring herself to a stop. "I'm sorry to trouble you. I'm usually inside by now, but Chip headed upstairs right away, so I came out here to think."

"It's no trouble. In fact, I'm glad it's you. I noticed things between you and Chip seemed strained at dinner. Is everything all right?"

"I don't know. We've always spent the evening together, but he headed up early tonight. He said he was tired, but I figure there's more to it."

The wooden support beam creaked as Tess rocked gently forward and back. "He's probably disappointed that they didn't catch the killers. Spencer is."

"Chip blames himself. I've never seen him like this. He's usually so easygoing, but he was quite upset."

"That's understandable. A man doesn't like to feel inadequate. He set out to capture the killers, but his plans didn't work out. Those he cares about are still in danger, and he can do nothing but wait until the murderers make their next move."

Chip had said much the same thing. "Isn't it possible they'll give up and move on?"

"It's possible but doubtful. They're probably planning

their next move. We're likely to have a reprieve, which is why I think it would be a good time for you and Chip to head to Placerville and place the final lumber order. Spencer agrees, so we'll watch the children for you while you make the trip up the hill."

"Why both of us? Chip doesn't need my help."

"No, but you two could use some time alone to mend your relationship."

Callie sighed. "There is no relationship. We're just friends."

"You might believe that, but the looks that pass between you tell a different story. You obviously care about him, and I believe he cares about you, too. Spending the day together could serve to move things along."

"I doubt that. He doesn't want me."

Tess stopped swinging and turned to Callie. "What makes you say that?"

She hadn't meant to voice her thoughts, but now that she had, Tess deserved an explanation. As quickly as possible, Callie summarized the accident and the doctor's diagnosis, along with Chip's desire to have children of his own.

Tess pushed her toes against the ground, setting her swing to moving again. "Sitting here reminds me of the day Luke taught me how to swing."

"Don't you mean you taught him?"

"No. I came when he was four and Lila was just a baby."

Tess wasn't the children's mother? The shock rendered Callie speechless.

"The orphanage where I grew up was in a large city. We didn't have a nice playground like this, so I'd never been on a swing. I didn't catch on as quickly as Luke

would have liked, and he got quite frustrated with me."
Tess chuckled at the memory.

"I had no idea you weren't their mother."

Tess's response was emphatic. "Oh, but I am. I love
Luke and Lila every bit as much as I love the children I
birthed, and they love me in return." Her voice grew soft,
her tone reflective. "It wasn't always that way, though.
Luke was quite angry when I arrived. He spent months
refusing to call me by name. When he finally did, I was
beside myself with joy. A few weeks later, Spencer married me and Luke called me 'Mama' for the first time.
My heart was filled to overflowing because the Lord
had given me the family of my dreams."

If only Chip saw things the same way. "I'm happy
for you. Not everyone is willing to take another person's
child as their own, although I think it's a wonderful alternative. Mom and Pop Marshall, who took me in when
my parents were killed, treated me like a treasured gift.
I'd never known love like that before."

"I can see why you would embrace the idea of adopting a child then. It might be forward of me to ask, but
does Chip share your views?"

Callie pressed her lips together and blinked to clear
the sudden moisture in her eyes. Thankfully, the darkness prevented Tess from seeing her moment of weak-
ness. "His experience was different than mine. He adored
his family and longs to carry on their legacy."

"I see."

Since Callie couldn't come up with a reply, she leaned
her head against the rope and listened to the sounds of
children being put to bed in the dormitories behind them.
Girlish giggles were followed by the muted voices of
group leaders attempting to quiet their charges. Each of

those children longed for one thing—a family. If only the Lord could make a way for her to provide a home for some of them.

Tess stood, and Callie did the same. "Have you considered visiting a doctor out here and seeing if there's anything that can be done?"

"I think I will." That was the only way to get the answers she sought. She would send Dr. Wright a telegram tomorrow and make an appointment to see him when she and Chip went up to Placerville. If the doctor knew of some way to reverse the damage that had been done when that horse kicked her, she'd be free to follow her heart. If not, she could accept the news, pour herself into her new job and make a difference in children's lives right there at the Double T. All would be fine—provided she didn't let herself dwell on what she'd lost.

The warm spring day, the jangle of his team's harnesses and the scent of Callie's perfume combined to create a pleasant atmosphere. The tension in Chip's shoulders eased more with each passing mile. He'd have to thank Tess for suggesting he and Callie get away from the Double T, just the two of them.

Out here on the main road he was enjoying a sense of freedom that he hadn't experienced since they'd discovered Jasper and Ruby huddled together that memorable morning. Callie's company added to the peaceful feeling. She, too, had shed the wariness of the past weeks and was her cheerful self. They'd spent the past nine miles talking, the conversation flowing as freely as the runoff in the Sierras.

"Your house sounds wonderful. I'm sure it will be a work of art when you're done."

"Would you like to see it? I could use a woman's input on where to put the shelves in the kitchen—and how many are needed."

She laughed, a light, airy sound he found quite appealing—as he did her. She looked particularly fetching in her pretty purple dress. "I doubt I could tell you anything you don't already know."

"Since the wife I plan to have someday is likely to be a good deal shorter than I am, having you there would help me visualize things. What do you say?"

"I'd be delighted to help."

He'd be delighted to have her help. She'd proven to be knowledgeable about woodworking, and she possessed a wealth of good ideas. Best of all, she had a way of chasing away the worries that had been his ever-present companions of late.

Chip pulled off the main road just west of town minutes later, parked in front of his two-story house and hopped from the wagon.

Callie gazed at his home with her mouth parted and her eyes wide. "It's magnificent! I like the Italian-influenced style you chose. It's quite popular now. The rich berry-red on the clapboards and creamy white for the trim are a switch from the light-colored siding and darker trim I'm used to seeing, but the bolder colors suit you. They're a nice reflection of your vibrant personality."

She saw him as bold and vibrant, did she? Interesting. His mother had used the same words to describe him when he was a boy, but he hadn't thought of himself that way in years. Callie had helped him rediscover that side of himself.

"The L shape is different, too, but I like the way you've staggered three sections of the house, with the second and third portions jutting out to the right beyond the ones before them. I presume the single-story section at the back that forms the long leg of the L is your woodshop?"

"It is." Although he completed his construction work at the job sites, he built furniture in his shop.

She climbed from the wagon and continued her perusal and running dialogue. No one had ever critiqued his work this way, and he liked it, especially since she seemed to appreciate the unique elements he'd added.

"With the plentiful windows, the interior must be basked in light. Those on the front with the bracketed crowns and moveable shutters are quite attractive. The decorative truss in the gable above the small attic window draws the eye upward nicely." She lifted her head higher yet, moved it back and forth and nodded. "The combination of the four gabled rooflines creates an appealing whole."

"I'm glad you like it."

"Who wouldn't? It's quite attractive…and expansive. I didn't expect a bachelor to have such a large home."

He surveyed the house with a touch of pride. It was large, but that was intentional. "I made it big enough for the family I'll have one day. If you're ready, we could go inside."

"By all means." She crossed the yard, climbed the three steps to the small porch and faced the double front doors. "These windows with their round arches are a nice touch."

She moved to the side, giving him access to the door. "Why don't you open it? Here's the key."

Her lips lifted in a playful smile. "If you insist." She held out a hand and focused her attention on it.

He placed one hand beneath hers and placed the key on her upturned palm, allowing his rough fingertips to graze her soft skin. She folded her fingers over the key and slowly lifted her head until their gazes locked. He leaned toward her and paused, gauging her response. Attraction flickered in the depths of her clear blue eyes, but she blinked, and it was gone.

She gave a decisive nod, turned away and slipped the key in the lock. The clunk of the tumblers caused his heart to sink. Although she'd opened the door to his house, it appeared she had shut him out. But why? She'd welcomed his kiss at her friend's orchard. Why not now?

The Plan didn't call for him to court a woman for another three years, but the more time he spent with Callie, the more the idea of pursuing a relationship with her appealed to him. She was bright and beautiful, and she had a way with children. Not only that, but she also admired his work and enjoyed participating in it. What more could a man ask for? He'd be a fool not to consider her as a possible partner in life. Their children would be beautiful, like her.

Now to figure out how to convince Callie to be a part of his plan and hope she'd be willing to wait until he was in a position to take a wife.

Chapter Eleven

The scent of roses greeted Callie. Scanning the foyer of Chip's magnificent home, she spotted a crystal bowl filled with potpourri, not something she'd expected to find in a bachelor's domain.

She lifted a handful of the fragile petals and let them drift from between her fingers. "What a nice touch."

"My mother said the fragrance of flowers makes guests feel at home. I forget to change fresh ones, so I opted for dried."

"It sounds like she was a wise woman."

A wistful look flitted across his face. "She was. Although she had four boys, she insisted on teaching us about the finer things in life. We took turns serving as her escort to our family's pew each week, and we practiced our table manners at Sunday dinners."

"You were obviously an apt pupil." And a devoted son. No wonder family mattered so much to Chip. He'd come from a loving one with parents who treasured their children as he would his.

Yes. *His.* As much as she'd hoped he would consider adoption, his desire to have a family of his own remained as strong as ever. Although the thought of seeing Dr. Wright and getting his learned opinion caused her chest to tighten, she must. To welcome Chip's attentions while keeping the diagnosis to herself would be unfair to him. He'd wanted to kiss her again on his stoop. She'd longed to let him, but she couldn't. Not until she found out if there was something that could be done for her. It might be foolish to hold out hope, but giving up without exploring all the options wasn't her way.

He held out a hand to the room on the left. "Why don't we start with the parlor?"

Venturing inside, her appreciation of his lovely home grew. Cornices crowned walls covered with rich wallpaper in William Morris's larkspur pattern—medium green sprays of foliage over a light green base. An assortment of chairs and settees in dark green and gold, complete with puffy pillows to match, offered ample seating. A painting of a field of California poppies hung over the rock fireplace. The elements created an inviting atmosphere.

"You've done a fine job. It's attractive but homey." She could picture herself spending evenings in the welcoming room with Chip. Their children would gather around them, filling the parlor with love and laughter.

Yes. Children. She would have as many as God chose to bless her with through whatever means He saw fit to use. The Lord knew her wish to experience motherhood, and He could remove the obstacles that stood in the way of her happiness.

Provided that was His plan. She prayed it was, because if it wasn't... She forced her thoughts back to the present and focused on what Chip was saying.

"I like it, although I don't spend much time here. Yet."

She chuckled. "Knowing you, you're out in your shop building things from morning to night."

"You're right, but that will change in a few years when I have my family."

His statement, delivered in that matter-of-fact manner, firmed her resolve to keep her appointment with Dr. Wright. In less than an hour, she'd know the truth about her situation and what could be done about it. She prayed she was strong enough to handle the news.

"If you're ready to move on, we can see the upper floor."

"Certainly." She took a last lingering look at the parlor and followed him up the stairs, her hand gliding along the smooth bannister as she made her ascent. The fresh scent of lemon oil hung in the air.

Four bedrooms came off the upper landing. She entered the one to her right and studied the headboard. "I've been impressed with your attention to detail on the utilitarian furniture we're making for Jack and Jill House, but your workmanship on these more involved pieces is exemplary. My parents were partial to the rococo revival style with its high relief carvings and dark stains. Like you, I prefer the new Eastlake designs." She traced the geometric patterns with a fingertip. "The modest curves, lightly incised carving and oiled finishes combine to create a simpler look that's refreshing and far more practical."

"I know you're well versed when it comes to types of woods, but I didn't realize you were so knowledgeable about furniture styles."

"That wasn't always the case. Working with talented woodworkers such as yourself has expanded my horizons. When I was a younger, I used to read fashion magazines and dream about my next gown. These days I read books on furniture making. I got a copy of Eastlake's *Hints on Household Tastes in Furniture, Upholstery, and Other Details* soon after it came out last year. You must have gotten a copy of the British edition released earlier since it wasn't available here in the United States until later. How did you manage that?"

He leaned back against the bureau and folded his arms. The fabric of his jacket strained to contain his muscular biceps. She forced herself not to stare at the alluring sight. "I trained with a furniture maker who'd come over from England, and he gave me a copy. I devoured it."

"If Mr. Eastlake could see your work, I'm sure he'd be pleased at how well you've incorporated his ideas into your lovely home. Every room is a shining example."

"I look forward to the day these up here are filled with children."

She struggled to keep her attention on what Chip was saying rather than admiring his manly physique. "You must plan to have a lot of them."

"At least four, but I could add on rooms if the Lord has more in mind." He shoved off the bureau to a standing position. "If you're done here, we could move on."

"I'd like that." She preceded him down the stairs.

She paused in the open doorway to her left. The large bedchamber must be his. The massive four-poster bed, made of oak, was magnificent, as were the matching wardrobes.

"You may go in if you'd like."

Although it felt strange to enter his room, she couldn't fight the pull. A stuffed toy dog rested its well-worn face against the pillow sham, just begging to be studied up close. Based on the sorry condition of the little jet-black fellow, he had evidently been much loved. The mental image she formed of Chip as a boy hugging the floppy-eared dog made her smile.

She rubbed a finger over the dog's cheek. Eager to learn more about the animal, she resorted to a thinly veiled query. "If Jasper were here, he'd have plenty of questions about your little friend."

Chip rested a shoulder against the door frame, staring at some point over her shoulder for the longest time. When he spoke, his speech was halting, as though forced through a throat thick with emotion. "When we prepared to head west, Mama and Papa said the trip would be too hard on our dog, so they found a new home for him. I didn't take that well, since Checkers and I had been such good pals. Mama made that little dog for me as a way to remember him." He swallowed, his Adam's apple bobbing. "It's the last thing she made, and it was for me."

His voice cracked on the final words, causing her chest to constrict. She blinked to clear her vision. Chip had told her about the tragic loss of his family, but this was the first time his grief threatened to overcome him.

She longed to throw her arms around him and ease his pain, but with his arms folded tightly against his chest and his eyebrows dipped into a scowl, he clearly didn't want sympathy. "Shall we go to the kitchen?"

Chip's features and posture relaxed, but the hollowness in her chest persisted. If only he'd let her offer what comfort she could.

He straightened, stepped in the hallway and held out a hand. "After you. I'm eager to get your input."

The next fifteen minutes passed quickly as Chip explained what he had in mind for his dining room and kitchen. He invited her to share her opinion of his plans, which she did. Freely and in detail.

She shouldn't allow herself to harbor dreams of being the woman who would prepare and serve meals in these rooms. If there was nothing that could be done to repair the internal damage she suffered all those years ago, she could be setting herself up for more disappointment and heartache, but she couldn't help herself. As happy as she would be working as a group leader and caring for children at the Double T, her desire to experience marriage and motherhood was strong.

Chip propped himself on the corner of a makeshift work surface fashioned from roughly hewn boards. "So, we agree that oak is the best wood due to its ability to resist scratches, as Eastlake says. And you recommend the larger decorative hinges over the smaller hidden variety in vogue today, as he does."

Callie nodded. "They would be better able to withstand the frequent opening and closing the doors on the sideboard and china cabinet would see. One of the things I like most about his style is the marriage of aesthetics and functionality."

"One last question. If this was your kitchen, is there anything else you would add?"

If only it could be. She could imagine the thrill of preparing meals in his beautiful kitchen, sitting down beside him at his expertly crafted dining table and taking his large hand as he gave thanks for the meal. "That's easy. I'd want carvings on the furniture in here similar to those on your wardrobes. Adding the decorative elements would create extra work, but a family spends several hours a day in these rooms. I think they should be as attractive as the others."

"I'll have to consider that." He stood. "We should get going. I've kept you long enough."

She didn't mind in the least. Being in his lovely home filled her with a sense of peace—and a sense of purpose. Although she'd had qualms about visiting the doctor, Becky said Dr. Wright had been college-educated and kept up on the latest developments. If anyone could give her a definitive diagnosis, Dr. Wright could. She would march into his office with confidence and leave with certainty.

"Miss Hunt?"

The feminine voice startled Callie. She jerked her head toward the doorway leading from Dr. Wright's waiting area to the rooms beyond. A round-faced woman stood there wearing a welcoming smile and an ankle-length white apron.

"I'm Callie Hunt." But who was she?

"Very well. If you'll follow me, I'll take you back."

Callie followed the woman, who walked at a brisk pace, her boot heels thudding on the pine floorboards. Becky had said the doctor worked alone, but obviously that wasn't the case.

"Here we are." The kindly lady stepped aside to let Callie enter. An examination table occupied the center of the small room. The distinctive scent of laudanum hung in the air. "You may take a seat, and then you can tell me why you're here."

Relief eased the tension in Callie's shoulders. Talking about such a delicate matter with another woman would be much easier than attempting to discuss it with a man.

She settled herself on the bentwood chair and smoothed her skirts. "I thought I'd be seeing Dr. Wright."

Not that she wanted to, but it would be nice to know who she would be confiding in.

The woman sat on a stool, facing Callie, and sent her an apologetic smile. "Forgive me for not introducing myself. I haven't been in town long and don't know who is aware of the news and who isn't. I'm his nurse—and his wife—Mable Wright."

"I'm the one who should apologize. I didn't mean to be so outspoken. My friend who recommended him hadn't mentioned you." Becky would be surprised to hear the news, but she'd also be happy for the doctor. She'd mentioned that Matthew Wright had taken an interest in her when she was caring for her husband's mother prior to her marriage and had felt badly about not returning the doctor's feelings.

Mrs. Wright's face flushed. "Ours was a whirlwind romance. I grew up back East. His sisters and I are good friends. I accompanied them on a visit to Placerville recently. When Matthew and I saw one another—" The color on the sweet woman's cheeks deepened to red. "What am I doing? You didn't come here to listen to a newlywed's prattle."

"It's fine. I'm happy for you." If the visit went as Callie hoped and Dr. Wright knew of something that could be done to repair the damage she'd suffered all those years ago, she might experience the same joy herself one day.

"Thank you. All the same, I should get down to business. The doctor didn't mention why you'd requested an appointment. What seems to be the trouble?"

As quickly as possible, she told Mrs. Wright about the accident, the diagnosis when she was six, the confirmation when she came of age and didn't experience the "monthly reminders of womanhood," as Becky had so tactfully put it, and her hope that a surgery or procedure might exist that would correct whatever it was that had gone wrong inside her.

"The best place to start would be for me to perform an examination. I could discuss my findings with my husband. That way you'd have two assessments—and the benefit of his expertise. He's a learned man and is well versed in the latest medical advancements, as your friend mentioned."

Mrs. Wright's reassuring smile eased Callie's fears somewhat. Even so, she felt her dream of a possible future with Chip slipping away.

"I'm fine with an examination, and I'd be happy to hear the doctor's thoughts, along with your own." She was open to any and all possibilities.

Twenty minutes later, Callie sat on a plush chair in the doctor's well-appointed office while he and his wife conferred in the examination room. With as much pressing and prodding as Mrs. Wright had done, surely she had been able to get all the information needed.

The clock on the floor-to-ceiling bookshelf that boasted an impressive collection of medical texts ticked off the seconds. Callie ran her hands along the smooth wooden arms of the chair. Minutes from now she would know if the faint hope that something could be done for her would have the opportunity to grow or whether it must be forever put to rest.

Dr. and Mrs. Wright entered the room a short time later. He took his place in the leather armchair behind the massive desk. His wife sat in the armless chair beside Callie's. Neither of their expressions revealed anything.

Callie braced herself for the news, whatever it might be. "What did you find out?"

A look passed between the couple that held…sympathy? Callie's mouth went dry.

Mrs. Wright placed a hand on Callie's arm. "I know this isn't what you wanted to hear, but based on your symptoms and my physical examination, the doctor and I believe the earlier information you were given is accurate. It appears you suffered some internal damage. I was able to the determine that your w…"

The nurse's lips continued to move, although Callie could hear nothing but the rushing of blood in her ears. A cold, hollow sensation filled her chest, and her skin turned to gooseflesh. She clenched her teeth to keep them from chattering.

At length, she became aware of Dr. Wright's deep voice. He was saying her name. "Miss Hunt? Are you all right?"

She nodded, a gesture that required an unusual amount of effort. Her head felt as heavy as a sadiron.

He continued, his tone filled with compassion. "I know the news is disappointing. The important thing to remember is that the inability to have a baby is no reflection on you or your worth. You're a beloved child of God, and He has plans for you."

Callie heard what Dr. Wright said, but he had no idea what it felt like to have your dreams of motherhood—and marriage—shattered. She knew for certain that Chip Evans, the finest man she'd ever known, would have no interest in her. She couldn't give him the one thing he wanted most—children of his own.

Somehow she managed to thank the Wrights, settle her bill and make her way to the Plaza, where she was to meet Chip. If only she didn't have to face him so soon after the crushing blow. He was sure to notice she wasn't herself and express concern. That she could handle, but what would she say when he asked the questions that were sure to follow? How would she feel when the man she'd grown to love rejected her?

Chapter Twelve

$\widehat{}$

As Chip prepared to finalize his order at the Blair brothers' lumberyard in Placerville, he inhaled deeply. The scent of freshly cut lumber had a way of making him feel invigorated, but never more so than today. Callie had seen his house, and even though it wasn't quite finished, she liked it. She'd even called it "magnificent."

To his surprise, he'd imagined what it would be like if she was his wife. As she'd stood in his parlor, he'd envisioned her sitting on the sofa with a baby in her lap and a toddler at her side. They'd ended up in the kitchen, where he'd pictured her standing at the stove wearing a ruffle-edged apron and turning to greet him with one of her warm smiles.

Those were pleasant images, but the one that had come to mind when she'd entered his room wasn't. Callie had seen the stuffed animal he'd been unable to part with, rushed over to it and cradled it to her, bringing back memories of him doing the same thing.

During the agonizing days after he'd lost his family, he'd been so sick with cholera that he was forced to ride in the wagon, enduring the swaying, jostling and unceasing bumps. He'd lain in the wagon the first night he was on his own without a single family member left, staring at the moonlit canvas bonnet overhead while clutching Checkers to his chest and willing himself to remain strong. The little dog had been his only friend for the remainder of the journey west.

The clerk returned, rescuing Chip from his reverie. "Looks like we have everything necessary for you to wind up the job at the Double T, Mr. Evans. We'll load as much as we can on your wagon. Mr. Blair said the rest of the order should be delivered tomorrow."

"And the wood I'll need for my place?"

"We'll have that order waiting for you when you're ready."

"Good. I'll be back for it as soon as I can." He had dormitory furniture to finish first and a kitchen and dining room to complete after that. Then he'd be free to locate as many carpentry and furniture-making jobs as possible. He could fill his bank account, ensuring that he could adequately provide for his future family. He would spare them the kind of financial worries that had led his father to embark on the trip west, resulting in Chip being left all alone in the world.

The thought of having a family of his own put a smile on his face and sent him striding down Main Street at a brisk pace toward the Plaza, where Callie would be waiting for him. Chip intended to make good use of their free day. Lunch first, and then a leisurely ride back to the Double T. If the afternoon went the way he intended, he could end up with a promise from Callie to wait the three years until The Plan called for him to begin courting. She might even allow him a kiss to seal their agreement.

Chip reached their meeting place a short time later

and scanned the area, searching for Callie and her light purple dress. He spotted her standing under the awning of the Placerville News Company with her shoulders drooped, her hands clasped and her gaze on the plank walkway. The pose was so unlike her that concern shot through him. If they'd been in Shingle Springs, his first thought would have been about the children. But they weren't. Callie had said she was going to see someone and do a little shopping, neither of which seemed a likely cause for her downcast demeanor.

He joined her and adopted a teasing tone in an attempt to lift her spirits. "You're here, but where are all the packages? I was sure your arms would be full of them by now."

"I haven't made it to the shops yet, but their shelves will be emptier once I do." Although she accompanied her reply with a smile, it appeared forced.

"I'll make sure to save room in the wagon then." His stomach growled, and he laughed. "I was going to tell you I was hungry, but I suppose you've figured that out. Would you like to join me for lunch? The café down the street makes the best chicken pot pie."

She pressed her lips together and looked up at the Bell Tower at the center of the Plaza as though seeking guidance from the wooden structure.

He waited for an answer, his uneasiness growing with each passing second. She wouldn't turn him down, would she? "It would be my treat, of course."

"I appreciate the offer, but I'm afraid I wouldn't be the best company." She lowered her gaze, fixing it on him. He'd expected to see wariness, but instead her eyes were filled with sadness. Not the sadness resulting from a minor disappointment, but the deep sorrow that followed a great loss.

His chest tightened. "Are you all right?"

She glanced around them and lowered her voice. "I'm fine. I just need some time. Alone."

He couldn't leave her like this. "It looks to me like you could use a friend, so we can go to the café. Once you have something to eat, you're sure to feel better." He held out an arm, took her hand in his and wrapped it around his elbow, holding it in place lest she try to pull away.

To his relief, she didn't, although she did stare at his hand for several moments before speaking. "Thank you, Chip. You are a good...friend."

Her hesitation didn't bode well. Something had happened while they were apart, and until he found out what it was, he would tread carefully.

Their mealtime was pleasant. Chip allowed her to lead the conversation. Talk centered around Jasper's latest antics and what she planned to buy for him and Ruby. Callie's love for the children ran deep. What would she do if, after the murderers were caught, a nice couple came along who wanted to adopt the children? Could that possibility be what was troubling her?

To Chip's surprise, she completed her shopping quickly, with a single stop at the Round Tent dry goods store. She selected fabric to make doll dresses for Ruby, a pair of chaps for Jasper and a new dress for herself.

The yards of white eyelet Callie chose caught Chip's attention. An image of her walking down the aisle toward him formed in his mind. Instead of shoving it away, as he would have in the past, he allowed himself to imagine what it would be like to stand at the front of the church wearing his Sunday best as he waited for her to join him.

A sense of excitement gripped him, spurring him to work harder than ever to achieve his goals and be in a position to go courting. Three years wasn't so long, was it?

"I'm ready to go whenever you are." Callie stood before him bearing a brown paper package tied with string.

"Here. Let me take that for you." He tucked the parcel under one arm and thought better about offering her the other. Until he found out what had brought about the change in her, he would respect her need for distance.

They returned to Blair Brothers Lumber Company, where Chip helped her into his wagon, now loaded with wood for the last of the dormitory furniture. He guided his team out of town. Callie sat beside him, silent, her gaze on her hands resting in her lap.

Two miles passed. He thought about the ideas Callie had given him for his kitchen and dining room and enjoyed the gentle breeze that fluttered loose strands of her hair. He resisted the urge to tuck them behind her ear for as long as possible but finally gave way to it.

She looked up at him, her eyes wide. "May I ask you a question?"

He smiled. "You just did."

Her slow blink brought him up short. She wasn't in a playful mood, so he adopted a serious tone. "Go ahead. Ask me whatever you want."

"Could you see yourself doing something that wasn't in your plan?"

He'd thought a lot about that lately, but he'd come to same conclusion every time. "I put it in place for a reason."

"I know, but sometimes circumstances change, and we must change with them." Her lovely face held an unspoken plea.

She'd asked about his plans for marriage. Could it be she was hoping he would consider courting her even though he wasn't ready? He reined in his team and took her hands in his. "Three years isn't forever, Callie. I'm willing to wait, and I hope you are, too."

Her answer was so soft that he had to lean close to hear it. "I would, but…"

"I understand." She'd given him his answer. He turned, took up the reins and started up again.

Another two miles passed in silence, save for the creaking of the wagon and the chorus of birds perched in the plentiful oaks. And then a sniffle. Chip glanced at Callie just in time to see her swipe at her cheek. Was that a tear she'd flicked away?

He pulled the wagon to a stop and faced her, keeping his voice low. "What's wrong?"

She dipped her head. "I can't say it. I thought I could, but I don't know how."

The anguish in her voice tore at him. "You can tell me anything, Callie, anything at all."

She clicked her handbag open and shut, open and shut.

He rested a hand over hers to still them. "You were fine when we reached town. What happened next? You said you were going to an appointment? Does it have something to do with that?"

She nodded. "I went to the doctor."

His stomach dropped into his boots. "Are you…sick?"

"No. It's nothing like that. I had a question about something a doctor told me when I was young. My friend Becky suggested I see Dr. Wright, so I did."

Callie continued to fidget with her reticule, running her fingers over the beaded bag. Although Chip wanted to press her for answers, he forced himself to wait. Whatever she'd learned had left her deeply shaken.

Her hands stilled at last, and she squared her shoulders. "Do you remember me telling you about being kicked by a horse when I was girl?"

"Of course. I wouldn't forget something like that." She'd fought for her life afterward.

"We got interrupted that day, and I didn't finish the story." She drew in a breath and rushed out her next sentence on the exhale. "The horse kicked me in the stomach."

Her eyes locked with his, and her brow furrowed. It was as though she was trying to send him a message, willing him to understand.

The realization dropped his jaw. "You can't have children."

"I can't bear any of my own, no." She blinked, and a tear streamed down her cheek.

"Oh, Callie." He pulled her into his arms.

She tensed.

He eased his hold enough to look at her. "I'm so sorry."

"I appreciate your sympathy, but I know what this means." She slipped out of his arms and averted her gaze.

What could he say? Callie knew he wanted children of his own and why having them was so important to him. For the past sixteen years, he'd vowed to carry on his family's legacy. For the past seven, he'd worked to make that dream a reality, faithfully following The Plan. He might have been willing wait for her, but the woman he married must be able to bear his children.

He cared about Callie. If he was honest with himself, he might even say he loved her. But he couldn't offer her anything more than friendship now, no matter how much she meant to him. "I wish it wasn't so."

"So do I." She straightened and gave a decisive nod. "But it's time for me to accept the truth. I'll never be a mother."

"You could be. There are other ways." Even though adoption wasn't an option for him, some people were willing to consider the idea.

"Perhaps, but at least I can love the children at the Double T." Callie hadn't said the words, but it was clear she knew her prospects of marriage were limited by her condition. Although she smiled, she couldn't hide the pain reflected in her eyes.

He might only be able to offer her friendship, but he would be the best friend to her he could. Perhaps, in time, his feelings for her would lessen.

"I really look like a cowboy now." Jasper marched around the woodshop wearing the chaps Callie had finished the night before. By putting a buckram lining under the dark brown chambray she'd bought when she was in Placerville the week before, she'd been able to mimic the stiffness of leather.

Chip leaned against his workbench and grinned. "That you do, pardner. Isaac is sure to be impressed."

Ruby skipped over to Callie. The little girl had relaxed over the course of the week, unlike Callie. Her shoulders were tight, and she'd awakened that morning with a slight headache. "Is it time for me and Jasper to see Mr. Isaac and wide the horsies, Miss Callie?"

"It is." Her brother was waiting for them. "Are you ready to go?"

"I got to give Daisy a kiss first."

"Who's Daisy?"

Ruby huffed out her exasperation. "Don't you 'member? She's my baby."

"That's right. I'm sorry I forgot, sweetheart." Ruby had told Callie the name she'd given her doll earlier in the week, but Callie had been so focused on her planing that the conversation had slipped her mind. "I'll wait here for you, and then we'll go."

It seemed all she could think about lately was the visit to Dr. Wright's office and her conversation with Chip afterward. Try as she might, she couldn't shake the melancholy that had settled over her. Pretending to be cheerful required a great deal of energy, and that was in short supply. What little she had, she poured into her work. The sooner she and Chip finished the job, the sooner he would leave.

Not that she wanted him to go. She would miss him terribly, but having him here was a constant reminder of what she'd lost. He'd made numerous references to their friendship and implied that it would continue, but she knew that things could never go back to the way they'd been. She'd seen his shock when she told him about her defect. He'd been so taken aback that his mouth had fallen open.

Chip lived his life by The Plan he'd written all those years ago, and it called for him to have children of his own. She understood why that was so important to him, but she'd hoped he would be willing to explore other options, such as adoption. There were many wonderful children like Jasper and Ruby waiting for families to take them in and give them the love they longed to have.

Just yesterday a couple had come to complete the process of adopting a child who had spent the past two years at the Double T. They'd all gathered for her Day of Celebration party. The girl, a shy seven-year-old with a lisp who feared no one would ever want her, had sat on the wagon seat between her new parents afterward, beaming as they rode off.

Callie had stood beside Tess, reliving the moment she'd ridden off with Mom and Pop Marshall. With Isaac away fighting, Callie hadn't known what would happen to her after the robbery that resulted in her parents' deaths. The uncle who owned the lumber mill where she'd spent every summer, a widower at that point, had enlisted early in the war. He'd perished a short time later, leaving her without a single relative to take her in.

The hours before the Marshalls had come for her had been hard. Callie sighed at the memory. Never before had she felt as frightened or as helpless as she had when she saw the robbers aim their revolvers at her parents. She'd cowered under the table, certain she, too, was going to die. When everything was over and the house grew silent, she'd crept out and wept over her parents' lifeless bodies. The servants had fled, so she was alone. God had been there for her, though. He'd placed her in a home where she was not just loved, but she was cherished, too.

Callie watched as Ruby fussed over Daisy. The little girl lavished such love on her doll. Callie felt that same protectiveness when it came to the children. They'd dealt with so much heartbreak in their young lives. She would do all she could to protect them and keep them from experiencing more pain.

Ruby rushed over to Callie and took her hand. Jasper grabbed hold of Chip's, and the four of them headed out to the stable for the children's riding lessons. A storm had passed in the night, leaving the ground soft. Callie lifted her skirts as she stepped over a small puddle in the path. Jasper tromped right through it.

"Careful, pardner," Chip called after him. "Ladies don't like to have their skirts splattered."

Jasper wheeled around, his chaps flapping against his legs. "Did you hear the thunder last night, Miss Callie? It scared me at first, but Mr. Chip told me a story about a posse catching some cattle rustlers. I pretended the sounds came from their gunfight, and then I wasn't scared no more."

"You two are much more adventurous than Ruby and I. We pretended we were riding in a stagecoach, where we were warm and dry, and hearing the crack of the driver's whip outside and his horses' hooves pounding the ground."

Jasper jammed his hands into fists. "You never told me you make up stories, too. I thought only Mr. Chip did that."

"I tell Ruby a story every night." It hadn't been easy to come up with stories the past week, but Callie wasn't about to let down the darling girl.

"What kind of stories?" Jasper asked.

To Callie's surprise, Ruby joined the conversation, something she rarely did. "About a little black doggie and the boy who loves him."

Heat rushed into Callie's cheeks. She cast a surreptitious glance at Chip, not willing to look at him outright.

She needn't have worried about him seeing her. His attention was on Ruby. "Is the doggie's name Checkers, perchance?"

Ruby shook her head. "It's Domino."

"So he *is* named after a game. I see." Chip did look at Callie then and sent her one of his most endearing grins.

If only he wasn't so charming. Keeping her distance was hard enough without him working so hard at maintaining their friendship, but she must. Her dreams lay shattered at her feet. Somehow she must pick up those pieces and forge a new life—without him. If she allowed herself to savor their final days together, that would only make the parting harder.

They reached the corral. Isaac hurried over to them as quickly as his limp would allow. "I thought I'd have Hardy take Ruby around today. Could I ask you to help Jasper, Chip? He'll need someone who can jog alongside him since he's getting to be quite the rider."

Chip readily agreed. "Certainly. I'm eager to see what my pardner can do. Besides, I think your sister would welcome your company over mine. She's been more interested in her work than her coworker this week." He winked at her.

Callie fought the urge to reward him with a smile. She mustn't encourage him. He had to understand that things were different. She certainly did. "Jasper will enjoy your company greatly." For as long as it lasted.

She dreaded thinking how hard it was going to be on the children when Chip left. They loved him dearly. Although he might deny it, he loved them, too. Would he miss them as much as they would miss him? If so, would he reconsider the possibility of adop—

No! She couldn't allow herself to hold out hope. Chip would find someone else, fill his house with children of his own and cross off every item on that precious plan of his. She certainly hoped his future wife understood how regimented her husband could be—and what a wonderful man he was.

Hardy helped Ruby onto her pony. Chip watched as

Jasper managed to mount his all by himself with the help of the mounting block. And then they were off, two ponies circling the corral with two beaming children on their backs.

Isaac slipped through the slatted fence, a tedious task due to his injured leg, and stood beside Callie. "What's going on with you and Chip?"

"What do you mean?"

"I'm not blind, Callie. I saw the way you were making eyes at him before, but things changed after you went to Placerville. You won't even look at him now. What happened?"

"I do like him, but he doesn't want me."

"What do you mean? He just winked at you."

"We're friends, but that's all we'll ever be." Isaac knew about the diagnosis, so there was no sense hiding things from him. "He wants children of his own, and I can't give them to him. I'd hoped that maybe something could be done for me, but I saw a doctor when Chip and I were in Placerville. He confirmed what the doctor told Mother after the accident. I'll have never children."

"Oh, sis, I'm so sorry." Isaac wrapped an arm around her and drew her to his side.

She rested her head against her brother's shoulder, recalling the many times she'd gone to him when they were children, stinging from another rejection or rebuke. He'd assured her that although their parents were too busy maintaining their social status to give her the love she craved, he loved her. She didn't know what she would have done without him. "I'll be all right."

"I know you will, but you must be disappointed."

Bitterly. "I have Jasper and Ruby and all the other

wonderful children here at the Double T. And I have you. That's enough for me."

If she said it enough times, she might believe it.

Chapter Thirteen

The sound of footfalls behind Chip stopped him. He paused, gouge in hand, and spoke over his shoulder. "Back already, Freddie?" The boy had come looking for Jasper a few minutes before, eager to eat lunch with him, but he was outside with Callie and Ruby. The children had grown restless, and she'd taken them for a walk.

"He's not. It's me, Spencer."

Chip wheeled around. "What can I do for you?"

"Tess said you're almost done with the job and suggested I come take a look at the rooms that are ready. If you have time to show me, that is."

"Of course." Chip untied his canvas apron, slipped it over his head and straightened his work area, as he did anytime he left it. With so many children around, he didn't want any accidents.

Spencer generally left the management of the orphanage to Tess and focused on running the cattle-ranching side of the Double T, but she always asked her husband to give his final approval as a project came to an end. In another day or two, this one would.

The thought stirred mixed feelings in Chip. He was

eager to finish and get back to his place and complete the kitchen and dining room, but he wasn't looking forward to saying goodbye to Callie and the children. She understood why he had to move on with his life, since he'd been clear about his plan to have his own children from the start, but Jasper and Ruby would have a harder time of it.

He'd miss them all, but he had to leave. The sooner he could, the easier it would be on all of them. The children would go on with their lives and forget about him in time. Callie might even heave a sigh of relief as soon as his wagon was out of sight.

Ever since they'd returned from Placerville the week before, she'd kept her distance. Clearly, she was upset, which made sense. The news she'd received had to have been devastating. Although he ached to see her hurting, all he could offer her was friendship. Nothing more.

Chip set the last tool in its box and spun around. "I think you'll be pleased with how everything's turned out."

"I'm sure I will. You do excellent work." Spencer scanned the wardrobe Chip had been working on and focused on the carving on the capital over the door. "What's that going to be?"

"Tess asked me to engrave each cabinet with a well perched on top of a hill. It's supposed to be the one Jack and Jill went up to."

"I see." Spencer walked over to take a closer look. "This brings back memories. Luke fell through the cover of an abandoned well a few months after Tess came. We spent an agonizing night at his bedside. It turned out he was fine, but I replaced that old cover in a hurry."

Chip struggled to make sense of what Spencer had said. "What do you mean after Tess came?"

"The Lord led her to Shingle Springs to work as my housekeeper after I lost my first wife. Lila was just nine months old, and Luke was four."

Chip shook his head. "She's not their mother? I had no idea."

"She's their mother, all right, in all the ways that matter. She adopted the children soon after we married and made it official."

"But she didn't—" Chip caught himself before stating the obvious.

"She didn't give them life, no, but she would give her life for them. They love her, too, but it didn't start out that way. Luke wouldn't call her by name for several months. Not until the day she rescued him from that dank, dark hole in the ground, in fact." Spencer shuddered at the memory. "I haven't thought about that in a long time. It's amazing how quickly the years go by."

"And the others? Are they…?"

"Our children? Yes. Along with every child who spends time at the Double T. Tess has a heart the size of Texas. She'd adopt every last one of the children herself, if she could." Spencer's tone held admiration, respect and love.

"She's a remarkable woman. I can see why Callie was eager to work for her."

"We're glad to have Callie. She cares for all the children, but it's easy to see that she has a soft spot for Jasper and Ruby. Seems to me you've become rather fond of them yourself."

He had, but that didn't change things. Tess might have been eager to adopt Spencer's children, but their situation was different than his.

Freddie popped in the door, breathless. "Mr. Chip."

"What is it, Freddie?"

"I looked for Jasper and Miss Callie," he said, resting his hands on his knees and gulping in air, "but I can't find them."

"They're not in the field where we flew the kite?"

Freddie shook his head and gushed out his answer between noisy breaths. "I checked there first. Then I went to the corral and the barn. I even checked the dining hall, but I couldn't find them anywhere."

The concern in the boy's tone raised the hairs on the back of Chip's neck. He did his best to sound calm, when he felt anything but. "Maybe Miss Callie took the children up to her room. Papa Spencer and I will go check there. Would you go see if they're in the big house with Mama Tess?"

"Yes, sir!" Freddie dashed out the door.

"You don't think that—" Spencer began.

"We should go." He had to locate Callie and the children.

"I'm right behind you."

Chip strode to Jack and Jill House and mounted the stairs. He took them two at a time, marched down the hall and rapped on the door to Callie and Ruby's room. There was no answer, not that he'd expected there to be.

He returned to the landing, where Spencer caught up with him. "I'm going to check our room, too. Jasper could have found a puddle left from the storm, taken an unexpected swim and muddied his clothes." Even though it hadn't rained since the night before last, there were still low spots with standing water.

"Good idea." Spencer followed Chip up the second flight of stairs.

A quick check of the room proved fruitless. Chip flew down the stairs, with Spencer behind him. Their thundering footfalls filled the empty building.

They reached the doorway just as Tess did. "Still missing, I see. What next?"

"I think we should—" Spencer said.

"Let's scour the—" Chip began.

She looked at Spencer, shook her head and shifted her focus to Chip. "What do you suggest?"

"We'll search the field and look for anything out of the ordinary."

Spencer clapped a hand on Chip's shoulder. "That's a fine plan."

He didn't wait for Spencer and Tess but sprinted toward the field.

"Chip!" Tess's call brought him to a stop. She closed the gap between them, her skirts rustling as she walked. "I know you're eager to find them, but we have to think about the other children. I can't have them alarmed."

"I'm sorry."

She rested a hand on his arm, her eyes filled with compassion. "I know you're concerned, but we'll find them."

If only he had her confidence. Images from the scene of Mr. Tate's murder bombarded Chip. The killers would stop at nothing to get what they wanted. If they'd taken Callie and the children…

No! He couldn't think about that. He had to focus on the task at hand.

Spencer stood at his wife's side. "Tess is right. They're out there somewhere."

"If we split up, we can cover more ground. I'll take the far side of the field. Ruby likes to serve tea in acorn cups. Callie might have taken them over by the oaks to look for some. Tess, if you would take the section closest to the playground, and Spencer, you can cover the middle. They might be laying in the tall grass watching the clouds. They've done that before."

Callie and the children had fun figuring out what the various formations resembled. Not that they would have much to work with today. The sky had cleared after the storm, leaving only a few scattered wisps of white.

Chip made his way to the area he'd chosen to cover with long, purposeful strides and began his search. In order not to miss anything, he walked down and back in straight rows, his attention focused on the ground in front of him, looking for anything amiss.

He'd been at it for several minutes when he came across a sight that sickened him. A soggy area at the edge of the field was filled with prints from both people and horses. One set of prints in particular sent a surge of fear through him. They were woman-sized and were attached to two long streaks, a sure sign of someone being dragged. Callie!

Chip stuck two fingers in his mouth and produced a piercing whistle, loud enough for Spencer and Tess to hear, but not loud enough to reach the playground beyond, where the children were enjoying their lunch recess. The Abbotts made straight for him.

Moments later the three of them stood huddled around the disturbed earth. Spencer squatted to study the troubling scene.

Tess drew in a ragged breath and released it in a huff. "I'd hoped they'd just wandered off, but…" She lifted her face to the bright blue sky. "Lord, be with our dear ones." She lowered her gaze and started. "What's that?"

Chip looked where she was pointing. A piece of paper had been stuck on a branch. He hustled over, grabbed the note and read the brief message.

If you want to see the lady and kids again, bring the jewels here at two o'clock. Come alone and unarmed.

His gut twisted. It was a good thing he hadn't eaten yet, because he would have lost his lunch. They had very little time to comply with the demands. Knowing what the murderous trio had done to Mr. Tate, it was clear they meant business.

Spencer and Tess joined him. Chip handed her the note without a word.

She read it aloud with a quaking voice. "I can't believe they came right onto our property and kidnapped Callie and the children."

Her anguish echoed Chip's own. He smacked a fist against his palm. "I have to go after them. I'll saddle my horse."

Spencer straightened. "I'll join you, of course, but let's talk to Hardy first. His father was a tracker during the war and taught Hardy everything he knew. If anyone can follow the trail, that young man can."

Tess gave the note back to Chip. "While you see to that, I'll have the group leaders get the rest of the children inside and keep them safe. I don't want them out here when those…those…ruffians show up."

Chip and Spencer headed for the corral, where they found Isaac brushing a pony.

"Where's Hardy?" Chip demanded.

"He's in the barn tending to the tack. Why? Is something wrong?"

He didn't have time to explain things to Callie's brother. Not now. He marched into the barn with Spencer on his heels.

Chip found Hardy at the bench oiling a harness. "I hear you're a good tracker."

"I do all right. Why?"

"Callie and the children have been kidnapped. We need you to follow their trail and find out where they're being held."

A voice, low and heated, came from behind Chip. "Those scoundrels have Callie?"

Chip spun around. Isaac stood a few feet away, gripping a saddle stand. The color had drained from his face.

"I'm afraid so, but we're going after them. We need your help. Could you get our horses ready?"

Isaac headed for the stalls, covering ground with more speed than Chip had ever seen the injured man achieve.

By the time Chip and Spencer had filled Hardy in, Isaac had the first horse ready. He handed Hardy the reins to his gelding and pinned Chip with a piercing gaze. "If I were you, I'd let Hardy go alone. A scout works best that way."

The certainty in Isaac's voice got Chip's attention. Callie's brother spoke with the authority of a soldier who had seen action. "You're right, of course. We'll do that."

Chip and Spencer took Hardy to the site of the abduction. The young ranch hand walked around the site, studying the ground from every angle. He stole through the grass nearby, his shoulders hunched. At length he straightened, nodded and returned to them.

"What did you find?" The question had burst from Chip before Hardy could say a word.

"It's as you suspected. Callie and the children were here, and they were accosted. There are three sets of hoofprints, but I only saw one set of men's boot prints. He must have handed the children up to the other two, and then—" Hardy's eyes filled with sympathy "—he grabbed Callie and dragged her. You can be right proud of her. She put up quite a fight."

The thought of the man who'd shot Mr. Tate laying hands on Callie only served to increase the roiling of Chip's stomach. A bitter taste filled his mouth. "Go find her—them."

"I'll do my best." Hardy mounted his horse and headed into the stand of oaks.

Spencer pulled out his pocket watch. "When did Callie and the children start on their walk?"

"Around eleven, I think, but I can't be sure. I lose track of time when I'm working." Why hadn't he paid more attention? Or gone with them? She'd asked him to, but he'd been so bent on getting the job done that he'd left her to face Mr. Tate's killers on her own.

"They can't be that far away if one of them is coming back to get the jewels at two," Spencer said. "We'll have Callie and the children with us again by dinnertime."

Chip would do everything in his power to make that happen. But what if they were too late?

Large hands gripped Callie's waist. The younger of the two men, whom the woman had called Nigel, pulled her from the saddle none too gently and set her on the ground. Although she'd been gagged, bound and blindfolded during the kidnapping, she could tell he wasn't as tall as Chip or as broad-shouldered.

Nigel took her by the elbow and shoved her ahead of him. "Look out for the stairs, girlie. There's three of 'em."

The warning came too late. Callie smacked her ankle against the first step and nearly fell forward. A muffled cry escaped her, but the pain was the least of her worries. She must get to the children and do everything in her power to keep them safe.

"Don't be making a ruckus. Zeke won't like that."

So that was the name of the brown-haired man who'd grabbed her. She'd fought to get away from him and call for help, but he was quite a bit larger than Nigel.

Zeke had clamped one hand over her mouth, the other around her waist and dragged her backward to his horse. He'd gagged her with a salty-tasting bandana he'd pulled from around his neck, bound her hands behind her with a piece of bristly rope and threatened to hurt the children if she didn't do exactly as he said.

She was forced to stand beside Zeke's horse, watch him snatch the children one after another and hand them to his cronies seated on their horses. He'd given Ruby to the woman and Jasper to Nigel. Zeke had then blindfolded Callie, stuffed her in front of him and clamped an arm around her waist, a most uncomfortable position since she was pressed against the pommel.

The children were ordered to keep quiet. The terror-stricken girl complied, as Callie expected. Jasper, bless him, had begged Zeke not to hurt her or his sister. The dear boy received a stern reminder to hold his tongue, coupled with a threat—if he said another word, he'd be sorry. Thankfully, he'd remained silent.

Callie lifted her foot and found the next two steps, a slow process.

"Get a move on, missy," Nigel snapped.

She aimed for the doorway, through which she could hear the woman talking to the children, although she couldn't make out the words.

Nigel shoved Callie into the room and whipped off the cloth covering her eyes, pulling her hair in the process. "You stay here with Virgie while I help Zeke. If you're a good girl, I'll remove this and the rope when I get back." He tapped the bandana Zeke had stuffed in her mouth, pushed her down beside the children, who were huddled in a dark corner, and left, yanking the door shut behind him with a bang.

Her tightly bound hands were numb, her shoulders ached and her ankle throbbed, but she scarcely noticed. All she cared about were the children. She must protect them from this thieving, murderous lot.

Ruby scampered across Jasper, crawled into Callie's lap and huddled against her.

Dust motes danced in the single shaft of light that pierced the darkness inside the tiny miner's cabin. The one-room shack looked as though it might topple if a brisk wind came along.

The woman, Virgie, stood with her hands on her hips in front of them. "You two little ones had better stay put and keep quiet. Don't be pestering Zeke. He's got a burr under his saddle, and you don't want to do anything to make him madder. He doesn't have much use for youngsters like you. If he didn't need you in order to get the jewels, you wouldn't be here."

She crossed the room and peered out the lone window, careful not to get too close to the jagged edges of the broken panes. "He and Nigel are taking care of the horses, but they'll be back soon. I'll see to lunch. Once they've had all they want, I'll try and sneak you all a bite."

Despite all that had happened in the last hour, Virgie's protectiveness gave Callie hope. Could she have insisted on putting the children out of the wagon the day their father was killed?

Virgie narrowed her eyes at Callie. "Why are you looking at me like that?"

Callie glanced from Jasper to Ruby, returned her attention to Virgie, dipped her chin and widened her eyes, her best attempt to gain the woman's sympathy while gagged.

Virgie moved away from the window and filled a pitcher from an old pump. She plunked it on the table, plopped down on the lone rickety chair facing Callie and began talking in a low voice. "Putting the children in danger was never our idea. Nigel and I just wanted to get married, but we didn't have two pennies to rub together. You have no idea what it's like to sell fancy jewels to rich people all day and receive a pittance in your pay packet. All of you in that fine orphanage sit down around your tables heaped with food, and you stuff your bellies with beef stew, pot roast and fried chicken. When I told Nigel about Mr. Tate's order, we got an idea. We were going to get the jewels. That was all. But his bossy big brother got wind of our plan and took over." She sighed. "Zeke's not one to cross. Nigel learned that the hard way."

A chill shimmied up Callie's spine. Virgie had just named the last three dinners at the Double T—in the correct order. The only way she could have known what had been served was if she or one of the men had been looking in the dining hall windows. Callie didn't even want to think about the fact that spies had been watching her every move, preparing to pounce. Had she known that, she would have insisted on having a well-armed ranch hand or two with her at all times. Now she was forced to protect the children from a bully, his browbeaten brother and a conflicted woman.

"Your fellow would have no trouble getting you a fancy ring, but I never could have hoped for one. Once we get those jewels, I'll have an engagement ring with a big ol' diamond in it, and this will all be over." Virgie held out her left hand to admire an imaginary stone, tilting it at various angles as though the gem was sparkling in the sunlight.

What would happen when Virgie learned that there were no jewels? Would she still be as concerned about the children's safety? It seemed more likely, from what she'd said, that she and Nigel would be worried about how Zeke would react and if he would take his anger out on them.

"Enough of my yammering. The fellows will be back soon, and I'd better have everything ready for them." Virgie stood, set some plates on the table and placed a platter in the middle. She whipped off the cloth covering it with a flourish, revealing a generous display of ham and cheese slices. "The larder back at your place is a wonderful thing."

Callie gulped. She knew they'd searched the bedrooms where she and Chip were staying soon after they'd arrived, but she didn't realize the trio had taken to breaking into the kitchen at Miss Muffet House and helping themselves. Tess would be incensed when she found out that everyone at the Double T had been in danger.

Jasper scooted closer to Callie. She longed to send

him an encouraging smile, but that was an impossible feat, given the wad of fabric in her mouth. Ruby had her face buried in Callie's shoulder, her doll clutched to her. The yellow gingham absorbed Ruby's tears and muffled her cries. At least the darling girl had Daisy with her to provide some comfort.

Virgie waved a fork at Callie. "You'd better get the girl to stop whimpering before Zeke gets back."

To do that, Callie would need to talk. She twisted her head from side to side, mumbled some unintelligible words and gave Virgie a pointed look.

"I'd help you if I could, but you heard Nigel."

Fine. She'd just have to wait a little while longer before the revolting thing was removed.

"I'll do it, Miss Callie." Jasper rose up on his knees and tugged on the bandana in Callie's mouth, but it was tied so snuggly it wouldn't budge.

Heavy footfalls thundered up the steps, and the men burst through the door.

Virgie visibly tensed. She whirled around to face Callie and the children. "Don't touch that, boy!" she snapped. "You heard Nigel. He's going to take it off."

The change in the woman was marked. Callie dreaded thinking how much danger she and the children were in if Virgie was that scared of Zeke.

Jasper sank back down and snuggled into Callie's right side, looking unusually subdued. Never had Callie longed for the use of her arms as she did at that moment. She was desperate to hug Jasper and Ruby.

Nigel and Zeke stood side by side. Although they had different builds and hair colors, it was easy to see that they were brothers. Zeke was tall and broad and had a menacing look about him. Nigel was shorter and thinner. He struck her as less sure of himself than he'd been when he visited the orphanage and posed as Mr. Smith. Even if Virgie hadn't eased her conscience with the unexpected confession, Callie would have had no trouble figuring out who'd fired the shot that took Mr. Tate's life.

Virgie handed a plate to Zeke. "I've got lunch ready for you."

"It's about time," Zeke snarled. "I'm as hungry as a grizzly." He scanned the shelves behind the pint-sized cookstove. "What did you do with the brandy?"

"You emptied the bottle last night."

He slanted a gaze at Nigel. "Why didn't you grab some liquor when I sent you to get the food?"

"There wasn't any. That place is run by a bunch of Bible lovers. I couldn't even find any wine."

Zeke muttered a word Callie was glad the children couldn't understand and wandered outside, leaving the door propped open. Based on the thud followed by a jangling of spurs, he'd plunked down on the steps.

Virgie held out a plate to her fiancé. "Here you go."

"Not yet. I told the girl I'd free her."

Relief surged through Callie. She'd been afraid Nigel would forget or change his mind. He stood in front of her, reached behind his back and whipped a bowie knife out of the leather sheath she'd noticed earlier.

Jasper gasped and Ruby buried her face against Callie's side. If only she could assure them that everything was all right. At least she hoped it was. Nigel didn't strike her as someone capable of harming a child, unlike Zeke.

Nigel huffed out his annoyance. "Don't be carrying on. I'm not going to hurt her. You young'uns need to move, though, so I can get to her hands and cut the rope."

Jasper let go of Callie, stood and pried Ruby loose.

"Here." Nigel grasped Callie by the arm, pulled her to her feet and slit the binding.

She reached behind her head, untied the knot and pulled the gag out of her mouth. It wasn't until she lowered her hands that she saw her wrists. The skin had been rubbed raw from the rough rope, not that she was concerned about that. As long as nothing happened to the children, she could bear whatever might come her way. Or so she hoped.

Ruby tugged on Callie's skirt. She leaned over, and the little girl whispered in her ear. Straightening, Callie addressed Nigel. "I need to take the children to the privy."

Suspicion furrowed his brow. "If you're thinking of sneaking off, you can think again."

"I'm not." At least not now when she was outnumbered three to one, but if an opportunity presented itself...

"I'll take them, and they won't get away." Virgie reached into her satchel, withdrew a holster and strapped it on. A revolver followed, a large model fit for a man.

Zeke's voice boomed through the open doorway. "If she gives you any trouble, Virgie, do what you have to."

"Right, Zeke." She used the barrel of her revolver to motion Callie to the back door opposite the front. "Let's go."

Callie took Jasper and Ruby by the hand and led them out back. Virgie stood guard while the children went about their business, her gun drawn the entire time. Callie was fairly certain Virgie had no intention of using it, but she wasn't about to test that theory.

While Callie held Ruby in her arms and waited for Jasper, she scanned their surroundings. The only thing she could determine, based on the location of the sun, was that they were a few miles north of the Double T. Since she'd heard splashing during the ride as the horses walked in water, they had to be somewhere along Dry Creek. But would anyone at the ranch be able to find them?

Virgie hustled them back inside, where Zeke stood waiting for them, plate in hand.

"You—" he motioned to Callie with the slice of ham he'd picked up "—take the children back to your corner, and make sure I don't hear a peep out of them." He shifted his attention to Virgie. "It's time for you to get going. Do you know what to do?"

She nodded. "If someone actually found the note and is waiting for me, I make sure he came alone, has the jewels and bring him back here for the exchange. If no one's there, I sneak around until I find the carpenter, deliver our demands and bring him back here—alone and with the jewels."

Fear gripped Callie's heart and squeezed. Hard.

Lord, please be with us—and with Chip. They're expecting him to pay the ransom, but we don't have the jewels!

Chapter Fourteen

Chip snapped his pocket watch closed and shoved it in his pocket. Hardy had been gone half an hour. If he didn't return soon—

The thundering of hooves across the field interrupted his thoughts. Chip folded his arms and tapped his foot as he waited for Hardy to reach the corral.

Spencer watched Hardy's approach. "We'll know what he found soon."

Not soon enough. Every minute Callie and the children were in the hands of the kidnappers was another minute in which things could go horribly wrong.

At last, Hardy arrived and reined in his horse. He slid from his saddle.

Chip closed the gap between them with three swift strides. "What did you find out?"

"I was able to follow the trail as far as Dry Creek, but they rode in the creek itself. I followed it a good half mile, but there were so many tracks that I couldn't find where they'd left it. I'm sorry, Chip."

"You did your best. That's all you can do."

Isaac joined them, his features drawn, and faced Chip. "What are you going to do now?"

"I'll have to show up at the meeting place." He had no other choice.

"Alone?" Hardy asked.

"I'd like you and Spencer to go with me, if you're willing to, that is."

Both men agreed without hesitation.

"I'll go, too."

Isaac's offer took Chip by surprise. He pulled Isaac aside and lowered his voice. "I'm not sure that's a good idea, but if you can ride, you could go for the sheriff."

"I can and I *will* ride—with you. Callie's my sister." Isaac locked his gaze with Chip's, his eyes filled with resolve. "I *have* to do this."

Chip didn't like bringing up Isaac's limitations, but a situation that could trigger memories of his wartime experiences could affect his judgment at a crucial time. "The lives of Callie and the children will depend on us. If we're fired on…"

"I'm well aware of that possibility and will do whatever I have to do."

"Very well." Chip raised his voice to a normal level. "There's been a change in plans. I'll meet whoever shows up, as per the demand, with Spencer and Isaac following me. Hardy, you'll go for the deputy, follow our trail and lead him to the hideout."

"Got it. What about the jewels? They'll want to see them, won't they?"

Hardy had raised a good point. "I'm not sure how to deal with that."

Spencer spoke up. "Since that's a woman's domain, let's ask Tess. I'm sure she'll have an idea."

Minutes later Chip stood in the Abbotts' parlor with Spencer and Tess, holding a box filled with necklaces, bracelets and brooches containing diamonds, emeralds, sapphires and more. "Are you sure you want to offer these, Tess? I can't guarantee I'll get them back to you."

She smiled. "Don't worry, Chip. They're not real. I don't invest in jewelry. I invest in children. Now let's get those bits of glass out quickly."

They went to work and soon had a small leather pouch filled with what appeared to be precious stones. They'd fooled Chip. Hopefully they would fool the kidnappers.

The next hour passed with the speed of a dull crosscut saw plowing through a slab of oak. Chip had planned, prayed, paced and prayed some more.

He got up from where he'd kneeled beside his workbench, brushed the sawdust from his trousers and returned to the corral. A quail darted across the path, followed by six chicks running as fast as their toothpick legs could carry them. The hen's shrill call sounded like the word *Chicago*, yet another reminder of Callie, who had grown up in that city.

Spencer and Isaac met him. They went over the plan one more time. Chip would get inside and do what he could to protect Callie and the children. Once all of the men helping him had reached the hideout, they would assess the situation and figure out how to mount the rescue.

"The horses are ready." Chip followed Isaac to the slatted fence, where five horses were tethered. "I've saddled one of the gentlest mares for Callie, and I put some peppermint sticks in your saddlebag for the children."

"Thanks. I'd best get moving." Chip mounted his horse and headed for the meeting place at the far edge of the field, with the mare tied on behind.

Not a person could be seen. Tess had given strict instructions that no one was to venture outdoors without an armed escort. The only sound was the creaking of the seesaw as the breeze gently shifted it from one side to the other. He thought of the times he and Callie had taken the children to the playground, where they'd ridden the seesaw, given Jasper lessons on the parallel bars and taught Ruby how to skip rope. Wonderful memories.

But now Callie and the children were in danger because of him and his preoccupation with work. If only he'd joined them on their walk…

He reached the oak where the note had been left and waited for what seemed like hours but was, according to his trusty pocket watch, only two minutes. A horse approached with a small rider. A woman. That meant the two men were with Callie and the children. *Lord, be with them.*

The blond woman rode up to him with her revolver drawn. She fit the description Callie had given of the so-called Mary Smith, who had played the part of the wife looking to adopt blond children. "You're alone. That's good. Are you armed?"

"No." Chip took off his jacket, revealing his empty holster. He shook the coat, patted his vest and lifted the legs of his trousers to show her that he didn't have any hidden weapons.

"Keep your hands where I can see them. I'm going to check your saddlebags." She looked in one, had him turn his horses around and checked the other. She pulled out a paper sack far larger than Chip had expected and peeked inside. Isaac must have quite a stash of peppermint sticks.

"Do you always carry this much candy?" Her voice held a hint of amusement.

"Only when I'm trying to sweeten up a deal."

She coughed, a suspicious sound he was sure was meant to conceal a burst of laughter. She quickly sobered. "Do you have the jewels?"

He'd anticipated the question and had come up with an answer that satisfied him. But would it satisfy her? "I'd be a fool not to, wouldn't I?"

She studied him so long that he fought the urge to look away. "You don't strike me as the foolish type. Show them to me."

With slow, careful movements, he pulled the pouch from his jacket pocket. He held it up and jiggled it, the fake gems clinking together in a decent impression of the real thing. Or so he hoped. He was no expert when it came to jewelry, although he had peeked in the window of Randolf Jewelers when he was in Placerville, curious about their selection of engagement rings.

"Open it. Those could be marbles for all I know."

He loosened the drawstrings on the bag, enlarged the opening and poured a portion of the "precious stones" onto his palm. He extended his hand toward her for a couple of seconds, just long enough for her to see that he'd brought the ransom payment, but not long enough for her to get a good look. He formed a fist to secure the colorful bits of glass, dribbled them back inside the pouch and tied it shut. "I've kept my end of the bargain, Mrs. Smith. Now take me to my friends."

"Not so fast. I have to blindfold you first. You'll leave it on, or you'll have Zeke to deal with. Take my word for it. You don't want that. He's got a mean streak five miles wide."

Callie and the children were with the ruthless murderer, because from what the woman had said, this Zeke fellow must have been the one who shot Mr. Tate. Chip tamped down his anger and responded as a lone rider would. "If I can't see the trail, how will I find my way back?"

She scowled. "That's your problem. I'm just following orders."

And she didn't seem too happy about it, a fact that could work in his favor. "I've got a bandana. If you're agreeable, I'll put it on myself. Save you the trouble."

"Aren't you the helpful one, carpenter boy?"

The trio had obviously been watching the orphanage. That explained them being on hand to grab Callie and the children. "My name's Chip."

"Fine, Chip. Do it."

He whipped out the navy square, covered his eyes and tied the blindfold securely. "All set. Can we go now? I'd like to get there and back before dark."

"Catch!"

He instinctively reached out but missed. Something hard pelted him. A pebble perhaps?

"Helpful and trustworthy. Hmm. No wonder Callie's sweet on you. Let's go." The woman set out, leading the two horses behind her.

Chip hadn't felt as helpless since he was lying in the wagon all those years ago battling cholera, but for the sake of Callie and the children, he must cooperate.

A good fifteen minutes passed with him gripping the pommel and listening for any signs of Spencer and Isaac. To his relief, he heard nothing but the sounds of the three horses in their party, along with the chatter of birds in the trees overhead. The woman must have continued north through the oak-studded area beyond the Double T.

The sound of running water a short time later told Chip that they'd reached Dry Creek, where Hardy had lost the trail. To Chip's surprise, the woman stopped, with his horse and Callie's mare coming to a standstill, as well.

"The going can be rough since we travel in the creek for a while. I'm not supposed to let you do this, but you can remove the blindfold and take the reins. I want to be sure I get you there safely. Your friends are counting on you."

He whipped off the bandana to find the woman studying him again. Doubt clouded her eyes. "You never meant for anyone to get hurt, did you?"

She stared at a distant point. "I didn't know Mr. Tate had children. When I saw them, I begged Zeke to drop them off. I was afraid he might rough up their father, and I didn't want them to see that. I never expected Zeke to…to do what he did." She returned her gaze to Chip. "I wish I'd never told Nigel about the shipment."

"How did you know about it?"

"As I told your sweetheart, I worked at the exchange in Sacramento City where Mr. Tate bought the jewels. His order was the largest I'd ever processed, which is why I told Nigel about it. He'd asked me to marry him, but he couldn't afford an engagement ring. He said that if we helped ourselves to Mr. Tate's bounty, I could pick the best diamond of the lot and have it set." She gave a dry laugh. "Me? Wearing a fancy ring like that? I'd never dreamed of such a thing, so I went along with the plan. But his brother, Zeke, got wind of it and took over."

"He's behind the kidnapping, then?"

"The kidnapping. The killing. It's all him." She lifted her chin. "My Nigel wouldn't do something like that."

No, he would just rob an innocent man of his future. Her love for the schemer might help Chip to free those he cared for, though, if he chose his words carefully. "It's good that he has a woman like you at his side. However, he's gotten himself in a lot of trouble. There's a posse being formed as we speak to come after you, with an excellent tracker at the lead. It's just a matter of time before you're all caught. Things could go better for you, if you agree to work with me."

"You have to understand. I was sick about what happened to their father. It was all Zeke. Nigel and I shouldn't have to pay for what his brother did." Determination straightened her spine. "What do you have in mind?"

"We'll have to stand up to Zeke, so I'll need to be armed."

She scoffed. "I'm not giving you my gun."

"I'm not asking you to. I have access to mine."

"That's not true. I made sure you didn't have any weapons."

"I don't. Not on me." He gave her time to process the information.

Wariness creased her brow. "We're not alone, are we?" She turned her horse and scanned the area behind them. "How many are there?"

"Just two, for now, but there are more on the way."

"If I go along with this, you'll put in a good word for Nigel and me?"

Chip nodded.

"Fine." She holstered her revolver. "Then call them."

He did.

She watched the trail for a minute and flicked her gaze back to him. "My name isn't Mary Smith, as you know. It's Virginia, but everyone calls me Virgie."

Chip nodded. "Good to know, Virgie."

Spencer and Isaac approached with caution, revolvers in hand.

"You can holster your guns. Virgie here is going to help us." Chip completed the introductions and filled in the other men.

They made their way to the hideout, with Virgie in the lead. A cabin came into view at last. Virgie answered questions about the layout of the ramshackle structure, and the four of them came up with a plan.

Chip looked at each person in turn. "You're all clear on what you're going to do, right?"

Three heads nodded.

"Fine. Then Virgie and I will be off."

Spencer moved his horse alongside Chip's. "We're being covered in prayer. Tess has seen to that."

"Then we're as prepared as we can be." Chip tied the bandana back over his eyes and prayed Virgie wouldn't betray them.

She led his horse and the mare into the yard and stopped. Her feet hit the ground. "I'm back, and he's got the goods!" she hollered loudly enough for those inside to hear.

A door creaked open. Heavy footfalls thudded down wooden steps.

Dried oak leaves crunched under Virgie's feet as she came alongside Chip. "Get down, carpenter boy," she barked.

Chip dismounted and stood with his hands in full view.

Virgie tapped the cold barrel of her gun against his temple. "You can take this off now."

He removed the blindfold. As planned, they were standing in front of the cabin, far enough to the left so that they couldn't be seen through the single window on the right unless someone inside was standing there.

A wiry fellow faced him. "You see the stones yet, Virgie?"

"Of course." Irritation gave Virgie's voice an edge. "Zeke sent me to do a job, and I did it."

Nigel grunted his acknowledgment. "He sent me out to get the jewels, so—" he shifted his attention to Chip "—hand 'em over."

"Not until I see Callie and the children."

"That isn't gonna happen until Zeke says so."

"I need some assurance."

Nigel sent an eyebrow toward his hairline. "You're mighty demanding for someone who's outnumbered."

Virgie intervened. "He's done everything I asked, so let him at least hear her voice. Zeke shouldn't have a problem with that. You know he's more than ready to be rid of the young'uns."

"Fine." Nigel stomped up the steps, shoved the door open and stuck his head inside. "Tell that feller of yours that you're here."

"Yes, I'm here," Callie called. "The children are with me. They haven't hurt us."

Nigel yanked the door closed and tromped back down the stairs. "All right. You heard her. Now give me them jewels."

Chip reached into his jacket pocket, cast a stealthy glance to the left to assure himself that Spencer and Isaac were crouched beside the porch and withdrew the drawstring pouch. "Here." He held it out, letting go just as Nigel reached for it. The bag landed at his feet.

Nigel swore. He bent over.

While Nigel was distracted, Spencer crept up behind him.

Nigel straightened, and Spencer clamped a hand over the shorter man's mouth.

Spencer pressed the barrel of his revolver in the small of Nigel's back and ordered him to march to the far side of the cabin.

Virgie lifted fear-filled eyes to Chip. "You promised you wouldn't hurt him," she whispered.

"We won't," he assured her, keeping his voice low, "but we can't have him alerting Zeke. You need to get over there with Spencer, too, so you're out of the line of fire."

"Do you really think it will come to that?"

"I hope not." His goal was to subdue Zeke first and rescue Callie and the children. "Now, go."

Virgie hesitated. "Keep them safe, Chip." She left.

He turned to Isaac. "Ready?"

"Yes."

"Give me a count of ten."

"Will do."

Chip stole around the cabin and got into position, his breathing heavy. Moments from now it would all be over.

The eerie silence didn't bode well. Callie hadn't heard a word from those in front of the cabin since Nigel had demanded the jewels. She dreaded the thought of Chip being confronted by Virgie and Nigel, both of them armed and intent on getting something Chip didn't have. At least she hadn't heard any gunfire. Yet.

She huddled in the corner and hugged the children to her. Ruby was clutching her doll and trembling, as she had been ever since Virgie had left. Jasper was doing his best to be brave, but he flinched every time Zeke said something. Callie could understand. Zeke scared her, too. She hadn't felt as powerless since the day she'd remained under the table frozen with fear while her parents were killed.

"What's keeping them?" Zeke rose from the rickety chair and strode across the room. He leaned over, took hold of Callie's upper arm and jerked her to her feet. "We're gonna go out there and make sure your fellow doesn't try any funny business."

They'd taken three steps, with him guiding her using his viselike grip to steer her, when the door was kicked open.

Isaac stepped inside, a revolver in his hand aimed at Zeke.

Zeke twisted her arm behind her, shoved her in front of him and put his gun to her head.

Anger unlike anything she'd ever seen blazed in her brother's eyes. "Let her go!"

"No one's leaving except me, and I'm taking the jewels, so tell your friend to hand them over."

Did he plan to kill them all?

Callie's knees threatened to buckle.

No! She refused to give way to fear. She would be strong. The children needed her.

She didn't dare look at them. She had to act.

Summoning all her strength, she slammed her boot heel down on Zeke's foot. Hard.

He cried out in pain and jerked forward.

Callie threw her head back, smashing into Zeke's nose with a sickening crunch.

He swore, and the gun left her temple.

A shot rang out.

Ruby screamed.

A heavy object crashed to the floor.

Callie broke free and raced to the children. She dropped to her knees and gathered them into her arms, shielding them from the violence behind her. "Jasper, Ruby, I'm here."

A scuffle ensued.

She tried to block out the sounds, but they intruded—boots thudding, the crack of a fist hitting a jaw, a body falling with a thud.

Footfalls approached.

Zeke!

Callie reached for the only weapon at hand—Ruby's doll—spun around and smacked the man in the knees.

"It's all right, Callie. It's me. Isaac."

No! She'd just hit his injured leg.

"Isaac. I'm so sorry. I thought you were—" She dropped the doll, jumped to her feet and threw herself at her brother.

He stumbled backward, caught himself and pulled her to his chest. "Thank the Lord, you're all right."

She tried to break free, but he held her tightly. "I am, but we have to get the children out of here. I can't let anything happen to them."

"Shh." He loosened his hold and pressed a finger to her lips. "They're fine. It's all over."

"It is?"

"Yes. Look." He stepped aside.

Zeke was sprawled facedown on the floor. Chip kneeled beside the murderer, tying his hands. Zeke's gun lay off to the side, where it had fallen. She searched for signs of blood but saw none.

Callie turned to Isaac. "I heard a shot. Who was hit?"

"No one. When Chip jerked Zeke's arm up, the gun went off." He pointed to a spot over Chip's head.

She looked at the roof. A shingle had been blasted away, leaving a hole. "How did Chip get in here? I didn't see him before." He'd come to their rescue, just as she'd known he would.

"He sneaked in the back door when I kicked open the front. After you'd tromped on Zeke's foot and just about broke his nose, Chip knocked the gun out of Zeke's hand. The brute threw a punch, but Chip dodged it. He was so angry that it didn't take him long to knock Zeke out."

"What about Nigel and Virgie? Where are they?"

"They're outside with Spencer and aren't going anywhere."

"Did you hear that, Jasper and Ruby? We're safe now." She opened her arms, and the youngsters ran into them. Callie held them close. *Thank You, Lord, for watching over us and sending help.*

Chip straightened and yanked a groggy Zeke to his feet, holding him by both arms. Their captor glared at her, but he said nothing, which suited her just fine, considering all the cruel comments that had rolled off his tongue already.

Zeke's nose was swollen and bloody. It would serve him right if she *had* broken it. That wasn't a gracious thought, but he'd killed Mr. Tate and kidnapped two innocent children.

Chip's gaze locked with hers. His eyes held an apology and something else. He looked away before she could determine what it was. "I'll get him out of here." He shoved Zeke forward.

Callie took the children outside, and Isaac led them

off with the promise of a special treat. Nigel and Zeke sat in the shade of an oak with Spencer standing guard over them. Chip was talking with Virgie, who, unlike her partners in crime, wasn't restrained. She said something to Chip. He nodded, and she started for Callie.

Moments later Callie found herself face-to-face with the woman who had come into the Double T under false pretenses and frightened Ruby so badly that the precious girl had withdrawn for weeks. "What do you want?"

"To apologize. I never meant for things to turn out this way. I just wanted to say I'm sorry for…everything. I hope things go well for you. You've got a fine fellow there and two wonderful children who adore you. Don't be taking that lightly." The wistfulness in Virgie's voice was unmistakable.

If only Virgie was right, but Chip wasn't Callie's fellow, as much as she wished that was so. In all likelihood, no man would be interested in her. But the children were part of her life, and she would shower them with love. "I'd like to be able to say that I forgive you, but you put those I care about in danger. I'll pray that the Lord will change my heart. In time, I trust that He will. That's the best I can offer."

"I understand." Virgie walked over to Spencer with her shoulders bowed.

Jasper bounded up to Callie waving a peppermint stick in each hand. "Look what Mr. Isaac gave me. He never let me and Ruby have two candies at once before."

"I think Mr. Isaac was mighty glad to see you." Callie joined her brother, who was sitting with Ruby on the cabin steps. Jasper plopped down on the far end of the porch. His heels kept up a steady beat as he drummed them against the side. Ruby scampered over, sat next to

Jasper and added her lighter thumps to the mix. Callie had expected Ruby to pull inside herself after the traumatic experience, but she was all sunshine and smiles. Perhaps she was old enough to understand that she had nothing to fear now that the bad guys had been caught.

Callie took the candy stick Isaac offered her. "Thanks. My stomach has been tied in knots for hours. Perhaps this will help settle it."

"I felt sick, too, when Chip said you'd been kidnapped. I insisted on being part of the rescue party, but it took some talking to get him agree. I've never seen him as worked up about anything before. He was barking orders like a drill sergeant."

"You were the last person I expected to see burst into the cabin. I know how difficult it is for you to deal with something so...unsettling."

"It's strange, but I didn't give it a thought. You and the children were in danger. I had to help. And I did."

Callie leaned against his shoulder. "Yes, you did. I've never been as happy to see you as I was at that moment."

He laughed. "And here I thought you'd be disappointed that it wasn't Chip."

"I wasn't disappointed, just surprised. And now that it's behind us, I'm feeling proud, too. You had to face your fears, and you did it."

"So did you, sis. You really laid into Zeke. He'll think of you every time he looks at his ugly mug."

Ruby dashed over and tugged on Callie's sleeve.

"What is it, sweetheart?"

"Daisy got hurted. See." Ruby held out her doll and pointed at the neck, where the rubber head was attached to the fabric body.

Callie took a closer look. Some of the loose stitches

from Mr. Tate's hasty repair job had come out. They must have broken when she'd smacked Isaac, thinking he was Zeke. "I'm so sorry, Ruby. I'll take your baby downstairs with me tonight and patch her up. She'll be as good as new."

Chip ambled over. "We'll be heading back as soon as Hardy shows up with the deputy. It shouldn't them take too long to get here since Spencer marked the trail."

Isaac stood. "You can have my place if you'd like. I'm sure Callie would be interested in hearing how things played out on our end."

She'd like that very much. He'd come to her rescue, and she was eager to thank him.

Chip rubbed the back of his neck. "We'll have to talk later, Callie. I should get back and help Spencer with guard duty." He doffed his hat to her and left.

Although his tone was friendly enough, the apologetic look she'd seen in his eyes earlier was still there, along with what appeared to be guilt. What did he have to feel guilty about? She was the one who'd taken the children on a walk and strayed too far afield—a mistake that could have cost them their lives.

"No, Miss Callie! I can't go to sweep without Daisy." Ruby clutched her doll, her lower lip trembling.

Callie sat on Ruby's bed and brushed a hand over the dear girl's face. "I'm sorry, sweetheart, but if I don't fix her now, more stitches could come loose in the night. You wouldn't want that, would you?"

Ruby shook her head.

"Fine. Then I'll get to work." She'd intended to see to the repair earlier, but she hadn't had a moment to herself since they'd returned to the Double T. Despite Tess's wish to keep the other children from hearing about the kidnapping, word had spread. Everyone was eager to make sure they were all right, and many had wanted to hear about the ordeal. She'd answered numerous questions, as had Chip, Spencer and the other adults.

Jasper had more questions than anyone else, which came as no surprise. They'd begun on the trip back to the Double T and hadn't let up. No doubt, Chip would have a hard time getting the inquisitive boy to settle down enough to sleep. Ruby had been quiet, as usual, but thankfully she seemed to have grasped that they were no longer in danger and had relaxed. Her primary concern was her doll.

Callie hadn't had a moment alone with Chip, but he said he'd be waiting for her on the playground. Although she tried not to, she couldn't help but hope that seeing the children in the hands of that horrid man Zeke had helped Chip to realize just how much Jasper and Ruby meant to him and revisit his stand on adoption. She'd heard the concern in his voice when he'd forced Nigel to give him an assurance that they were all right and had seen the love in Chip's eyes after he'd rescued them. If only he'd looked at her with as much love as he had the children, but he'd avoided making eye contact with her since the rescue.

Callie took the doll Ruby reluctantly released, crossed the room and got her sewing kit out of her wardrobe. She sat on her bed and threaded a needle.

"You won't take Daisy away, will you?"

"Of course not, sweetheart. I'll stay right here." With her back to Ruby, of course. It wouldn't do for the tender-hearted girl to watch her doll's head being reattached.

Callie picked out the broken stitches that had held the

rubber head to the fabric body. She attempted to shove the escaping stuffing back inside, sticking her fingers up into the head, but met with resistance. Something was in the way.

Working carefully, lest she tear out more stitches, Callie probed the area until she encountered a piece of coarse fabric. She managed to get a second finger inside and, using the two as tweezers, pinched the cotton and felt something hard beneath it.

No. Not something. Some *things*. Small, hard things.

A tingling sensation swept over her. Could it be…?

Working as quickly as possible, despite the awkward position, she tugged the fabric toward the opening and pulled out a small pouch. Her fingers trembling, she loosened the drawstrings, poured the glittering contents onto her palm and gasped.

"What's wrong, Miss Callie?"

"N-nothing, sweetheart. I just, um, pricked my finger with the needle. I'll be fine." She would, once she could breathe again.

"Will you be done soon? I want Daisy back."

"I'll be quick, all right." She couldn't wait to show Chip what she'd found.

Chapter Fifteen

Chip sat in the tree house overlooking the playground and scanned the area below. The sun had dipped low on the horizon, bathing the area in warm yellow light. All was quiet, except for a cricket choir that was warming up.

It wasn't like Callie to be late, but perhaps she was having a hard time getting Ruby to sleep after their trying day. Jasper had asked a million questions before he'd unwound enough for Chip to tell him a story. Revisiting every detail didn't sit well with Chip, reminding him anew of his failure to protect Callie and the children, but Jasper had witnessed something no child should ever have to see and needed answers.

Five more minutes passed. Chip couldn't sit still another second. He climbed down the ladder and dropped to the ground. The parallel bars beckoned. He mounted them and performed a series of swings, moving on to rolls, releases and catches. He'd just lifted into a handstand when he heard someone coming. He completed a hasty dismount and spied Callie with her skirts hitched above her boot tops, sprinting toward him and clutching the shawl draped over her shoulders.

Fear gripped him momentarily, but he quickly dismissed it. The children were no longer in danger, so it had to be something else. But what?

She reached him, her face alight, and gripped his arm. Her words tumbled out, bright and breathy. "I'm sorry I'm late, but I have the most incredible news. I found Mr. Tate's jewels!"

Chip's jaw went slack. "Are you serious?"

"Yes. I'll show you. Hold out your hand." She reached into her skirt pocket, pulled out a small white handkerchief that was tied shut and set it on his palm.

"When did you find them? Where were they? How do you know they're the real ones?"

She shook a finger at him in schoolmarmish fashion, but the smile tugging at the corners of her mouth undermined her attempt to appear stern. "Patience, Mr. Evans. You're as full of questions as Jasper."

"And as impatient for answers as he always is, so fire away."

"I found them a few minutes ago. It turns out they were here with us all along."

Must she keep him waiting? He waved his hand in a gentle beckoning motion. "Answers, Callie, please."

"Of course. Ruby refused to go to sleep until I fixed her doll, so I got out my sewing kit and set about making the repairs. I removed the broken stitching at the neck. When I went to shove the cotton batting back inside the head, I felt something odd. I pulled that out—" she inclined her head toward the little bundle he held "—took a look inside and couldn't believe my eyes. Holding in my excitement wasn't easy, but I remained calm for Ruby's sake. Now I can finally show you."

She gently undid the knot and pulled back the corners

of the simple white square, revealing a striking assortment of gems in a variety of shapes. "It's too dark now, but wait until you see them in the light. They sparkle and shine so beautifully."

"They're pretty, all right. You're sure they're genuine, then?"

"See for yourself. Hold this in your left hand and compare them." She produced a pouch that looked like the first and gave it to him. "I put an amount of Tess's cut glass pieces in one of my handkerchiefs equal to Mr. Tate's stones."

Chip held out the two, as though weighing them on the twin pans of a miner's scale.

"You can feel the difference, can't you, even though it's not marked?"

"The stones that were in the doll are slightly heavier than those Tess took out of her jewelry."

Callie smiled. "Exactly. I performed another test that Mother taught me when I was a girl. The diamonds that were in the doll didn't fog up when I breathed on them, but the clear glass stones Tess gave you did. We can take the ones from the doll to a jeweler to confirm my findings and determine their value, but it appears Mr. Tate hid his shipment inside Daisy when he sewed her up that day."

Chip went back over everything Jasper had told them about Mr. Tate's stop in Clarksville. Understanding dawned, and he laughed. "He told Jasper he'd hidden them and didn't need a map because the location was in here." He tapped his head.

She clapped a hand to her chest. "That's right! So he had given Jasper a clue, after all. He must have put them in there when he went out to the barn that day. But why would he?"

That was a good question. "It's possible he suspected that someone was following him. If so, the safest way to ensure that the jewels didn't get in the hands of robbers would have been to put them in the one place they wouldn't check."

Callie slid the handkerchief containing the fake stones into one of her pockets. "I hope it gave him comfort in his final moments to know that he'd left his most valuable items with his children. Tess can save them to give to Jasper and Ruby when they're older. They could finance a college education for Jasper. Ruby could have one put into a ring as a reminder of her father. I don't know how she'd choose between them, though. They're all beautiful."

"Seems to me she'd want a ruby, but maybe not. Which is your favorite?" He liked the light blue one that reminded him of Callie's eyes.

"Hmm." She brushed a fingertip over the gems. "The diamonds are stunning, but I was drawn to this one." She'd picked the same one he had. "I think it might be a blue topaz."

So that's what it was called? He would have said sapphire. Showed how much he knew about such things.

Callie tied the corners of the handkerchief together and slipped the tiny bundle into her other pocket. "I'll get these to Tess. I'm sure she'll want to put them in the safe."

"Don't you want to talk first?"

She glanced at the horizon, which was now ablaze with orange, pink and purple as the sun bid the day farewell. "It's getting late, so I'll run them over to the main house and come back. Where will I find you?"

"I thought we could sit on the tree house's porch. We'll have a good view of Jack and Jill House from there, not that I expect either of the children to stir. Jasper was quite tired, even though getting him settled took me longer than usual." And since he would follow Callie up and sit by the ladder, she wouldn't be able to leave until he moved out of the way. He'd chosen the location for that reason since she'd been avoiding him. He had things he needed to say.

She glanced at the oak where he'd built the small structure. "I'm not fond of heights."

"It's only ten feet off the ground, and I'll be there to keep you safe." No sooner had the words left his mouth than he regretted them. He'd sent her and the children into danger mere hours before.

She drew in a breath and released in it a long, slow exhale. "All right. I won't be long."

Chip watched as each step took her farther away. She'd brought sunshine and smiles into his life, making him feel fully alive. He'd enjoyed himself more in the past five weeks than he had since he'd lost his family. Although he laughed and joked with people at times, life had become a serious business.

Callie could have changed that, had she been the woman for him. She would have seen to it that he didn't bury himself in his work and forget to have fun. She would have been happy to help him with his woodworking projects, too. They could have mixed business with pleasure. More than once, he'd imagined chasing her around his workbench, intent upon claiming a kiss, her beautiful blue eyes alight as she playfully evaded him. But that would never happen.

He picked up a pebble and rolled it between his fingers. The smooth surface reminded him of the jewels she'd found. How long might they have remained hidden inside Ruby's doll if Callie hadn't used it to defend herself from her supposed attacker? But she had. Thanks to her willingness to do whatever it took to keep them safe, the children had an inheritance that could make a difference in their lives, giving them some of the things their parents would have wished them to have.

But Jasper and Ruby wouldn't have what mattered most—family. Nothing could take the place of that. At least the children had each other.

Chip heaved a sigh. The years he spent on his own had been lonely at times, but they would be over in another three. All he had to do was pray that the Lord would bring the right woman into his life—a woman who could give him the family he'd been preparing for ever since the day he'd written The Plan.

Images of a woman marched through his mind—in the kitchen preparing a meal, in the parlor reading a book to a passel of attentive children, in one of the bedrooms upstairs tucking a little one into bed. In every scene, the woman and children had hair the color of honey. Try as he might, he couldn't envision a brown-, black- or red-haired wife.

Callie's return minutes later rescued him from his reverie. She didn't run, as she had before. Her steps were slow, her gaze downcast, as though she was reluctant to spend time with him, sensing what was coming. Perhaps that was best. Her acceptance would make their upcoming parting easier.

They climbed the ladder to the tree house. Although

she'd expressed fear, she made it up quickly and only hesitated when stepping from the top rung to the landing. Once she was seated on the front porch with her back to the elevated cottage, looking through the rungs of the railing, she relaxed—until he sat beside her. She pulled her skirts closer to her, as though wanting to put as much distance between them as she could.

He refused to scoot farther away. They were friends, after all, and he intended to keep it that way. "What did Spencer and Tess say?"

"They were surprised to find out the jewels had been here all along, just as we were, and admired Mr. Tate's cleverness. Spencer pointed out what a good thing it was that we found them. They could have been lost forever. He thinks Mr. Tate had no idea what fate awaited him because, if he had, he would have told someone where the stones were. Tess thinks he was more concerned about the children than the jewels, which is why he didn't tell them. He didn't want to put Jasper and Ruby in danger. We all agreed that the Lord knew where they were and when He wanted them to be found."

"By a bright, brave woman who risked her life for the children."

She adjusted her shawl. "I didn't do much—except put them in danger in the first place. It's my fault they were taken. If I'd been paying more attention..."

"You didn't do anything wrong." He jabbed a thumb at his chest. "I'm the one to blame. You asked me to join you on the walk, but I was too busy rushing to get the job done to join you. If I'd been there, things could have turned out differently."

"I'm glad you weren't. You would have fought back,

and who knows what could have happened to you. There were three of them." She shuddered.

He resisted the urge to wrap his arm around her. "Instead, I left you to deal with them on your own. Fine job of protecting you I did."

She rested a hand on his arm, a gesture he appreciated but shouldn't encourage. "You're not to blame. We had no way of knowing they were lurking about, waiting to kidnap us. They might have succeeded, but you came to our rescue. Isaac told me you planned the whole thing."

He didn't deserve the admiration in her voice. "I had plenty of help. Every person played a role, including you. I've never been as surprised or as proud as I was when you took on that bully. Zeke has to be three times your size, but you didn't let that stop you. I think you could have disarmed him yourself if I hadn't stepped in."

She gave his arm a playful swat before pulling her hand away. "Don't be so sure of that. You have no idea how scared I was, but I couldn't stand there and do nothing—" her voice softened to a strangled whisper "—like I did before."

He hastened to reassure her. "It's normal to be afraid. I was. Any number of things could have gone wrong, but I did what you always do—prayed and hoped things would turn out all right. And they did."

She twirled the fringe of her shawl around her finger. "This time, yes, but when my parents were being held at gunpoint, I froze. If I'd done something…"

"You were a child."

"I was twelve." Her tone held unwarranted self-reproach.

"That's a year younger than Luke. You wouldn't expect him to go charging at a gun-toting madman, would you?"

Her fingers stilled, and she slowly turned to face him. Even in the fading light, he could see her wide eyes and gaping mouth. "I never thought about it like that, but I couldn't have done much to help back then, could I?"

"Except put yourself in danger. I'm sure your parents were thanking the Lord that you stayed out of harm's way. That's what I was praying Jasper and Ruby would do."

"I was, too, and they did, bless them. Now they're safe, and Ruby is happy. I love seeing her smile. Since that whole ugly episode is behind us and things have settled down, I look forward to seeing many more. Don't you?"

Callie had given him an opening. "About that. It will only take us another two days to finish the furniture, and then I'll be going."

She was silent so long that he wondered if she was going to answer. Finally, she did. "It won't be easy on the children, but from what I've seen, youngsters are often more resilient than we adults are. They'll miss you, though."

"Will you?" The words were out before he could stop them.

"Of course, but I know you have other jobs waiting for you. There's a house up in Placerville that needs its kitchen and dining room completed. I'm sure the rooms will look lovely when you're done with them. And then you can move on to the next item in your plan."

Was it his imagination, or was her voice thick with emotion? It had grown too dark for him to see if her eyes were glistening. He didn't want to cause her pain, but it was nice to know she cared for him as much as he cared for her. If only things were different...

* * *

If only things were different… Callie stood in the field watching Chip and the children and sighed. That thought had run through her mind countless times since they'd spent those memorable few minutes in the tree house and he'd told her he was leaving. She'd known the end of his stay at the Double T was coming, but having him say it had brought up a swell of emotion. It had been all she could do to keep tears from streaming down her cheeks. The only thing that had kept them from falling was remembering the vow she'd made when Zeke had held the gun to her head—she must be strong. And she would.

"I got mine." Jasper displayed a blade of grass proudly. "How do I make it whistle like you done, Mr. Chip?"

Ruby took her time choosing a specimen that satisfied her. Even though they were in the field not far from where Zeke had grabbed them, Ruby didn't seem to care. She'd said several times since then that the bad men were all gone and couldn't hurt anybody else. Seeing the darling girl at peace warmed Callie's heart.

Chip squatted beside Jasper and demonstrated how to position the blade. "Put it between the bottoms of your thumbs, and then press the tops of them together. Make sure to keep the grass straight. If it's kinked like mine is, pull it up with your fingertips, like so. Once you have it in place, blow into the little window between your thumbs."

Jasper worked to get his piece of grass in place, concentrating so hard that the tip of his tongue peeked out the corner of his mouth. Could the dear boy be any cuter?

His first attempts at making a sound were fruitless, but he persevered and finally managed a faint squawk. He rushed over to her, beaming. "Did you hear that, Miss Callie? I did it!"

"You sure did. I'm proud of you."

"Now you try."

"Me? All right, but I'm not sure I can do as well as you did." She plucked a blade of grass, placed it between her thumbs and proceeded to make all manner of silly sounds. As she'd hoped, they made Jasper laugh. The longer she could keep the children from thinking about the parting soon to come, the better. She didn't want to think about it, either.

Chip yanked a long piece of grass from a nearby clump and brushed her cheek with it. "Come now, Miss Callie. I don't think you were trying hard enough. Give it another go."

Jasper joined in, encouraging her, as was his way. "Yes, Miss Callie. You can do it. I know you can."

She wasn't sure about that, but she would do her best. She blew as hard as she could and was rewarded with a piercing squeal that rivaled those Chip had produced.

He sent her one of his lopsided smiles that had first endeared him to her. "Well done, Callie! You're a champion grass-blade whistler."

Longing clamped its hands around her, squeezing so hard that it was all she could do not to turn into Chip's arms and beg him to reconsider. When he climbed aboard his wagon minutes from now and drove away, he would be taking a large part of her heart with him— as well as putting an end to her dreams.

She forced herself to breathe. "You're a good teacher." And a good man, the finest she'd ever met. But he didn't want her because she was…broken.

"Lookee, Miss Callie!" Ruby skipped over to her waving a piece of grass so wildly that it was a green blur. "I founded a good one."

"You surely did. Do you want me to show you how to make it whistle?"

Ruby shook her head. "I'm a big girl. I can do it myself."

The show of independence, although unusual, was encouraging. "I'm sure you can."

Ruby managed to get the grass in place without any assistance. She pressed her mouth to the tiny opening between her thumbs and blew. No sound came out, aside from a soft whoosh.

Jasper bounded over. "Blow harder, Ruby, like I done."

Chip draped an arm across Jasper's shoulders. "Patience, son. She's doing fine."

Callie watched the two of them, wide-eyed and wary. She'd heard Chip call Jasper *son* once before, and Jasper had balked. Seconds passed with no sign of protest on Jasper's part. She wasn't even sure if the endearment had registered with Jasper or with Chip. It seemed so natural that neither of them had noticed.

She rested her chin on her clasped hands and savored the sweetness of the moment, imprinting it in her memory. Her dream of being a wife and mother would probably never come to pass, but she'd enjoyed something close to it over the past five weeks.

Ruby huffed and puffed until her round cheeks were red, but at long last her efforts resulted in a squeak. She gave a joyful shout and spun in circles, her arms flung wide.

Chip put out a hand to catch her. "Whoa, there, princess. I don't want you to get so dizzy that you take a tumble."

"I'm not." She took a series of zigzagging steps, plopped down on the ground and laughed, a musical

sound Callie relished. "Yes, I am. Hold me, Mr. Chip."
She lifted her arms to him.

He scooped her up, rested her on his hip and planted
a kiss on her cheek.

She patted each of his. "I don't want you to go away."

"I know, but I have to. Other boys and girls need furniture, too, and they need someone to make it."

Jasper raced over, wrapped his arms around Chip's
waist and pleaded with him. "Can't you stay a little longer? Mr. Isaac said I'll be ready to ride a pony all by
myself real soon. Don't you wanna see that?"

Chip ruffled Jasper's curly locks. "I'll come visit you
sometime, and you can show me then."

Jasper peered up at Chip. "When?"

Callie answered before Chip could. She couldn't
stand by and let him make a promise he might be unable to keep, no matter how well intentioned he might
be. Children didn't take disappointments like that well.
Her parents had made many of them. "He comes whenever Mama Tess has a job for him to do, so we'll just
have to wait and see when that is."

"Miss Callie is right. I come to the Double T a few
times a year, so you'll see me again. In the meantime, I
have a little something for each of you in my wagon. The
first ones to reach it get to open their packages first."

"Me!" Jasper took off running. He stopped, dashed
back to Ruby and grabbed her hand. "Come on. We can
beat Miss Callie. Grown-ups are slow."

Callie accepted the challenge, admiring Chip's clever
ploy to ease into the goodbyes soon to come. "Not this
grown-up. You'd better watch out, or I'll beat you." She
hitched up her skirts and took off, staying a few feet behind the children all the way to the barnyard.

Jasper and Ruby reached the wagon and jumped about, cheering.

Callie arrived moments later and leaned over with her hands on her knees, breathing noisily in a feigned display of exhaustion.

Ruby sent Callie a triumphant smile. "We beated you here, Miss Callie."

"Yes, you did beat me. I guess I'm not as fast as I thought."

Chip arrived and congratulated Jasper and Ruby. "Now close your eyes and hold out your hands, and I'll give you your surprises."

The children waited, eagerness shining in both their faces, as Chip handed each of them a tissue-wrapped package. "All right. You can open your eyes and your presents."

The youngsters tore off the paper, revealing loaf-pan-sized pine boxes with their names carved in the lids in easy-to-read capital letters.

Jasper traced each letter of his name with a fingertip. "It says *Jasper*, doesn't it?"

Chip nodded. "And your sister's says *Ruby*. These are treasure boxes. You can keep special things in them. Go ahead and open yours. I put something inside for you to remember me by."

Jasper opened his box and pulled out a wooden horse and four cows. His mouth gaped as he admired the tiny creatures. Callie could see why. The detail on the saddled horse was amazing. Chip must have spent hours on that animal alone. "This is a cowboy's horse, isn't it, Mr. Chip?"

"It is. And that's the tiny herd the cowboy who rides it takes care of."

"What did Ruby get?"

Callie wondered the same thing. "I'll hold your box, sweetheart, so you can look inside."

Ruby handed it over, lifted the lid and squealed with delight. "Lookee!" She held up a tiny teapot and two acorn-cap-sized cups and saucers in turn, oohing and aahing over each item.

Callie studied the tea set. "Those are adorable. You and I can have a tea party this afternoon and use this wonderful gift Mr. Chip gave you." She straightened. "What do you say to him, children?"

Jasper and Ruby chorused their thank-yous.

"That's good. Now we need to say goodbye so Mr. Chip can leave. He has a special job waiting for him, and we don't want to keep him. I'm sure he'd like your hugs, though."

"I sure would." Chip squatted and opened his arms. Jasper and Ruby flew into them, holding on to him tightly. Jasper was the first to pull away, followed by Ruby. He sniffled as he tried to hold back his tears, but hers flowed freely.

Chip wiped Ruby's cheeks with his freshly laundered handkerchief and tucked it back in his pocket. "What happened, princess? You're leaking. Where did that beautiful smile of yours hide?" He peeked behind her head and lifted her arms. "Or maybe it's even farther away." He removed Jasper's cowboy hat and grabbed at the area above his head. "Would you look at that? It's right here. Let's get it back where it belongs." He pretended to hold the smile stretched between his thumbs and forefingers, moved it over to her and put it back in place. "Much better. Now let me see it so I know if I got it on straight."

Ruby's lips lifted. Although the smile was wobbly,

Chip had succeeded in getting her to produce one. He had a knack for making difficult situations more bearable with his well-timed jokes and gentle teasing.

Callie could use a dose of his humor right now. Sadness had welled up inside her, causing her eyes to sting and her chest to tighten. Despite the extra time she'd spent on her knees that morning asking the Lord to help her get through the goodbyes without an emotional display, she struggled to maintain control.

"Jasper! Ruby!" Luke crossed the yard with his long strides. "Mama wanted me to tell you that there's a game of leapfrog getting started on the playground. We could use some more players. How about it?" He held out a hand to each of them.

They looked to her, and she nodded. The children gave Chip one last hug and left without a fuss, for which Callie was grateful.

The curtains in the Abbotts' parlor fluttered. Tess had been watching and had created a timely interruption. Thanks to her, Callie would have a moment alone with Chip. Not that she knew what to say, but she appreciated the privacy.

She returned her attention to Chip. He held another tissue-wrapped package out to her, the same size as those he'd given the children. "This is for you."

"Oh!" She hadn't been expecting anything but took the gift. "Do you want me to open this now or later?"

"Now, please."

She removed the paper and gasped. "This is incredible." He'd given her a box, too, but hers was made of oak and had an inlaid top with the letter *C* in the center. The workmanship was exemplary. "I... I don't know what to say. 'Thank you' seems inadequate. I'll treasure this."

He grinned. "That sounds fitting. After all, it is a treasure box. Look inside."

"There's more? Goodness." She opened the box and pulled out an exquisitely carved flower. It looked like—

"It's an apple blossom."

"It's beautiful. Thank you very much for it and the box."

He rubbed the back of his neck. "I wanted you to have something to remember me by and thought of those few minutes we shared at your friend's orchard. I'll carry that memory with me all my days."

"So will I." That was when Chip had kissed her, before she'd known for sure that nothing could be done to repair the damage from the accident. She'd been so happy and filled with hope.

He took a step toward her, reached out a hand toward her face, paused with it in midair and slowly dropped it to his side. "I'm sorry things didn't turn out the way I'd planned. I care for you, Callie, and have enjoyed the time we've spent together. I wish things could be different, but…"

"I understand." That didn't make this any easier. "I wish you all the best as you finish your house and—" the words lodged in her throat, but she forced them past the lump "—and see to all the other items in The Plan. You'll be a fine father one day." And he'd make some woman a remarkable husband.

"You'll be a wonderful group leader and will enrich the lives of many children." He stared at her for several seconds, his gaze sweeping over her face. Finally, he heaved a sigh. "I need to get underway. Goodbye, Callie."

"Goodbye, Chip, and Godspeed." She turned and walked away, not trusting herself to look back. She pasted on a smile and headed to her room. The Lord had a plan for her, and she would embrace it—even if all she felt like doing was flinging herself on her bed and soaking her pillow.

Chapter Sixteen

Sitting on a hill overlooking Main Street, the Church of our Saviour, with its cross-shaped layout, steeply pitched roof and four-story belfry, added grace and elegance to Placerville's skyline. Chip admired it each time he headed up Canal Street, but what he most looked forward to was seeing the interior. The wooden pews that smelled of lemon wax, the diffused light streaming through the tall, thin stained glass windows and the expertly carved altar flanked by brightly colored bouquets made him feel welcome.

He stood between the pews and the steps leading to the chancel, toolbox in hand, looked overhead and turned in a slow circle. The sight took his breath away every time. Built to look like the inverted hull of a sailing ship, the ceiling showcased the skill of the woodworkers who had created the work of art. What he would have given to have been a member of that crew.

The squeaking of a door to the left drew his attention. Mr. Parks entered the sanctuary. He was dressed in trousers, a cotton work shirt and a vest, such as Chip wore. The auburn-haired minister didn't want anything getting in the way of drawing people to the Lord, so he didn't wear a clergyman's collar or use the title Reverend. His heartfelt concern for those who had yet to find their way into the family of faith was one of many things Chip admired about the humble man.

Mr. Parks smiled. "I thought I heard someone. Welcome, Chip. I appreciate you coming to see to the matter so quickly, but that wasn't necessary. I know you're a busy man."

"I didn't want to keep you waiting." He was also curious why the minister's dragging study door had suddenly become so important to him since the problem had developed some time ago. Knowing Mr. Parks, he had something he wanted to discuss, which was why he'd mentioned the repair job when he greeted Chip on his way out of church the day before. "I should be able to fix it in no time."

True to his word, he had the door off and the bottom planed in a matter of minutes. He oiled the hinges and rehung the door so it swung freely once again. "You can try it now."

Mr. Parks pulled the door closed and reopened it. "Good as new. What do I owe you?"

"There's no charge. I'm happy to help." Chip picked up his toolbox. "I'll be going now—unless there's something else I can see to while I'm here."

"No other projects, but if you have a minute, I'd like to ask you something."

"Sure."

Mr. Parks took a seat on one of the front pews. Chip sat and plunked his toolbox at his feet, eager to hear what was on his minister's mind.

"Ever since you returned from Shingle Springs three

weeks ago, you've seemed even more serious than usual. I sense an underlying sadness that concerns me. What happened while you were away?"

Chip quickly summarized the events, from finding the children alongside the road to rescuing Jasper, Ruby and Callie from the hands of Mr. Tate's murderer.

"I'm glad to hear Callie got the position. She did a fine job at the Blair brothers' lumberyard, but I can't think of anything she's more suited to than caring for children. She has a real way with them that has blessed the youngsters in our Sunday school program. The ordeal had to be hard on her and your young charges. Where do things stand now?"

"Zeke will receive the stiffest penalty because he pulled the trigger. The sheriff requested leniency for Virgie since she helped us." Things could have turned out differently if she hadn't waged a battle with her conscience. "He's considering a lesser charge for Nigel, too, since it's evident that the kidnapping and murder were never his idea."

"Our sheriff is a fair man, so I trust justice will be administered with a balance of wisdom and grace. How are Callie and the children faring after the ordeal?"

Chip ran his hand along the pew's smooth back. "They seemed fine when I left them. Jasper's a bright boy. Even though he's young, he grasped the situation from the beginning. Knowing that he was a big help when Virgie returned with Nigel for the second interview gave him some peace. The change in Ruby after the rescue was remarkable. Once she realized the danger was past, she relaxed and became the bubbly girl I thought she'd be."

"You neglected to mention our dear sister, Callie. How is she?"

"She was shaken, of course, but she handled herself well." Remarkably so. He experienced a surge of fear every time he relived the experience, followed by a swell of pride. "She's an exceptional woman."

"Interesting." Mr. Parks stroked his neatly trimmed beard, which, like his temples, had hints of silver. "Although I've seen you three times since your return, this is the first time you've said anything about her. I take it things didn't work out the way you'd hoped."

The minister's gentle manner loosened Chip's tongue. "I care for her, but all I can offer is friendship."

"What's holding you back?"

How could he answer without revealing Callie's... limitation? "I've told you how eager I am to carry on my family's legacy. While some might see adoption as a way to do so, that's not something I've considered."

Mr. Parks reached for a pew Bible, flipped through the pages until he found what he was after and handed the book to Chip, opened to the third chapter of Hebrews. "I think I understand what you're not at liberty to say. Perhaps I can offer a new perspective. Would you read the fourth verse, please?"

He didn't have to because that particular verse was one of his favorites, and he knew it by heart. "'For every house is builded by some man; but he that built all things is God.'"

"You build beautiful houses, Chip, but God's in the business of building families. If you'll turn to the first chapter of Ephesians, the fourth through sixth verses, you'll see how He goes about it."

Chip found the passage and began reading. "'According as he hath chosen us in him before the foundation of the world, that we should be holy and without blame before him in love: Having predestinated us unto the adoption of children by Jesus Christ to himself—'" He stopped and stared at the words.

"You see it, then?"

Chip swallowed. "We're adopted into the family of God. You mentioned this in one of your sermons earlier this year, but I'd never thought of it in relation to my own family before."

"There are many stories in the Bible about men eager to carry on their lines, some of them with surprising outcomes. One of my favorites is in Luke. I mention it in a sermon each December."

"You're talking about Joseph, aren't you?" The heaviness that had settled on Chip the day Callie had told him she couldn't have children lifted. "He didn't want to honor his engagement to Mary when he found out she was expecting, but that changed when he learned the child was God's own Son and that he'd been chosen to be Christ's father—his *adoptive* father."

Mr. Parks nodded. "Perhaps that knowledge will help you with your decision."

"It has. I know just what to do. I only hope it's not too late."

Sounds of laughter drew Callie to the window of her room in Jack and Jill House. Children had gathered on the playground below, clad in their Sunday best. Their group leaders were busy keeping them contained to a small area so they wouldn't muss their clothing before heading to church. She didn't envy the leaders. Keeping fifty active children corralled wasn't easy.

The ache that had filled her chest ever since Chip had left had intensified the past Friday. When that heart-breaking day began, there had been fifty-two children at the Double T. That was before Tess had pulled Callie aside at breakfast and told her Jasper and Ruby were being adopted and would be picked up shortly afterward. Tess had gone on to explain that the interview process had been handled swiftly because of the family's unique situation. She'd assured Callie the children would be in a home where they would be well loved.

Callie tore herself away from the window, only to have her gaze come to rest on the wardrobe that had held Ruby's clothes. Packing her little outfits had been so difficult. Tess had kept the children with her while Callie completed the task, which had been wise. She'd been in a state of shock as she gathered Ruby's things and put them inside the cute little trunk her adoptive parents had sent. Jasper's new group leader had seen to his things, sparing Callie that task, at least. Somehow she'd gotten through the goodbyes before the tears fell. At least she hadn't been asked to meet Jasper and Ruby's new parents. She didn't know how she could have endured that.

A sob threatened, but she choked it down. She had the other children to think about. Come tomorrow morning, five of them would be in her care. Tess had assigned Callie the task of filling in for one of the other group leaders who was going to visit her family up in Grass Valley.

She stooped and took one last look in the wall mirror mounted at child height. A rap on the door brought her upright. She opened it. "Tess! What a surprise. Did you need something?"

Tess glanced from Callie's simple chignon to the toes of her boots and gave a cluck of disapproval. "My dear girl, I know you're feeling blue, but you don't need to wear such a dark shade of it. I'm certain you have something more suited to a glorious spring day like today. Let's take a look, shall we?"

Callie stepped aside to allow Tess to enter. The determined woman flung open the doors of Callie's wardrobe and pulled out her new white dress. "This is just the thing to lift your spirits. I'll step outside while you change, and then we can walk to church together. I want to tell you about the girls in Amanda's group."

The dress was finished, thanks to Tess. She'd invited Callie to the Abbotts' ranch house while Isaac and Hardy were giving the children their riding lessons earlier that week and had suggested she bring a project to work on, so she'd had more time for sewing than usual. Talking with Tess as she tended to some of her family's mending had helped Callie keep her mind off Chip, who entered her thoughts countless times each day. Losing him had been difficult, but she'd been doing her best to carry on. Losing the children...

No! She couldn't think about that now. Tess was waiting.

Minutes later, Callie stepped into the hallway wearing her new eyelet dress. She'd chosen a simple princess design with a slightly higher waist, around which she'd added a wide pink ribbon tied into a fluffy bow in back. The ruffles at the cuffs and bottom of the skirt added a feminine touch. Although she did look less somber, the heaviness in her chest remained.

The large group from the Double T started out, walking rather than riding in wagons since it was a warm day with not a single cloud in the brilliant blue sky. Wildflowers dotted the fields alongside the road, and mother birds scolded as they protected their nests tucked in the branches of the plentiful oaks. Spring was bursting forth all around her, at odds with the dreariness inside.

Despite Tess's animated descriptions of the girls in Amanda's group, Callie had to force herself to concentrate. She wanted to learn all she could about the children who would be in her care, but images of Ruby holding acorn-cup tea parties and Jasper racing around the woodshop on his stick horse with chaps flapping intruded. They'd only been in her life two months, and yet they would remain in her heart forever.

By the time they reached the church, Tess had told Callie everything there was to know about the girls in Amanda's group—or so it seemed. Before they headed inside, Callie asked the questions that had been foremost in her mind ever since leaving Jasper and Ruby with Tess and trudging back to Jack and Jill House. Alone. "Why didn't Jasper and Ruby didn't get their Day of Celebration?"

"They will. The family was headed out of town, but they'll be back soon, and we'll hold it then. The parents are both looking forward to it, as are Jasper and Ruby."

So was she, although it could become the final farewell, unless… "Will the family ever return to the Double T after that, or is it possible for a group leader to a visit a child after an adoption has taken place?"

"We encourage families to visit us here at the Double T after the children are settled into their new families so they can see their friends, but it's up to their new parents. If they do come back, we usually see them about three months after the adoption took place—although a few children have asked to visit before that."

Three months? How could she wait that long? She'd

just have to hope Jasper and Ruby missed her as much as she did them and asked to see her sooner.

The children trooped inside the white clapboard church, which was larger than one would expect for such a small town. Spencer and Tess had donated funds for a church expansion several years before in order to accommodate the group from the Double T. Isaac came in with Freddie and smiled at Callie as he and his new sidekick slipped into a pew.

As she did each week, Tess chose a pew in the row behind all the children from the Double T. Her own six children were sprinkled among the rows, sitting beside their friends. She said that helped the orphans feel as though they were part of a big, happy family, which they were. Even those children who were never chosen for adoption would have a good life thanks to Spencer and Tess.

Tess held out a hand to the pew. "Why don't you join me this week, Callie? I don't like the thought of you sitting by yourself."

Although Callie would have preferred to do just that, politeness demanded she accept Tess's kind offer. Callie sidestepped her way down the row and took a seat beside two-year-old Lucy, who sat next to her father.

Spencer leaned over his daughter's head and whispered, "The past couple of days have been rough, but the Lord has a way of bringing joy from heartache." He would know, having lost his first wife.

Callie summoned a smile. "I'm sure He has a plan for me." It wasn't the one she'd envisioned. Somehow, someday, she would have to make peace with that, but right now just she had to get through her first service without Jasper and Ruby sitting on either side of her.

The pianist began the prelude. Tess took her seat,

and the service got underway. As the final strains of the opening hymn faded, Reverend Josephs, a small man with a voice befitting someone twice his size, pushed up his spectacles and took his place at the pulpit. The minister's messages thus far had been inspiring, but Callie's mind wandered so many times during that particular one that she would have a hard time telling anyone what it was about, should someone ask.

Before she knew it, the congregation was on their feet singing the closing hymn, a new one. "What a Friend We Have in Jesus" had fast become one of her favorites. The Lord must have known she could use a reminder that He was there for her in the midst of her sorrows. He would be there for her as she grieved and help her move beyond the pain.

The hymn ended, and Reverend Josephs stepped to the front and delivered the benediction. Callie waited for the pianist to begin the processional and the minister to dismiss the congregation, but he stood there smiling. Heads turned all around her, the questions on others' faces surely mirroring the puzzlement on hers.

"Brothers and sisters," Reverend Josephs began, "a gentleman who has worshipped with our church family on a number of Sundays came to me with a special request, and I was happy to grant it. Mr. Evans, if you'll please come forward, you may address the congregation."

Callie inhaled sharply. Chip was here?

He strode up the aisle, his gaze forward, his expression schooled, looking as handsome as ever in a short black frock coat, matching trousers and white shirt with royal blue puff tie. What could he possibly have to say? Would he leave right after his announcement, or would he look for her? Did she trust herself to talk to him without turning into a puddle of tears?

Chip joined the minister at the front. "Thank you for granting my request, Reverend." He turned to face the congregation. "Ladies and gentlemen, boy and girls, I enjoyed my time here in Shingle Springs. Leaving was one of the hardest things I've ever done."

Callie could understand. Saying goodbye to Jasper and Ruby was like tearing out a part of her heart. Did Chip even know the children were gone? If he'd come expecting to see them, he would be disappointed.

"When I rode off that day, I returned to Placerville ready to complete my house, which was my plan. What happened next was God's."

Had Chip finally relinquished The Plan? If so, had he found the peace she longed for him to experience?

"As I put the finishing touches on the home I looked forward to sharing with a family one day, I realized my definition of family was limited."

Hope took root inside Callie. She leaned forward, eager to hear more.

"Our Heavenly Father chose the Israelites to be His people, but He didn't stop there. He'd planned all along to welcome into His family people from 'every tribe and language and people and nation,' as it says in Revelation. Those of us sitting here weren't born into the family of God. We were added to it when He adopted us. Those of us who have welcomed the Lord into our lives are God's children and part of His family."

Callie clung to Chip's every word, her hope growing with each one.

"Once I understood these truths, I faced another. I was following The Plan, which I'd written. It specified when

I would start my family, but I'd left God out of my plans. I'd also left behind the very people I wanted to be part of my family because of my insistence on doing things my way, so I set about remedying that. The first thing I did was visit Spencer and Tess and see about adopting two children who found their way into my heart. Jasper and Ruby, would you come to your new papa?"

The children raced up the aisle and flung themselves into Chip's open arms.

Callie covered her mouth to keep from shouting with glee. Not that she needed to worry. Applause filled the sanctuary, along with whoops and hollers from several of the children. Despite the undignified response, the adults smiled at the jubilant outburst.

When the room finally quieted, Chip continued, with Jasper and Ruby standing on either side of him. "I'm happy to be a father to these wonderful children— my pardner and my princess—but they're in need of a mother, and I can think of no one more suited than the woman who captured my heart long before the children did, Miss Caroline Hunt." Chip held out a hand toward her. "Callie, would you please join us?"

Joy unlike anything she'd known before washed over her. She slipped past Tess, who sent her a conspiratorial smile. Clearly, she and Spencer had helped Chip plan this incredible surprise, for, if Callie wasn't mistaken, Chip planned to propose. The very thought caused her to be so light-headed that she had to concentrate on walking in a straight line. *Just look at Chip, and you'll be fine.*

Then again... The love in his eyes was unmistakable. If she wasn't careful, she might forget how to put one foot in front of the other. Somehow she managed to reach the front without falling on her face.

Chip reached out and took her hands. "I'm a man of action, not words, so I'll keep this simple. I love you, Callie, and have for a long time, even though I didn't know it. If I'm honest, I fell in love with you the first time you helped me with an order at Blair Brothers Lumber Company. You were as knowledgeable about wood as any man, but when I left, you sent me a smile filled with sunshine. I was smitten."

Callie sighed, along with half the women in the pews.

Chip dropped to one knee, and her heart did a jig. "Will you marry me and be my wife and my partner in all my endeavors?"

Before she had time to answer, Jasper and Ruby dropped to their knees, too, and spoke in unison. "And our mama?"

"Yes, yes and yes!" Callie kneeled and hugged the three people dearest to her in the world as the sanctuary erupted in applause once again.

Chip stood, pulled her to her feet and helped the children up, too. "Now that we've settled that, I have another surprise."

She stared at him, speechless. There was more?

"If you're agreeable—" he gazed into her eyes, his own filled with eagerness "—I'd like to marry you right away."

She found her voice. "Where and when?"

"Here and now, with the congregation serving as witnesses of our vows. I figured you might like Mr. Parks to perform the ceremony since he's our minister, so I invited him to join us. He's got the license and is ready, if you are. Please, say you are. You'll make me a mighty happy man if you do."

"I am."

Minutes later, Callie stood at the back of the sanctuary with Isaac. The pianist began the "Wedding March."

Her brother held out an arm, and she slipped a hand around his elbow. He leaned close and whispered, "You've got a fine man there, sis, and wonderful children. It's a privilege to hand you over to them. Just see to it that you don't get so busy enjoying your new family that you forget about your old brother." He kissed her cheek, and they set off toward Chip, who stood to the right of Mr. Parks with Jasper at his side. Ruby waited on the left, holding a bouquet of wildflowers like those in Callie's hands, which the children had picked. No bride had ever had a bouquet chosen with such love, she was sure of it.

The ceremony was short but oh, so sweet. Before Callie knew it, Chip reached for her hand and slipped a beautiful ring on her finger with a blue topaz similar to the one she'd admired among Mr. Tate's jewels. Mr. Parks announced them man and wife and gave Chip permission to kiss his bride. The brush of her groom's lips on hers was brief, but his eyes shone with the promise of kisses yet to come.

Reverend Josephs joined the wedding party at the front and addressed the congregation. "In honor of this special occasion, Spencer and Tess Abbott have asked me to extend their invitation to a wedding luncheon at the Double T for Chip and Callie Evans, along with the Day of Celebration party for their children, Jasper and Ruby Evans."

The afternoon flew by in a flurry of fun. Callie's cheeks were sore from all the smiling she'd done. Not that she cared. This had been the most wonderful day of her life.

Chip found her and grabbed her hand. "Come with me."

"Where are we going?"

"To the woodshop. I haven't had you to myself all day, and I can't wait any longer for a kiss. A real kiss."

Neither could she.

The kiss they'd shared in the orchard was delightful, but there'd been a tentativeness to it on both their parts. This time Chip took her head in his hands, lowered his mouth to hers and claimed her lips in a kiss that started out tender but turned into something so incredible that she clutched his jacket to support herself. If she'd had any doubt Chip loved her and wanted her as his wife, he'd convinced her otherwise.

He pulled away and loosened his hold enough to look into her face. "Tess and Spencer have offered to watch Jasper and Ruby for us tonight so we can have an evening to ourselves. We can go anywhere you'd like, within reason. There's still time for us to make the last train down to Folsom or Sacramento City and rent a room in fancy hotel, or we could head up to Placerville and stay at the Cary House, if you'd prefer."

"I'd like to go to Placerville, but I don't want to stay in a hotel. I want to go to your house."

"It's *our* house now. I'll gladly take you there, but I'm surprised you passed up the opportunity to be pampered."

"Oh, I will be. Our house—" she smiled "—was built by a gifted carpenter, and I happen to know what a kind, caring, loving man he is."

"I'm not sure he deserves all that praise, but he loves you dearly and looks forward to a lifetime spent showing you just how much."

She did, too, but love went both ways. "In case you're wondering, I'm a wee bit smitten myself. Shall I show you?"

He grinned. "By all means."

Epilogue

One year later

All her life Callie had dreamed of having a baby to love. Wonder of wonders, she did. The adorable infant in her arms, just one week old, couldn't be any more beautiful. From her fine blond hair to her ten tiny toes, she was flawless, at least in Callie's eyes. The dear girl did have a piercing cry when she was hungry, though, as she was now.

Jasper looked up from where he and Ruby were building a block tower. "She's loud."

"Chip," Callie called, "could you hold the baby while I get her feeding bottle ready?"

Hurried footfalls announced his arrival in the parlor of their lovely home. "I've taken care of that already." He held out the glass bottle with its India rubber tube and teat.

"Did you wash everything first and boil the pieces the way Mrs. Wright told us?" The nurse midwife had left a short time before, after a helpful session in how to care for a newborn. Her husband, Dr. Wright, was an advocate of boiling syringes and other implements prior to use.

"Of course. And, as Mrs. Wright suggested, I will always hold our little primrose when it's my turn to feed her rather than leaving her alone with the bottle." Her handsome husband smiled one of his teasing smiles. "Provided you'll let me feed her on occasion. As smitten as you are, I'm not sure you'll ever put her down."

Jasper grabbed another block from the pile and paused. "Mama said babies need lots of help 'cause they can't do things the way big boys and girls like me and Ruby do."

Callie positioned the bottle and popped the mouthpiece between her new daughter's rosebud lips. "Since we've only had her with us two hours and this is her first feeding, I thought I'd go first. But since you're obviously as taken with our unexpected gift as I am, I'll let you give her the second half of the bottle."

Tess had shown up hours before with the baby and said that the little girl's mother, a heartbroken young widow, had been so weakened by the delivery that she'd passed on before even naming the baby. Chip had offered to take the child in without a second thought.

Callie smiled as she recalled his eagerness. It wasn't until moments later that he'd sheepishly turned to her and apologized for not asking her opinion first. She didn't mind a whit. Chip had so embraced adoption that he'd let Tess know he and Callie were eager to expand their family. He'd asked Tess to remember them should she come across a child she felt would be a good fit for their family. She had, and now Callie was holding her third child, with a promise of more to come.

When she'd sat in Dr. Wright's office a year ago and

learned that she couldn't bear children, she'd felt useless and broken. Since then she'd come to realize that God had a way of using broken people to do His work in the world. She and Chip were able to provide a loving home for children desperate for one.

The tiny girl's eyes locked with Callie's. They held such trust. She trailed a finger over her daughter's cheek. "You're a beautiful baby, but you need a name."

Ruby looked up from the block tower. "Papa called her primrose."

Callie smiled. "That he did, and I'm sure he will many times, just as he calls you princess. But those are nicknames. Your little sister needs a real name."

Chip sat beside Callie and gazed at their little girl with love and awe. "I think we should call her Hope, because her mama hoped for children, and now she has them."

"That's true. I do." She lowered her voice to a whisper and leaned close to Chip. "Thanks to you and the Lord, because together you've granted my motherhood wish."

* * * * *

If you enjoyed HER MOTHERHOOD WISH,
look for these other books by Keli Gwyn:

FAMILY OF HER DREAMS
A HOME OF HER OWN
MAKE-BELIEVE BEAU

Dear Reader,

I hope you enjoyed Chip and Callie's story. The idea for it came about as a result of two incidents from my own family that dealt with infertility and adoption. Callie's accident is based on my great-aunt's experience. She was kicked by a mule when she was very young. As a result, she was unable to bear children. I asked myself what it would have been like for a woman in the 1870s to deal with such a diagnosis.

Adoption has played an important role in my own life. My mother was already pregnant with me when she began dating the man I knew as my father. Although she was young and had been pressured to give me away, she'd chosen to raise me herself, for which I'm very grateful. Since my parents married when I was a baby, I don't remember life without Dad. I never considered him my stepfather, although legally that's what he was. Thirty years after he came into my life, we entered the historic courthouse in my Gold Rush–era town, where he adopted me. That was a milestone day!

As I created this story, I asked myself what would happen if a woman who was given the same diagnosis my great-aunt received, and who embraced adoption as a way to form a family, was to meet a man intent upon having children of his own. The possibilities were intriguing, and the story took shape. Setting the story at the Double T, where my first Love Inspired Historical, *Family of Her Dreams*, took place, was fun. I enjoyed revisiting Spencer, Tess and their children.

I love hearing from readers. You can contact me through my website at www.keligwyn.com or write to me at PO Box 1404, Placerville, CA 95667.

Warmly,
Keli Gwyn

COMING NEXT MONTH FROM
Love Inspired® Historical
Available April 4, 2017

THE RANCHER'S SURPRISE TRIPLETS
Lone Star Cowboy League: Multiple Blessings
by Linda Ford

After stumbling on triplet orphans abandoned at the county fair, rancher Bo Stillwater's not sure what to do with them. But when he leaves them in the care of the town doctor's lovely spinster daughter, Louisa Clark, he finds he can't stay away—from her or the babies.

COWBOY HOMECOMING
Four Stones Ranch • by Louise M. Gouge

When cowboy Tolley Northam returns home, he's determined to finally win his father's approval. Perhaps a marriage to family friend Laurie Eberly will help him earn it. But when Laurie discovers *why* he began pursuing her, can he convince her that she holds his heart?

UNDERCOVER SHERIFF
by Barbara Phinney

After a woman, a child and Zane Robinson's small-town-sheriff twin all go missing, the woman's friend Rachel Smith has a plan to find them. But for it to work, Zane must pose as his brother and draw out anyone involved in their disappearance.

FAMILY OF CONVENIENCE
by Victoria W. Austin

In need of a father for her unborn child, mail-order bride Millie Steele agrees to a marriage in name only with single father Adam Beale. But as she grows to love her new children—and falls for their handsome dad—can their convenient family become real?

———————

Get 2 Free Books,

Love Inspired HISTORICAL

Plus 2 Free Gifts—

just for trying the Reader Service!

SPECIAL EXCERPT FROM

Love Inspired HISTORICAL

When local rancher Bo Stillwater finds abandoned triplet babies at the county fair, the first person he turns to is doctor's daughter Louisa Clark. But as they open their hearts to the children, they might discover unexpectedly tender feelings for one another taking root.

Read on for a sneak preview of
THE RANCHER'S SURPRISE TRIPLETS,
the touching beginning of the series
**LONE STAR COWBOY LEAGUE:
MULTIPLE BLESSINGS.**

"Doc? I need to see the doctor."

Father had been called away. Whatever the need, she would have to take care of it. She opened the door and stared at Bo in surprise until crying drew her attention to the cart beside him.

"Babies? What are you doing with babies?" All three crying and looking purely miserable.

"I think they're sick. They need to see the doctor."

"Bring them in. Father is away but I'll look at them."

"They need a doctor." He leaned to one side to glance into the house as if to make sure she wasn't hiding her father. "When will he be back?"

"I'll look at them," she repeated. "I've been my father's assistant for years. I'm perfectly capable of checking a baby. Bring them in." She threw back the door so he could push the cart inside. She bent over to look more closely at the babies. "We don't see triplets often." She read their names on their shirts. "Hello, Jasper, Eli and Theo."

They were fevered and fussy. Theo reached his arms toward her. She lifted him and cradled him to her shoulder. "There,

there, little man. We'll fix you up in no time."

Jasper, seeing his brother getting comfort, reached out his arms, too.

Louisa grabbed a kitchen chair and sat, putting Theo on one knee and lifting Jasper to the other. The babies were an armload. At first glance they appeared to be in good health. But they were fevered. She needed to speak to the mother about their age and how long they'd been sick.

Eli's wails increased at being left alone.

"Can you pick him up?" she asked Bo, hiding a smile at his hesitation. Had he never held a baby? At first he seemed uncertain what to do, but Eli knew and leaned his head against Bo's chest. Bo relaxed and held the baby comfortably enough. Louisa grinned openly as the baby's cries softened. "He's glad for someone to hold him. Where are the parents?"

"Well, that's the thing. I don't know."

"You don't know where the parents are?"

He shook his head. "I don't even know *who* they are."

"Then why do you have the babies?"

For an answer, he handed her a note and she read it. "They're abandoned?" She pulled each baby close as shock shuddered through her. He explained how he'd found them in the pie tent.

"I must find their mother before she disappears." Bo looked at Louisa, his eyes wide with appeal, the silvery color darkened with concern for these little ones. "I need to go but how are you going to manage?"

She wondered the same thing. But she would not let him think she couldn't do it. "I'll be okay. Put Eli down. I'll take care of them."

Don't miss
THE RANCHER'S SURPRISE TRIPLETS by Linda Ford,
available April 2017 wherever
Love Inspired® Historical books and ebooks are sold.

www.LoveInspired.com

*Returning to her Amish community, Lizbeth Mullet comes
face-to-face with her teenage crush, Fredrik Lapp. As he
builds a bond with her son and she falls for him all over
again, will revealing the secret she holds turn out to be their
undoing—or the key to their happily-ever-after?*

Read on for a sneak preview of
HER SECRET AMISH CHILD by *Cheryl Williford*,
available April 2017 from Love Inspired!

"Lie still. You may have broken something," Lizbeth
instructed.

His hand moved and then his arm. Blue eyes—so like
her son's—opened to slits. He blinked at her. A shaggy brow
arched in question. Full, well-shaped lips moved, but no
words came out.

She leaned back in surprise. The man on the ground was
Fredrik Lapp, her brother's childhood friend. The last man in
Pinecraft she wanted to see. "Are you all right?" she asked,
bending close.

His coloring looked normal enough, but she knew nothing
about broken bones or head trauma. She looked down the
length of his body. His clothes were dirty but seemed intact.

The last time she'd seen him, she'd been a skinny girl of
nineteen, and he'd been a wiry young man of twenty-three.
Now he was a fully matured man. One who could rip her life
apart if he learned about the secret she'd kept all these years.

He coughed several times and scowled as he drew in a

deep breath.

"Is the *kinner* all right?" Fredrik's voice sounded deeper and raspier than it had years ago. With a grunt, he braced himself with his arms and struggled into a sitting position.

Lizbeth glanced Benuel's way. He was looking at them, his young face pinched with concern. Her heart ached for the intense, worried child.

"*Ya*, he's fine," she assured Fredrik and tried to hold him down as he started to move about. "Please don't get up. Let me get some help first. You might have really hurt yourself."

He ignored her direction and rose to his feet, dusting off the long legs of his dark trousers. "I got the wind knocked out of me, that's all."

He peered at his bleeding arm, shrugged his broad shoulders and rotated his neck as she'd seen him do a hundred times as a boy.

"That was a foolish thing you did," he muttered, his brow arched.

"What was?" she asked, mesmerized by the way his muscles bulged along his freckled arm. It had to be wonderful to be strong and afraid of nothing.

He gestured toward the boy. "Letting your *soh* run wild like that? He could have been killed. Why didn't you hold his hand while you crossed the road?"

Don't miss
HER SECRET AMISH CHILD by Cheryl Williford,
available April 2017 wherever
Love Inspired® books and ebooks are sold.

www.LoveInspired.com